THE TOP OF THE ROSTRUM
SUDDENLY SPLINTERED

The governor froze, his fingers clamping on the edges of the podium.

Lyons's mind raced as fast as his body as he took two steps and dived into the air. It was impossible to pinpoint the sniper's location from the lone shot, but he recognized the weapon's make and caliber. The distinctive sound had come from an M-16.

The shooter had missed, but another round would be on its way.

The Able Team commando heard the second explosion and twisted in the air, turning to face the source of the attack as he fell over the podium between the governor and the sniper. As his side hit the top of the wooden rostrum, he felt the round strike him full in the chest.

DON PENDLETON'S
MACK BOLAN®
STONY MAN

ASIAN STORM

A GOLD EAGLE BOOK FROM
WORLDWIDE®

TORONTO • NEW YORK • LONDON
AMSTERDAM • PARIS • SYDNEY • HAMBURG
STOCKHOLM • ATHENS • TOKYO • MILAN
MADRID • WARSAW • BUDAPEST • AUCKLAND

First edition March 1997

ISBN 0-373-61911-1

Special thanks and acknowledgment to
Jerry VanCook for his contribution to this work.

ASIAN STORM

ASIAN STORM

PROLOGUE

Beijing, China

Hand behind his back, Kosuke Yamaguchi drew the Randall Model 1 fighting knife partially out of its sheath and ran his thumb across the edge just above the choil. He watched the back of Ming Long's balding head as the Chinese politburo member poured drinks at the table in the tiny kitchen.

No, the time was not yet right. The back of the bar was mirrored, and while Ming's attention was on the bottle and glasses, he would notice any movement behind him.

The delay didn't matter. There was time. Yamaguchi dropped the knife back into the sheath and let his black suit coat fall back to his side.

Ming turned, saw the smile on Yamaguchi's face and returned it. He handed the Japanese a tumbler of whiskey and nodded an informal toast. Both men drank.

Yamaguchi let the alcohol burn his throat. It tasted

like bad Scotch whiskey, but it did warm his stomach. He dipped his head slightly in appreciation, remembering that the Chinese custom of bowing was slightly different than his own. The whiskey might be Japanese, and in reality, he might be, too. But Ming knew Kosuke Yamaguchi as "Low Sing," and it was important that Yamaguchi keep up the ruse that he was a fellow Chinese.

At least for a little longer.

"Low Sing," Ming said, "shall we move to the couch? We have much to discuss."

"Certainly," Yamaguchi said in a well-rehearsed Manchurian accent. "Much to discuss," he agreed, "and so little time."

Ming nodded and pushed his glass toward the living room of the small one-bedroom apartment. Yamaguchi turned and stepped over the warping kitchen tile and onto the frayed carpet. Ming's little "home away from home" was a hovel by Japanese standards, but in a Communist country, such as the People's Republic of China, Yamaguchi knew it would be regarded as a castle, and it afforded the fat politburo member a place to conduct private meetings.

The men took seats on the stiff leather sofa, Yamaguchi careful to position himself to Ming's right. From where he sat he could produce the Randall in less than a second and drive it through the man's heart in little more.

Ming took a long drink from his glass, then turned

toward his guest. "I have summoned you for one reason." He looked down at his feet. "It is not easy to admit. But I am afraid."

Yamaguchi reached across the back of the couch, patting the minister of defense on the shoulder. "Do not be ashamed, Comrade," he said. "Valor is not the absence of fear. It is the courage to overcome it."

Ming nodded. "Two of our government's high-ranking officials have already died under mysterious circumstances. Yao Hongwen's house burst into flames. The police suspect arson." He paused for another sip from the glass. "Kwong Li's automobile ran out of control and might have been tampered with."

"The police will find their suspicions correct on both counts," Yamaguchi said bluntly. "Neither of the deaths was an accident."

Ming looked up quickly, his face turning pale. "You believe so?"

"I *know* so. It is my business to know such things. I am sorry—I am not at liberty to discuss how I know, even with a politburo member such as yourself. But let us just say this. One member of the politburo dying violently might be considered bad luck. Two in one week? Too much coincidence."

Ming nodded. "Precisely. Which is why I wanted you as my personal bodyguard. Although we have never met, you are known to be among the finest warriors in the People's Republic."

Yamaguchi smiled modestly as his mind traveled

briefly to the shallow grave where the real Low Sing now fed the worms. Perhaps the man had been a great warrior. Yamaguchi would never know. He hadn't given the man a chance to prove it, firing one round into the back of the Manchurian's head from a hundred yards away.

Ming turned to face Yamaguchi. "Who is doing this?" he asked. "The Russians? Americans? Perhaps the Japanese are using their famed *ninja*s."

Yamaguchi chuckled politely. "*Ninja*s? Do you mean the men in the silly black pajamas who climb walls with grappling hooks and throw steel stars? They are rumored to be capable of making themselves invisible." His face took on a look of mock horror, and he looked quickly around the room. "Be careful! One might be here now!"

Ming threw back his head and laughed at the performance.

Yamaguchi patted him on the knee. "I do not mock your concern, Ming Long," he said. "It is justified. But there have been no *ninja*s for hundreds of years."

Ming's laughter dropped to a chuckle. "I suppose you are right," he sighed. "But then who could it be? The Russians? For five hundred years they have carried on their imperialistic expansionism regardless of what government they were under."

"The Russians are a possibility," Yamaguchi acknowledged, "but an unlikely one. Moscow currently has too many problems at home to go after more territory."

"The United States, then," Ming said, nodding. "They are behind the assassinations?"

"That would be my guess."

The Chinese turned back to the front, twirling the whiskey in his glass in circles. "The CIA," he said. His head twisted back to the man at his side. "You will stay with me? You will take over as my chief of security until this mystery is solved?"

"Of course. What loyal comrade would turn down such an opportunity to be of service to the people?"

Ming relaxed visibly. "I will make it worth your while."

"I have my government stipend," Yamaguchi said.

Now it was Ming's turn to chuckle. "Yes, of course. But you have been in our government long enough to know that much money changes hands under the table. And some of it will become yours."

"I am grateful," Yamaguchi said, looking down at the floor.

"It is *I* who am grateful," Ming said. A lecherous smile started at the corners of the man's mouth. "And I have arranged a little gift to show my appreciation." He stood, crossed the room to the bedroom door, then turned and beckoned for Yamaguchi to follow.

The Japanese stood.

Ming opened the door, and Yamaguchi saw the surprise the politburo man had promised. Tied to the bed were two nearly nude Caucasian women. Both struggled against their restraints, their voices muffled behind tight ball-gags. Their eyes stared at the men in horror.

Ming licked his lips as he turned to Yamaguchi. "They are American," he said proudly. "Big breasts. Large posteriors. I get them from a man I know who deals in exotics. Do you see how they feign horror? They are good." He unbuckled his belt and had begun to unzip his pants when he suddenly stopped. A puzzled look replaced the smile. "But I did not tie them up. So how...?" His voice trailed off.

Yamaguchi shrugged. "This man you deal with," he said. "Their manager, so to speak? He knows of your tastes, of course. Perhaps he bound them for you before he left?"

"Of course," Ming said. "You see how the assassinations have upset me? I am a fool for not realizing that myself." He began removing his clothing again.

Ming turned to Yamaguchi, who was still clothed. "You do not wish to indulge?" he asked, frowning.

Yamaguchi shrugged. "Why not?" He took off his jacket, then his pants, careful to keep the Randall fighting knife out of sight. He glanced toward the closet and saw the partially open door. He chuckled at the opening as he moved to the bed. Reaching to the back of his pants, Yamaguchi drew the knife from the sheath. With two quick steps he was behind Ming, his left hand grabbing a handful of the man's thinning hair. A quick jerk snapped the Chinese's head back to expose his throat.

Yamaguchi drew the blade across the soft flesh, severing both the carotid artery and jugular vein. Blood gushed forth from the deep laceration. Ming tried to scream, but the effort came out in a low gurgle.

The fat brunette stared up in horror as Ming's blood fell to soak her hair, face and breasts. Yamaguchi shoved the corpse to the floor and looked down at the terrified eyes above the ball gag. Smiling, he raised the knife high over his head in a reverse grip, then brought it down.

The sturdy clip point penetrated the prostitute's ribs and moved on through the heart. Her abdominal muscles convulsed in death, sucking tightly around the blade, and Yamaguchi had to use both hands to withdraw the knife. He turned his attention to the blonde, driving the knife deep into both of her kidneys.

The Japanese didn't bother to turn when he heard the closet door open behind him. He knew who it was. Takaka had taken up his position in the apartment long before Ming or Yamaguchi had arrived. He had been there to act as backup in the unlikely event that Ming proved tougher to kill than expected, or anything else went wrong.

"Did you have fun, Kosuke?"

Yamaguchi chuckled. "I have no particular fondness for fat women," he said. "But if you close your eyes, they all look the same."

"Had I been in your position," the other Japanese said dryly, "*I* would have been the one who had to be tied down."

Yamaguchi chuckled as he got off the blonde and turned to face Takaka. "May I assume that they were here when you arrived?" He noted that the man's face seemed unusually taut.

Takaka nodded. "Tying them to the bed seemed appropriate in light of Ming's appetites. I knew it would appear that their pimp had left them that way, and that their struggles were simply the acting of professionals."

"You were able to hear our conversation in the living room?"

A faint smile crept onto Takaka's face. "Yes. Already the Americans are suspected. That is good." He paused, snorting lightly. "Your discourse on the foolishness of believing in *ninja*s was particularly good. Climbing walls? Invisible? Really!"

Yamaguchi laughed. "*Ninja*s were the invisible warriors because they blended in," he said. "During feudal days, they wore black *gi*s and carried swords and the weapons of that time. Today we wear business suits and carry Uzis in briefcases." He looked down to the knife in his blood-soaked hand. The weapon had been created during World War II by W. D. "Bo" Randall, and had been popular with Americans ever since. It might not be quite as American as apple pie or baseball, Yamaguchi thought as he dropped the knife to the floor and started for the shower, but to anyone in the know, the blade would point directly across the Pacific toward the United States.

And certainly not toward members of the Iga-ryu *ninja*s, as were Takaka and himself.

CHAPTER ONE

Vietnam

Sweeping cedars, thick pines and shorter vegetation that looked almost as if it had been plotted by a landscaper spotted the emerald green grass. The valley below would have flattered the most talented artist's canvas.

It would be a lovely place to die.

High atop one of the hills surrounding the valley, and hidden within the thick boughs of the cedar he had just climbed, Mack Bolan looked down at the bushes hiding the portable satellite dish. A faint light on the side of the apparatus flashed vaguely through the leaves, indicating a call was on its way.

He wrapped the headset around his ears and pushed the VOX button on the battery unit at his waist. Now connected to Stony Man Farm, America's top-secret counterterrorist organization hidden in the Blue Ridge Mountains, he heard a familiar voice.

"Striker," Hal Brognola said, using Bolan's mission code name, "Are you in position and set up yet?"

"Affirmative as to position, Hal. I'm getting set up as we speak. Give me a second." He swung the Galil rifle off his back and slid his arm through the sling, twisting it tight around his elbow to secure the grip. Raising his eye to the scope, he positioned the cross hairs on the trail below and glanced to the range finder: 785 meters. He'd be pushing the far end of the sniper rifle's effective range.

But pushing the far end was nothing new for Mack Bolan, better known to the world at large as the Executioner. He had earned that appellation as a U.S. special forces sniper years before, only miles from the tree where he now sat. Since the war he had returned to Vietnam on several occasions. Each time, including this one, it was almost an experience of déjà vu.

Bolan double-checked the combination compensator-muzzle brake on the Galil and rammed a 20-round magazine into the receiver. Lowering the rifle to his lap, he spoke again into the face mike. "Okay, Hal, it's all over but the waiting." His mind wandered to Aaron "the Bear" Kurtzman, and for a moment he flashed a mental picture of the computer genius at his long row of monitors, hard drives and keyboards in the Stony Man computer room.

"Does the Bear have General Nguyen spotted yet?"

"Affirmative, big guy," Brognola said. "We're

watching our favorite heroin pusher on the satellite screen right now. Still several miles from you. Nguyen's men are having trouble with one of the donkeys. Slowing them down. He just slapped the animal across the face. Looks like he's angry.''

The distant crack of a gunshot sounded on the other side of the valley, and Bolan looked up.

"Well," Brognola said, "that's one way to get an animal's attention, I guess."

"How about General Pham?" Bolan asked. "Any sign of him yet?"

"Not yet. But he has to come through some pretty thick undergrowth to get to the meeting spot. Probably just hidden from the satellite."

Bolan shifted in the tree as he studied the valley spread out below. The infamous Golden Triangle area of Southeast Asia was an intriguing labyrinth of hills and valleys that provided drug-dealing warlords like Nguyen and Pham with hidden paths on which to conduct their trade. According to data Kurtzman had secretly gleaned from DEA files, Nguyen's caravan was loaded down with heroin and on its way to meet with another warlord calling himself General Pham. Pham would purchase the load of death-dealing white powder. From there it would be cut and begin its journey to the United States, where it would end up in the veins of American citizens.

Bolan's jaw set firm as he continued to study the trail below. That in itself was enough reason to kill both Nguyen and Pham. But on this mission, the Executioner's motives for long-range rifle justice went even deeper.

Over the past several months, while the attention of the U.S. had been diverted to Haiti, Somalia, the former Yugoslavia, and other hot spots around the globe, a strange coalition of countries had suddenly appeared in Southeast Asia. Laos, Vietnam and Kampuchea—formerly Cambodia—had united their militaries into one huge United Nations-like force, and were half a step away from consolidating into one nation. Calling themselves the Confederation of Southeast Asia, they had purchased massive amounts of land and sea weapons and were currently running naval maneuvers in the South China Sea.

All of which had the Philippines and other neighboring countries scared out of their wits.

The Confederation—or CSA—had made no public mention of any imperialistic intentions. They didn't have to. Actions spoke louder than words.

As director of the Sensitive Operations Group at Stony Man Farm, Harold Brognola had been after the President to authorize clandestine strikes against the new military alliance that looked as if it might threaten stability in a sensitive area of the world. But the President had dragged his feet.

The Man had an election coming up and was trailing dismally in the polls. Memories of America's last sojourn into Southeast Asia were still painfully fresh, and in the Oriental sections of New York and Los Angeles, demonstrations against U.S. intervention had already turned into full-fledged riots. Even now Able Team—Stony Man's stateside team—was on its way to San Francisco, where protestors were already gathering.

To intervene or not to intervene—that was the question. And the President knew that the wrong decision could cost him a second term. So he had authorized limited intervention on Stony Man's part, with a strict reminder that the Oval Office would disavow all knowledge of a clandestine operation. As usual.

"Kurtzman got any new leads?" Bolan asked.

"Negative," Brognola answered. "But he's got Akira working his probability program."

"How about Wethers and Delahunt?" Bolan asked. "We need to find the money behind the CSA and we need to find it fast."

"Hunt and Carmen are busy trying to find out who's really responsible for the Chinese assassinations."

Bolan nodded to himself. In his focus on the Confederation and the Golden Triangle warlords, he had temporarily ignored the other problems going on in the world. Someone was taking out Chinese politburo members and making it look as if the U.S. were behind the assassinations. The People's Republic was threatening retaliation, and Phoenix Force, the Stony

Man team that operated internationally, was in Beijing investigating.

"Do all these questions mean you still don't believe the warlords are behind the Confederation?"

"They do," Bolan said. "Sure, the money to expand militarily like the CSA has done has to come from somewhere. The warlords are rich, and they're a possible source. But something about it just doesn't add up."

"What?"

"I don't know yet. But since I'm here, I might as well find out. A drug deal like this is worth stopping anyway, and even if Nguyen and Pham aren't involved with the CSA, they might know something."

"Affirmative. Wait a minute." Several seconds went by, then he said, "Okay. The caravan's moving again."

A few moments later the Executioner saw a half dozen men on donkeys round a grassy hill and start down the trail that crossed the valley below. All carried AK-47 automatic rifles slung across their backs. Four Indian elephants followed, their backs packed high with leather saddlebags. Another group of armed men followed on donkeys. A final elephant, carrying an elderly Oriental, brought up the rear.

The leather saddlebags told the Executioner that the caravan had to belong to Nguyen. Keeping his voice low, he whispered into the face mike. "Have you seen Pham yet?"

"Negative," Brognola replied. "And he should have come into view somewhere by now. I don't—" He stopped talking suddenly.

The Executioner heard Kurtzman's voice in the background. "We've picked something up on radar, Hal," the Bear's voice said. "Looks like Pham's coming in by chopper."

"You get that?" Brognola asked into the phone.

"Affirmative, Hal." By the time the words were out of Bolan's mouth, he could hear the rotor blades nearing the valley.

By now Nguyen's caravan had come to a halt in the middle of the large clearing. Through the scope Bolan saw the men dismount and look up into the air as a Bell OH-58D scout helicopter appeared on the horizon. The Executioner squinted through the scope. As the chopper neared, he could make out twin Stinger missiles mounted on the starboard side.

Bolan's plan until now had been simple: take out the men below with rapid sniper fire, leaving only Nguyen and Pham wounded but alive for questioning. He had known he'd get off several shots before the drug dealers would pinpoint him in the tree, and it would take even longer for them to decide where in the branches he was hidden. Even then, their assault rifles didn't have the effective range and accuracy of his Galil.

Now things had changed; the Stingers complicated matters. If whoever sat over the button could locate his general vicinity, pinpoint accuracy would be unnecessary. The Executioner would experience a very unpleasant end to the mission.

He could fire a few rounds, then change positions. But each time he did that, he would give the men below a chance to take cover.

No, he'd have to chance it, pull the trigger as quickly and accurately as possible, hoping as he did that the guards below didn't fix on his position before he was finished.

The Bell's skids hit the ground a hundred feet from the caravan, causing the donkeys to bray and the elephants to raise their trunks in alarm. Bolan watched four men jump down from the chopper and walk forward. They held MAC-10 machine pistols at the ready, and stayed clear of the path the Stingers would take if the man behind the controls decided to fire.

Seated next to the pilot was a well-dressed man Bolan took to be Pham. Four of Nguyen's hitters walked forward to meet the men with the submachine pistols. Neither side appeared to trust the other, and a new idea flashed across the Executioner's mind. If he played his cards right, he knew he could get the men below to do most of his work for him.

But it would be tricky if he wanted someone left alive for questioning.

Swinging the rifle toward the helicopter, Bolan positioned the cross hairs on the bubble front. He held no illusion that his medium-velocity 7.62 mm rounds would penetrate the heavy safety glass and take out either Pham or the pilot. That wasn't his purpose.

The Executioner just wanted to get things started with a bang.

Squeezing the trigger, Bolan sent his first round sailing smoothly into the center of the glass. The men below froze momentarily, and he took advantage of the delay to swing the Galil toward Nguyen's caravan. As the weapon moved, it chambered another round, and the Executioner's second shot took out a guard still sitting astride his donkey.

World War III erupted below as both sides became convinced the other had snipers hidden in the trees. Bolan watched the four men with the MAC-10s fire point-blank into the bellies of the men with the AK-47s. As Nguyen's men jerked and spasmed, they triggered their own weapons, blasting 7.62 mm rounds into the drug guards with the MACs. The sudden hailstorm of lead spooked the rest of the donkeys and elephants, and the men still atop the animals were hurled into the air.

A high-velocity rifle barked as the men hit the ground and the stampede for safety started. This rifle—whatever it was—was enough to do the job the Executioner had known his Galil couldn't. The glass in the helicopter shattered.

Bolan watched one of Nguyen's men jump back to his feet. He raised his weapon to fire, unaware that death would come from his own camp, rather than

Pham's. He heard the pounding behind him and half turned a moment too late. Even across the valley and above the roar of the rifles, the Executioner could hear the man's scream as he disappeared beneath the feet of the frightened elephants.

The terrorized animals led the donkeys across the site, taking more of Nguyen's and Pham's men in their stampede, and they didn't slow as they started back up the trail in the direction they'd come.

Only a few guards still stood as the Executioner dropped down from the cedar and stepped out of the thick boughs. As he did, he heard a roar and saw the first of the Stingers blast from the helicopter. The second Stinger followed a moment later.

By the time Bolan had made it down the slope to the valley, the smoke and dust had settled. Very little remained of the Golden Triangle warlords, their men and animals, or the heroin.

Beijing, China

DUSK HAD FALLEN over the city, and with the semi-darkness came an eerie feeling of impending violence.

The two police taxi vans stopped in front of the Beijing Plaza Hotel. Five young men jumped down from the first and began unloading suitcases. The men wore light green uniforms, and their faces were covered with the soft peach fuzz of youth.

To have guessed them to be exactly what they

looked like—Chinese police cadets from the People's Security Institute—would have been correct.

Five older men stepped out of the second van. They wore well-cut business suits and deadpan expressions. To have guessed them to be Southern Police Institute graduates who were agents of the United States Department of Justice—as their visas stated—would have been incorrect.

These were the men of Stony Man Farm's Phoenix Force.

Former British SAS officer and Phoenix Force leader, David McCarter, followed Hong Chei, the cadet who had been assigned as their host, up the concrete steps toward the hotel lobby. Behind him McCarter could hear the footsteps of Calvin James, Rafael Encizo, Gary Manning and Phoenix Force's newest member, Thomas Jackson Hawkins. Hong set down McCarter's bags and opened the door to the lobby, then turned and waved the party past with a smile.

McCarter entered the stark lobby and watched the other members of his team parade past. They were followed by Hong and the other four police trainees who carried their luggage. They struggled with the bags, and the Briton could tell by the looks on his friends' faces that they were as uncomfortable letting the others do all the work as he was.

He followed Hong to the registration desk, then listened as the young man spoke rapidly in Mandarin.

The desk clerk eyed the Westerners with smiling lips but suspicious eyes as he handed Hong a room key.

Hong turned to McCarter. "The management regrets we will have to take the stairs, Special Agent Green," he said, using McCarter's alias for the mission. "The elevator is out of order."

The Briton replied using the drawl of a man who might well have grown up under the very shadow of the Southern Police Institute in Louisville, Kentucky. "A little exercise'll do us good," he said. "You just lead the way on in there, son."

Hong smiled and did as suggested. The procession moved past the sign posted on the closed elevator door, and started up the stairs.

Four flights later the young cadets were huffing and puffing under their heavy load. But they had refused every offer of help from the members of Phoenix Force. McCarter followed Hong out of the stairwell and past the floor desk where an elderly Chinese woman sat watching a tiny transistor television.

"She will be here all night in case you need anything."

McCarter nodded and waited until the cadet had turned around again to smile. And to make sure they didn't leave, he thought as Hong stopped in front of a door.

The young man unlocked the door, then used the Phoenix Force leader's bags to brace it open. Stepping back, he ushered the others inside the suite.

McCarter glanced quickly around as he entered the living room. The place was simple by American or European standards, but in Red China it would be considered top-of-the-line. The Communist cops were going out of their way to treat their American visitors well.

The cadets carted the luggage inside the suite, set it carefully in the middle of the living-room floor, then assembled against the rear wall and stood at attention.

"If there is anything else you need tonight," Hong said, "please do not hesitate to ask the hostess at the end of the hall. If she cannot provide it, she will summon me immediately. We will call for you before the first meeting in the morning."

"Thank you," McCarter said in his Southern drawl. "But I'm ready for some shut-eye and I reckon the other boys are, too."

The five cadets snapped into stiff salutes and filed out of the suite behind Hong.

As soon as the door had closed behind them, Hawkins shook his head. "Those are nice boys. Mannerly. A little stiff, though. You suppose they run a steel rod down the back of each cadet when he enters the academy?"

"Remind me to get them to do the honor guard at my funeral," Gary Manning said.

"What do you mean, honor guard?" Rafael Encizo asked. "As far as the government is concerned, we don't exist."

"Okay, let's get down to business," McCarter directed, replacing the Kentucky accent with his usual British intonation. He turned to Hawkins. "T.J., sweep the place, then get the phone assembled."

Hawkins pulled a bug detector from his suitcase and began to search the suite for hidden transmitters while the other men knelt on the floor, unzipped their bags and dug through false bottoms and other secret compartments for the cellular components they had smuggled into China.

Hawkins finished his duties, said, "We're clean," then took a seat at the wooden table by the living-room window. Almost as proficient with electronics as Able Team's Hermann "Gadgets" Schwarz, he put the pieces of the phone together as fast as they were handed to him.

"What's to keep the ChiComs from picking up on our calls?" asked Calvin James, former Navy SEAL and Phoenix Force's edged-weapons expert.

"This baby's got a built-in scrambler," Hawkins replied. "Anybody snooping won't be able to understand what they hear. But even if they could, they won't know where it's going. Each call—incoming or outgoing—gets routed through about four different continents before it hits Stony Man. It'll bounce from here to Australia, then to Munich and Rio de Janeiro before it sees our little home-away-from-home in Virginia." He turned proudly to McCarter.

McCarter looked away to hide his grin. Hawkins

was a good, mature, levelheaded man who'd seen combat in Panama, Grenada and Somalia. He'd led a Delta Force recon team deep into Iraqi territory to locate SCUD missiles during the Gulf War, and received the Silver Star for leading his men to safety after their helicopter crashed on the outskirts of Baghdad. Of course, those kind of qualifications weren't unique; James, Encizo and Manning had their own, equally impressive histories. What made Hawkins different was the boyish enthusiasm he sometimes exhibited, which was a breath of fresh air for the older warriors.

By the time McCarter turned back, Hawkins had removed his coat, shirt and tie, and was cinching the Velcro closure on the belly band that would carry the cellular phone hidden beneath his clothes. If Stony Man called, the phone would vibrate against his skin rather than ring and alert all others in the area to its presence.

McCarter watched the man insert the phone into the elastic and position the instrument under his arm. The Phoenix Force leader noted the empty pistol pocket on the other side of the elastic band. John "Cowboy" Kissinger, Stony Man Farm's chief armorer, had provided the members of Phoenix Force with lightweight Hungarian-made FEG .380 automatics for the mission. Leo Turrin, the Farm's top undercover man, had flown into Beijing carrying fake papers and a diplomatic pouch that contained the weapons.

McCarter glanced out of the window. Dusk was turning to darkness, but there was still too much light. He needed to meet with Turrin as soon as possible to pick up the pistols—traveling unarmed was as uncomfortable to the men of Phoenix Force as traveling naked—but he'd have to wait a little while longer. Right now his six-foot-plus frame and Caucasian features would stand out too much on the streets.

The suite contained three bedrooms off the living room, two to the right and one to the left. Manning and Encizo had already moved their things into the one closest to the hall, with James and Hawkins taking the one on the other side of the living room. McCarter lifted his bags and took them down a short hall to the final bedroom, which faced the street. Inside he found twin beds that looked as if they'd come from the police-academy dorm. He dropped his bags on one, sat on the other and began to remove his suit.

Hawkins appeared in the doorway. "It's Leo," he said, handing his leader the phone.

McCarter pressed the phone to his ear after glancing to the light that assured him the call was being rerouted and scrambled. Turrin, he knew, would be calling from a similarly equipped phone. "Yes, Leo?"

"Santa's here, and he's brought presents."

"Where are you?"

"Place called the Palace," Turrin replied. "My escort just got me checked in and took off for the night." He paused, chuckling. "Only baby-sitter I've got at the moment is the old lady in the hall."

"We've got our own here," McCarter said. "Can you shake her?"

Turrin's voice held mock irritation. "Can you shake yours?" he asked. "I'm sure I can pull off anything you're capable of."

In a serious tone, Turrin added, "It won't be a problem. I just plan to walk out. I'll be gone before she can get anyone up here to stop me, and with diplomatic immunity all they can do is send me home. I fly back tomorrow anyway." He paused. "You spot any place we can meet where we won't stand out like nuns in a whorehouse?"

McCarter racked his memory of the trip from the airport in the vans. Their cadet guides had taken special pains to make sure they saw Tiananmen Square before they arrived at the hotel, and of course the drive-by had included a quick speech about how the Western press had distorted the massacre of student demonstrators by government troops several years before. During the discourse McCarter had happened to glance across the street to a small café. Men and women in Western dress sat at the tables behind the glass.

"We passed a café about a block from Tiananmen that looked like a tourist joint," he said. "Catty-corner from the Monument to the People's Heroes. Don't know the name. Think you can find it?"

"I'll find it," Turrin said. "How long will it take you?"

The old woman at the desk by the stairs wasn't just there to fetch toilet paper if they ran out. Her real job was to report any of the team who decided to leave during the night. She shouldn't be that hard to distract, but she might report a distraction, which meant Hong or one of the other guides returning to check on them. If he did, he'd find McCarter gone. "I'll have it a little tougher than you," he said finally. "Give me an hour." He hung up.

The Phoenix Force leader changed quickly into jeans, a plain black T-shirt and an OD green Army fatigue jacket. That had appeared to be standard dress for many of the Chinese he'd seen on the street, and if he kept to the shadows the darkness should hide his Caucasian features. His size was what worried McCarter. But short of cutting his legs off above the ankles, there was nothing he could do about that.

The Briton stuck his head out of the room and spotted Encizo coming out of the bathroom. "I'm going after the guns," he said. "Tell the others I'll be back as soon as I can. At least by morning."

Encizo grinned. "Remember it's a school night," he said. "You're scheduled to speak on international terrorism in the morning. You need your sleep so you can be fresh."

McCarter grunted. He had known that the Justice-agent-crime-symposium cover would be a pain in the ass. But as Occidentals in an Oriental country, they had needed a reason to be there. "I'll make out."

Encizo's face and voice turned serious. "Want me to go with you?" he asked.

McCarter shook his head. "One can hide better than two if anything goes down," he said, and turned back into the bedroom.

Through the window the Briton could see the street four stories below. Pedestrian traffic had lightened, but there were still too many eyes to simply shinny down the wall. The Plaza was five stories, which meant if he went up instead of down, he could reach the roof and then come down the wall in the alley, unseen.

At least he hoped he would be unseen.

With a deep breath David McCarter opened the window.

San Francisco, California

AFTER THE RIOTS in the Oriental sections of New York and Los Angeles, San Francisco had known it was just a matter of time before the same thing happened in the Bay Area. When the permit to demonstrate had been applied for the day before, city officials knew that time was up.

Stony Man Farm's Able Team leader Carl "Ironman" Lyons stood next to the ballroom window on the sixteenth floor of the Knox building, where the SFPD command post had been hastily set up. His right hand was in the side pocket of his suit coat, where he absently fingered the U.S. Justice Department special agent credentials the Stony Man operatives carried as cover.

Behind him Lyons could hear the chatter of roughly two hundred cops. Some plainclothes officers inhabited the desks that had been hurriedly wheeled into the room. A few were speaking on the phone lines already hooked up, while others waited impatiently for the installer to finish his work.

At least three-fourths of the SFPD officers were on one side of the ballroom slipping into riot gear and preparing to go below if ordered. So far, the orders had been just the opposite. Word had come down from the chief of police that no uniforms of any kind were to be seen below. The mayor didn't want anyone accusing him of hampering a peaceful demonstration in San Francisco, the bastion of permissive liberality.

Through the glass Lyons could see Coit Tower, and at its base the edge of Chinatown. It was here, on San Francisco's famed Telegraph Hill, that the demonstration against U.S. involvement in the escalating Confederation of Southeast Asia problem was about to take place.

Lyons stared through the glass. Peaceful demonstrations didn't bother him—as a former L.A. police officer, he had seen more than his share. Freedom of speech was a fundamental American right, and peaceful protests often "got the bugs out" of people's systems, then everything returned to normal for a while.

But the demonstrations in New York and Los Angeles had quickly turned into full-blown riots. In New York seventeen people had been injured. Two had died. L.A. had been even worse, with forty-three taken to the hospital and eight dead.

Lyons dropped his gaze to the streets, where men and women of every race, color and creed were beginning to assemble. He didn't like the feeling he was getting in his gut. It told him the impending peaceful demonstration had great potential for making the first two riots look like a Sunday school picnic by comparison.

Lyons felt a presence move in at his side and heard Rosario "Politician" Blancanales's voice. "What do you think, Ironman?"

"I think we've got problems."

Vaguely Lyons heard an angry voice behind him. He continued to stare out the window. A moment later he felt a rough hand on his shoulder and turned to see a pudgy man with soft features and thick lips. The man's hair had been carefully cut and blow-dried and was rinsed a medium brown. It was time for another rinse job, Lyons thought—gray was starting to creep out at the roots.

"You *are* the riot-control experts the Justice Department sent, aren't you?" the man asked belligerently as he stared up at Lyons.

The big ex-cop looked down at the angry face. The skin around the man's mouth was wrinkled, and his entire face was flushed. "We are," he replied calmly. "And who the hell might you be?"

A larger form stepped in next to the little man. Lyons hadn't met him, but he recognized the uniform. "I'm Chief McBain," the man said, his voice reflecting his own barely controlled rage. "This is Mayor Bridgewater."

The mayor didn't wait for Lyons to introduce himself. Moving quickly to the glass, he looked down at the street, then turned back. "So what are you planning to do?" he asked, his voice rising at least an octave as his frustration mounted.

"Right now, nothing," Lyons said.

"Nothing?"

"Nothing."

"Then why in the hell did the Justice Department send you?"

"That's what I'd like to know," McBain chimed in. "We're perfectly capable of handling this ourselves without any help from our heroes in Washington."

"Do something!" Bridgewater ordered.

Lyons turned back to face the window. He had formed an instant dislike for both men. The Able Team leader had never been known for tact or diplomacy, but he knew if he intended to quash what could turn into a killing field he would need the cooperation of both the mayor and chief.

Taking a few deep breaths to calm his temper, Lyons looked down at the growing crowd. There had to be at least a thousand people marching up and down the street with signs and banners now, and more were joining them from the side streets.

When he had a grip on his anger, Lyons turned back to the mayor. "You want me to break up what so far is a perfectly peaceful demonstration?" he asked. "How do you think that's going to look for you in the press?"

The reality of the political trap he was in suddenly dawned on Bridgewater, and his face froze.

"Okay, no problem," Lyons said. He turned to the third member of Able Team, Hermann "Gadgets" Schwarz, who had just entered the room carrying a large suitcase. "Gadgets," Lyons said, "the mayor wants this cut short. Tell the boys to break out the pepper spray."

"No!" Bridgewater shouted. "You can't use that on peaceful demonstrators!"

"You'd prefer live rounds?" Lyons asked.

"No!"

"Then I'm sure you have a better idea. I'll be glad to hear it."

The mayor fell silent.

"Okay, then," the Able Team leader said. "Let's

identify your goals. You want the people below to disperse before things get out of hand, right?"

The mayor nodded.

"But you don't want it to look like the police had anything to do with that dispersal because it would reflect badly on you."

Putting his political concerns into such unpolitical, no-nonsense terms made the mayor wince. Bridgewater's nod was slow in coming, and self-conscious when it did arrive.

Lyons couldn't resist twisting the knife a little further. "Let me make completely sure I understand," he said. "What you want to do is get rid of everyone below but make it look like it's someone else's fault they had to leave."

This time when he nodded the mayor had to turn his head.

"Okay," Lyons said. "No problem. Get me a hundred plainclothes officers up here."

Five minutes later forty of the men and women in riot gear had switched back into civvies. They were joined by detectives, undercover narcs and other plainclothes officers.

Lyons assembled them along one wall of the ballroom. "Everyone here have a knife of some sort?" he asked.

He got a hundred curious looks.

"Those of you who have knives, cut the right front pocket out of your pants. If you don't have a blade, borrow one from someone who does. Ladies, if you're wearing dresses or slacks without pockets, we'll need a hole in the bottom of your purse."

Pocket knives and several pairs of scissors appeared, and the sound of cloth being severed filled the ballroom. An attractive brunette in a short skirt stepped forward, holding up her purse. "This thing cost me two hundred bucks, pal," she said. "If you think I'm going to—"

"The mayor will be happy to reimburse you, won't you, Mayor?" Lyons said, shooting Bridgewater a wolfish smile.

The little man grumbled as he reached into his pocket and produced a gold money clip.

When the pockets had been cut, Lyons stepped to the side and let Schwarz take charge. Gadgets set his suitcase on the floor in front of the assembly and flipped the lid. The faces of the plainclothes officers looked puzzled again as they stared down to see what appeared to be a case full of crushed paper drinking cups, the likes of which could be seen on any street or sidewalk in the world.

Schwarz lifted one of the cups and held it high. "If you'll look closely," he said, "you'll see a small button mounted to the bottom of each cup. Pushing it will start a timer that's preset for five minutes. Each of you will hold one of these in your pants—" he turned to the brunette "—or purse, as you enter the crowd. We need to synchronize our watches." He glanced at his wrist. "Everyone set your timepiece at 1145 hours exactly." He paused while wristwatches came off wrists, then said, "Now." After another pause, he said, "After you enter the crowd, just walk along and be part of the show. But at exactly 1215 hours, I want you to press the button and then drop the cup. Let it fall out the cuff of your pants so no one sees you drop it."

"Then what?" a voice at the rear of the room asked.

"Then I suggest that you get the hell out of there just as fast as you can. Come back up here, and be very careful not to accidentally push the button beforehand."

Mayor Bridgewater stepped forward. "What's going to happen?" he asked. "What's in the cups?"

Blancanales patted him on the shoulder. "Mayor, believe me," he said, "it's better that you don't know."

One hundred men and women filed past the open suitcase and reached down to take a crushed paper cup. Most looked as if they believed they'd just been transferred to security at a mental hospital. They made their way out of the ballroom and down the elevators to the street.

Lyons, Schwarz and Blancanales stood by the window and watched them enter the crowd of protestors from every angle. Bridgewater and McBain stood talking in hushed tones, casting occasional nervous glances at the men of Able Team.

At 1214 hours the mayor could take no more. He hurried to the window and confronted Lyons. "You've got to tell me!" he said. "Will there be any way to trace this back to me? Will anyone be injured?"

Schwarz smiled. "Ah," he said. "You asked those questions in the order of importance for a true politician, didn't you?"

Bridgewater ignored him. "Will people find out I was behind this?" he asked again. "What's in those cups?"

Lyons glanced at his watch and saw it was 1215.

At 1220 on the dot, a few people began leaving the throng. Then gradually more and more began walking swiftly away from the protest. Within sixty seconds people were scampering down side streets, and in two minutes the street below was not only quiet—it was deserted.

The plainclothes officers began drifting back into the ballroom as the mayor finally blew his stack and grabbed Lyons by the arm. "What was in those cups?" he demanded. "Will it lead back to me?"

Schwarz spoke up immediately. "I'll answer your second question first," he said. "It's unlikely anyone will make the connection to you, Mayor," he said, "although I'm afraid there will be one clue that might link you to it."

"What's that?" Bridgewater demanded.

"The answer to that is the same as to your question about what was in the cups," Schwarz said. He turned to Blancanales. "Tell him, Pol."

It was Blancanales's turn to grin. "Concentrated skunk scent," he said. "You can get it at any outdoor-gear store."

Just then, one of the phone lines rang. Chief McBain picked it up. "Yes...uh-huh..." He turned to Lyons. "One of the men accidentally activated the device while he was up here," he said. "It went off in his pocket. In the elevator."

"Tell him to try tomato juice," Schwarz said as Lyons led his men out of the ballroom.

"Hey, Ironman," Blancanales said as they stepped into the hall. "What do you say we take the stairs?"

CHAPTER TWO

The Executioner made his way carefully down the slope, stepping through colorful clusters of orchids and other flowers growing wild in his path. He couldn't ignore the natural beauty of the terrain; it contradicted the violence that had just taken place in the valley, yet seemed at the same time to emphasize it in the serenity it presented.

The elephants and donkeys that had comprised Nguyen's caravan had stopped running a half mile from the scene and, curious, were now returning to the destruction. The wild animals in the area had silenced as soon as the fighting began, but by the time Bolan reached the bottom of the valley, birds had returned to the treetops and monkeys chattered in the limbs over his head.

Bolan held his rifle in front of him as he neared the area where bodies lay scattered across the ground. Due to its sniping role, the Galil had been modified for semiautomatic fire only. But the Executioner hardly felt undergunned. Controlled fire in the semiauto mode would do nicely ninety percent of the time, and was even preferable to full-auto in most cases. But in case the Israeli weapon let him down, the Executioner carried his two trademark pistols—the sound-suppressed 9 mm Beretta 93-R and the mammoth .44 Magnum Desert Eagle. The pair rode under his arm in shoulder leather and on his right hip, respectively. In addition to the guns, and extra magazines for all three, Bolan carried a blade for close, and silent, work. The Benchmade 800S Advanced Folding Combat Knife was clipped inside the right front pocket of his fatigue pants.

The Executioner slowed as he neared the first body. Keeping an eye on the battleground in general, he focused on the corpse before him. The man lay facedown in the grass. He'd taken multiple rounds in the back as he attempted to flee to cover.

Bolan moved on. The next body he came to had been one of Pham's men. He looked to have fallen from a single 7.62 mm bullet through the heart. He lay on his back, staring blindly at the sky.

A low sigh came from Bolan's left, and he swung the Galil's barrel instinctively that way. On the ground twenty feet away was a legless man. His shocked eyes stared in wild fascination at the stumps on which he sat. His AK-47 was still gripped in both hands as the lifeblood drained from his body, but he made no attempt to raise the weapon toward the Executioner.

Bolan held the sights on his chest. A moment later the guard closed his eyes and fell backward in death.

The Executioner moved on through the killing ground, checking each body individually for signs of life. With some he had to press his index finger into the carotid artery to feel for a pulse. With others the procedure was unnecessary.

The Stinger missiles left little doubt as to whether the men in their path had survived.

Bolan shook his head. The valley had become a graveyard of unburied corpses. He had hoped there would be at least one survivor who could be questioned, but it didn't look as if there had been.

Moving toward the bullet-riddled helicopter, the Executioner saw a flash of movement through the shattered glass. He raised the Galil's sights to eye level. Someone *had* survived—inside the chopper.

Bolan moved to the side slightly, keeping the Galil's barrel aimed at the two men in the seats of the helicopter. The pilot had slumped over the controls, half his head splattered across what little remained of the glass shards in the frame. That meant the movement had to have come from the other man sitting next to him. Pham himself.

The Executioner called out loudly in Vietnamese. "Open the door and get out, Pham. Keep your hands in plain sight."

He got no response.

Bolan repeated the orders, but again there was no reply.

Moving cautiously forward, the Executioner saw Pham through the shadows in the chopper's front seat. The warlord had taken several rounds through the chest and was slowly bleeding to death. He seemed paralyzed; one of the rounds had to have severed his spine.

Slinging the Galil, Bolan drew the Desert Eagle and stepped up to the gaping windshield. Pham was a small, wizened man who looked to be in his seventies. His tired eyes followed the Executioner's every move.

"Can you talk?" Bolan asked in Vietnamese.

"Water," came the hoarse whisper.

The Executioner unhooked the canteen from his web gear, twisted the cap and held it to the old man's lips. Pham choked on a mouthful, most of it running down his chin. When he had recovered his composure, he looked at Bolan again. His eyes narrowed slightly, as if some half-remembered recollection was trying to creep into his brain. "What is your name?" he whispered.

Bolan eyed the man. Had they met years before during the war? Had their paths crossed later during the Executioner's ongoing war against crime and injustice?

He didn't know and probably never would. From the looks of the wounds in Pham's chest, the man wasn't going to live long enough for them to figure it out.

"Bolan," the Executioner finally said. "Mack Bolan."

The name brought remembrance to Pham's eyes. "The Executioner," he said. "I remember you."

Bolan didn't answer.

Pham's expression shifted from memory to terror. "I am dying?" he asked.

Bolan nodded.

"Can I be saved? Can you help me?"

"There's nothing I can do."

A look of resignation replaced the fear on Pham's face. He closed his eyes.

"But there's something you can do," Bolan said. "You've made a life of hurting others. Now, before you die, you have the opportunity to do something to help."

Pham's eyes opened again.

"Tell me about the Confederation of Southeast Asia," the Executioner said. "Are you and the other warlords behind it?"

Pham's head shook slowly and painfully. "No."

Bolan studied the man. Pham knew he was dying. Unless he had sons or other family involved in the drug trade, he had no reason to lie. More importantly Bolan's gut reaction was that the man was telling the truth.

"Water," Pham said again, and Bolan gave him more.

"Who's the money behind the Confederation?" Bolan asked.

"I do not know."

Again the big American believed him. He leaned closer to the old man. Pham's face showed the pain he had to be feeling, and every few seconds he grimaced. "I need to know who is backing the CSA financially," Bolan said. "Where can I get that information?"

Pham coughed, tried to drink again, then gave up as the water mixed with blood in his mouth and ran down his chin. "Mr. Vu," he sputtered. "If anyone would know, it would be Vu."

The Executioner knew the name. Vu was a Ho Chi Minh City character who'd been around since before the war. He bought, sold and traded information and was loyal only to the highest bidder. Bolan had never met Vu, but he had known countless others like him. True scum of the world, they appeared from under rocks near all troubled spots around the globe, providing Intel to government agencies, terrorists, criminals or anyone else who wanted it and was willing to fork over enough cash. And they were always involved in other criminal activities. Besides dabbling in drugs and gambling, Mr. Vu was reported to do a flourishing trade in the white slave market, kidnapping Western women for the pleasure of Oriental and

Mideastern men while shipping Oriental and Mideastern women forced into prostitution to the West.

"Go...see...Vu...." Pham whispered.

Bolan turned away from the warlord. He dug through the packs and saddlebags of the nearby donkeys and elephants, and within ten minutes twenty million dollars of Southeast Asian white heroin had blown away in the breeze.

He had started to leave when he heard Pham's faint voice. "Bolan...Bolan..."

The soldier turned back to the demolished helicopter. Pham's face was now a constant mask of pain as he continued to die a tortured death.

"Bolan..." the drug-dealing warlord whispered again. "The...Executioner..." His voice trailed off and he closed his eyes. For a moment Bolan thought he had died. Then the eyes opened again. "You had...one other name during the war," Pham choked out.

Bolan knew the name, and knew what Pham was asking of him. Slowly he lifted the Galil to his shoulder, sighted on Pham's chest and pulled the trigger.

The lone 7.62 mm round ended the warlord's life and suffering.

Bolan flipped the weapon to safe and started back up the hill. The next stop would be Ho Chi Minh City, where he had an appointment with a Mr. Vu. "Sergeant Mercy" had disappeared. He was once again the Executioner.

STANDING ON THE windowsill outside his bedroom, McCarter was able to stretch up and grab the stone ledge that circled the building between the fourth and fifth floors of the Beijing Plaza Hotel. With a deep breath he pulled himself upward, got a knee over the edge and worked the rest of his body onto the narrow platform. He glanced down quickly to ascertain that no one below had chanced to look up and take notice, then across the street to the buildings there. It was impossible to tell. The windows were dark.

McCarter reached up, grabbed the bottom of the sill of the window above him and pulled himself up. When he'd reached the next foothold, he looked through the grimy glass to see a man and woman asleep in the room above his own. Overhead he could see the roof, just out of reach.

A low retaining wall ran the perimeter of the hotel's roof. There was only one answer. He'd have to jump and hope he got a good enough grip on the edge of the wall that he didn't plummet the five stories to the sidewalk.

The Phoenix Force leader didn't think any further about the consequences of failure. More deliberation would be useful only if the decision to act hadn't yet been made, and McCarter had already elected to risk the jump.

So he did.

The first joints on the fingers of both his hands slid

just over the stone wall and clamped down like the claws of a bird. His body settled back at the ends of his arms, and for a moment he felt the burn in his back and shoulders. Then, like a man doing chin-ups, McCarter pulled himself up and over the wall onto the roof.

Taking a moment to catch his breath, the Phoenix Force leader looked over the wall. The people on the streets were scurrying home, their heads down, intent on reaching their destinations before the curfew set in. None appeared to have noticed that a human fly had just scaled the face of a wall above them, or if they had, they didn't consider it important enough for a second look.

McCarter felt his breathing return to normal and stood. Still, it wouldn't do to waste time. Some good comrade might have seen him and decided it would be a feather in his cap to report that unusual occurrence. The sooner he met with Turrin, picked up the pistols and returned to his room, the better.

Crossing the roof, McCarter found a four-story building on the other side of a ten-foot alley. He turned back, paced off a ten-step running start, then sprinted for the span between the buildings.

The Phoenix Force leader left the edge of the hotel roof like an Olympic-class long jumper, flying through the air across the alley and down one story to the tar roof of the shorter building. When his athletic shoes hit the surface, he immediately rolled forward to break the fall before rebounding to his feet.

A door to the stairway stood in the center of the roof, and McCarter made his way toward it. As he neared, he could see in the soft moonlight that a rusty padlock secured the entrance. The clasp to which the lock had been secured had been screwed into the splintery wood of the door and frame. There didn't appear to be an alarm of any type.

The screwdriver blade of McCarter's Swiss Army knife made short work of the latch. He placed the hardware carefully to one side of the door where he could find it on his return trip.

On the other side of the door, McCarter found what appeared to be a warehouse of some type. As he descended the open steel staircase, he saw stacked boxes and crates covered with plastic tarps, as well as forklifts and other machinery. On the ground floor he found a door that had to lead to the alley. This time, however, he saw the movement detectors installed above the lintel. Crude and only partially effective, they would nevertheless alert someone if the door began to open. He had started to disarm the device when he glanced to his side and spotted the window.

The glass was obscured by years of dust and grime, making it difficult to see in the dim illumination inside the warehouse. McCarter walked over and found it was unguarded by any monitoring device. It was even unlocked.

Opening the window, he slipped through into the alley, then closed his exit behind him.

The Phoenix Force leader jogged quietly across the bricks beneath his feet to the end of the alley, then turned onto the street. He moved quickly across the open area to another path between buildings and hurried on. Gradually, keeping out of sight in the alleys and taking to the streets only when he encountered a dead end, he made his way toward Tiananmen Square and the café where he hoped to meet Turrin.

When forced to take to the sidewalks, McCarter kept his face down in the collar of his field jacket and slumped low, doing the best he could to appear shorter. He encountered a few stragglers on their way home, and a few of them eyed him inquisitively. But none seemed curious enough to investigate further.

Pedestrian traffic had thinned substantially by the time McCarter finally spotted the famous Gate of Heavenly Peace. From there he got his bearings, and angled down another alley in the general direction of the café. Looking both ways before stepping out of an alley, he saw that the way was clear and emerged to the sidewalk—just as a young man wearing the dark green uniform of the Chinese National Police rounded a corner one storefront away.

The young officer stopped in his tracks, eyeing the figure that had just come from the alley. McCarter turned away from the man and walked on, slouching lower than ever now. He heard the voice call out behind him, sounding first friendly, then authoritative when it got no response.

McCarter stopped but didn't turn. He could run for it, but that would draw other police who would comb the area. The search would include the café, not only precluding his meeting with Turrin but risking the other Stony Man agent's safety, as well.

No, the Phoenix Force leader thought as he finally turned toward the officer and smiled. There was only one way out of this predicament.

The young cop walked briskly forward, his hand on the baton in the ring on his belt. McCarter took note that he wore no gun, but he wasn't surprised. Only about five percent of the Chinese police carried firearms on a regular basis, mostly drug and special tactical units. Guns were rarely needed in Red China. The nation's weapon was tyranny itself.

When he was directly in front of the Phoenix Force leader, the young cop spoke again, repeating whatever words McCarter had heard earlier. Slowly the Briton raised one hand and tapped his lips, shaking his head. He began moving his fingers in the sign language used by hearing-disabled people the world over.

The Chinese officer stared at him in naive surprise. He seemed not to have realized that the man in front of him had been facing the other way when he had spoken his orders and wouldn't have known to stop had he been deaf.

McCarter didn't mind the young man's inconsistency in logic at all. It gave him the time he needed.

The spelling fingers suddenly closed into a fist and drove into the young Chinese cop's chin. Taken by surprise, the cop crumpled from the force of the blow.

McCarter knelt next to the unconscious man as he studied both sides of the street. No one appeared to have witnessed what had just happened. Grabbing the cop's heavy black boots, the Phoenix Force leader dragged him into the alley.

The Briton whisked the cop's tunic over his head and tore the T-shirt from his chest to fashion a gag. The young man's whistle lanyard effectively bound his wrists, and by punching a new hole through his belt with the Swiss Army knife's leather punch, McCarter was able to make it fit tightly around the unconscious man's ankles. Hiding the sleeping form behind a large white trash receptacle, McCarter returned to the street.

The cop would wake up in a few minutes. It wouldn't take him more than an hour to work himself free.

But by then the Phoenix Force leader planned to have picked up the guns from Leo Turrin and be back at the Beijing Plaza.

Turning a corner, McCarter saw the well-lit café just down the street. Through the glass window in the front he could see Leo Turrin at a table facing the door.

Tokyo, Japan

HOLDING THE KNIFE in a forward cutting grip, Yuji Tanaka adjusted his fingers slightly and twirled the knife into a horizontal thrusting position. A quarter turn moved the blade to a vertical thrusting grip. Tanaka moved automatically through the twenty-six-step *tanto bujutsu* blade-manipulation drill, finally ending with the knife in a reverse cutting grip.

With his other hand, he pressed the phone tighter to his ear. "Yes, Nori," he said. "What were you saying?"

As Yuji unconsciously started the grip-change drill again, Nori Tanaka spoke over the wire from Ho Chi Minh City. "I was saying, brother, that I expect the Vietnamese politburo to decide upon consolidation sometime this week. When they do, Laos, Burma and Cambodia will soon follow suit."

Yuji smiled and let the knife stop halfway through the drill in a reinforced blocking grip. The middle brother of Sekichi Tanaka's three sons had taken on the role that many middle children did—he had become the diplomat of the family. Highly skilled in the art, his tongue had worked as if cast in gold as he moved back and forth across Southeast Asia in an attempt to convince the governments of Vietnam, Laos, Cambodia, and Burma that they should move beyond the military merger the Confederation repre-

sented and consolidate in one united regional super-
power. Combining Nori's art of persuasion with the
millions of dollars in graft he had spread among government officials in the four countries had resulted in
little resistance to the idea.

Outside his seventh-story office, Yuji watched a
rope-supported wooden scaffolding rise through one
of the windows. A middle-aged man wearing coveralls doused the pane with a watery blue substance and
began running a squeegee down the glass. Yuji gave
the window washer little thought.

As head of the wealthy Tanaka family since his
father's death, Yuji had grown to think of both his
younger brothers almost as sons. And although he
would never voice the words, his chest swelled with
pride when he thought of what Nori had accomplished
in so short a time.

"Yuji?" Nori said into the line.

The head of the Tanaka family realized he had been
silent too long, lost in his thoughts. He mindlessly
twirled the knife into a vertical striking grip. "I am
sorry," Yuji said. "I had a momentary lapse in concentration. Please continue."

"That is all," Nori said. "I fly to Phnom Penh in
a few minutes. I will contact you from there." He
paused for a moment. "What do you hear from
Ichiro?"

Yuji felt the warm feelings he had for his middle
brother suddenly evaporate and turn his stomach sour.

As if to punctuate the sudden swing of emotion, the window washer's squeegee squeaked irritatingly on the glass.

Ichiro, the youngest of the three Tanaka brothers, was still in America stirring up resistance to U.S. action against the Confederation's military exercises. He had done a fine job in New York and Los Angeles, and the fat, lazy American public, which shied away from anything unpleasant that didn't directly and immediately affect them, had grown even more convinced that their government should not involve itself in another losing battle in Southeast Asia.

But something had gone wrong in San Francisco. What had promised to develop into the most destructive riot yet had fizzled. Yuji pressed the phone tighter against his ear, and with lightning speed twirled the knife into a fist thrusting grip. Slowly his fingers ran up and down the smooth eel-skin handle.

"Yuji?" Nori said again. "Another lapse in concentration?"

Yuji chuckled. "Yes," he said into the receiver. "I am afraid so. I am afraid thoughts of our hotheaded younger sibling often affect me like that."

Always the diplomat, Nori said, "Ichiro has gained more control of his temper recently, I believe. And he appears to be thinking more with his head than his loins. I think the responsibility you have assigned him is behind his new self-control."

"Perhaps," Yuji said. "But his flamboyance is annoying and someday may prove costly. His actions scream, 'Look at me! Look at me!' He would be better off remaining low-profile." He paused, then went on, "Something went wrong in San Francisco, Nori, and I cannot help wondering if Ichiro's disposition had anything to do with it."

"Do you know what caused the crowd to disperse?"

Yuji snorted. "Ichiro said that skunks invaded the crowd. It is nonsense." His eyes followed the window washer as the scaffolding moved to the center office window and the man dipped his huge brush into a bucket. "In any case he goes from San Francisco to Oklahoma City. It remains to be seen what will happen there."

"Ichiro will do well," Nori said. "I will call you from Cambodia."

Yuji cradled the phone, shoved the knife back into the wooden sheath and set it on his desk. For a moment he stared at the weapon. Well over seven hundred years old, it had been forged by the famed swordsmith Yoshimitsu for one of Yuji's samurai ancestors and had been in the Tanaka family ever since. He kept it on the desk ostensibly as a letter opener and conversation piece. But Yuji knew it served a far more valuable function—it soothed his nerves when he practiced the many drills he had learned as a young child of the samurai caste.

He snorted as he lifted the phone again. He used

the knife as an Oriental version of the "worry rock" Western businessmen rubbed to relieve stress. Pressing the intercom button that would ring his secretary in the outer reception area of Tanaka Enterprises, he said, "Yoko, has Yamaguchi arrived?"

Yoko spoke quickly. "Yes, sir." Her voice lowering slightly, she added, "And Takaka is with him."

Yuji frowned silently. As a samurai, he had a basic aversion toward the lower-caste *ninja*. But as the samurai had for countless generations, he followed the Code of Bushido, which precluded the utilization of the deceitful techniques *ninja* could employ. So, again like his ancestors, he found it necessary to employ the *ninja*s to do the dirty work his code forbade he do himself.

That there might be no moral difference between conducting treacherous acts and employing someone else to do them never occurred to Yuji Tanaka.

Yuji sighed. Dealing with one *ninja* was distasteful enough. The thought of two such underhanded assassins in his office at the same time was completely unpalatable.

"Send Yamaguchi in," he finally said into the phone. "I have no need to see his second-in-command." He hung up and watched the window washer as the scaffolding swung to the last window in the corner of his office.

Yoko opened the door, and Kosuke Yamaguchi walked in. The *ninja* leader wore a plain black business suit, black shoes and tie, and a white shirt. His coal black hair was cut in an impeccable flattop, and he wore black wire-rimmed glasses.

Yamaguchi knew a thousand and one ways to kill people. But on the surface he looked like a Japanese accountant.

The *ninja*'s eyes moved immediately to the window where the man in coveralls was brushing the pane. He frowned, then took a seat across from Yuji's desk.

Yuji glanced at his knife, then decided not to pick it up. Yamaguchi was so perceptive that the man seemed to have a tuning fork in his brain. He would recognize the tanto drill for just what it was—a method for relieving anxiety. And Yuji had no intention of letting the *ninja* know that his presence induced such anxiety.

"All went well, I presume?" Yuji said.

Yamaguchi nodded. "In a day or so, Ming will be found in the company of two dead prostitutes," he said. "The other members of the politburo will attempt to keep it quiet. But they will know."

Yuji nodded. "Who is next?"

The *ninja* glanced to his side as the window washer began the squeegee portion of his ritual. "Lee," he said. "Comrade Kwon Lee." His eyes returned to the window.

Yuji followed the *ninja*'s gaze but thought little of it. He remembered Lee's file. The stalwart Communist was another politburo member Yuji had decided wasn't likely to be "cooperative" and should there-fore be eliminated. "Lee will present no problem?" he asked.

"No more so than the others. There have been no changes, I assume, in the long-range plans?"

Yuji shook his head, realizing too late that he had done so too emphatically. He stared back at the *ninja* and forced a chuckle. "Of course not," he said. "When the Republic of Tanaka has been established, you will have your place on the council. You will rank evenly with my brothers, answering only to me." He paused. "You will be wealthy. You will wield more power than you can imagine." He blew air suddenly between his lips and waved his hand in front of his face. "But you already know that."

The smile that stretched the *ninja*'s lips was as forced as Yuji's had been earlier. "Yes," he said, his voice devoid of emotion. "But it is nice to hear again occasionally, particularly since your word is my only assurance."

An awkward moment of silence followed, during which Yuji turned away to look at the window washer. Did Yamaguchi suspect that he would be killed when he was no longer useful? Or had he al-lowed his ego to force reality from his brain and ac-tually believed that a *ninja* would be allowed to rise to equal footing with a samurai family?

It was impossible to tell. But it would do to watch him closely. The deceitful peasant *ninja*s had a tendency to turn nasty when they found *they* had been deceived.

"So," Yuji said, "you will be returning to Beijing to oversee this Lee business personally?"

"Of course. Takaka and I returned only because you requested it."

"You had no need to bring Takaka here," Yuji said.

Yamaguchi glanced once more to the window. "He has been behaving unusually lately," he said. "I am keeping an eye on him."

"A problem?" Yuji asked.

The *ninja* shrugged. "Perhaps, perhaps not. But there is the possibility that he is losing his nerve. We will see."

"Do not allow it to become a problem," Yuji said. He glanced to the door.

Yamaguchi recognized the glance as an indication that the meeting was over. He stood. "I will take care of it," he said, bowing low. "With all due respect, sir, taking care of such things is what I am good at." He smiled pleasantly, then turned to the window where the man in the coveralls was gathering up his tools and preparing to move to another office. "Did you hire this man to wash the windows?"

Yuji frowned. "Of course not. The building manager would have done so."

"Then you have never seen him before?" the *ninja* asked.

"No."

Yamaguchi bowed again, then moved to the window. "Then, once again with all due respect, you could not possibly know if the fact that he chose to wash your windows at the exact time of our meeting was coincidence or in order to listen to what we had to say."

The man in the coveralls saw Yamaguchi through the glass and stopped, a surprised look on his face.

Yamaguchi smiled as he opened the window.

The *ninja* was still smiling as both hands shot through the opening and shoved the window washer off the scaffolding.

The closing window muffled the screams of the falling man.

Yuji stared at the man in the black business suit as he walked toward the door to the reception area. "He *was* a spy?"

Yamaguchi shrugged. "In my business...*our* business," he said, "it is not wise to take chances."

CHAPTER THREE

Saigon, now known as Ho Chi Minh City, had changed since the war in Vietnam.

Bolan had returned to the country several times over the years and he had watched the transfiguration, sometimes fast, sometimes slow. The city, which had once reminded visitors of Paris with its tree-lined streets, smart shops and happy people, didn't make anyone think of the French capital anymore. Trees still lined the streets and the shops were still there. But the people had lost the vitality that had spawned the comparison to "Gay Paree."

Bolan nodded his thanks to the driver, handed the man a hundred *xu* and watched the surprised look on the man's face as he pocketed the money before driving away. A quick glance up and down the street told the Executioner what he needed to know.

The majority of men and women were native—short, dark and obviously Oriental. But the collapse of the Soviet Union and Eastern Bloc had meant hardcore party members had to flee somewhere, and Vietnam was one of the last bulwarks of communism in the world.

In short, the streets contained enough Caucasians to allow the big American to blend in without drawing undue attention.

Bolan started casually along the streets of the harbor area. Ho Chi Minh City lay at the end of a forty-mile inlet from the Pacific. Far across the water, sailing into harbor on the incoming tide, he could see a large cargo ship. Closer to the docks, sampans and river junks poled along the banks, disappearing now and then along the narrow channels that led to nearby villages.

Bolan caught the eye of a cyclo driver, handed the man some money and climbed aboard the chair on wheels. "Liberty Street," he said in Vietnamese, and the man steered the strange vehicle away from the harbor.

Bolan double-checked the buttons of the long black raincoat that hid the Desert Eagle and Beretta. He had been forced to abandon the Galil when he'd seen the ox cart coming down the road and decided to flag a ride. The driver had seemed to buy Bolan's story that he was Russian, and asked no more questions. They had chatted about the weather and the current rice crop, staying carefully away from politics, religion or anything else that might cause a difference in opinion.

The warrior had done so because he hoped the driver would forget him. The man in the cart, who had learned much about political survival since the fall of the city, had the same motive; he hoped to make no lasting impression on a former Soviet who might have some ranking even now in the Communist government.

The cyclo driver stopped on Liberty Street, and Bolan stepped onto the curb. The area was thick with people hurrying toward whatever appointments they needed to keep. The women, almost invariably, wore the traditional *ao-dai*—an overdress that was form-fitting to the waist with tight sleeves and a high Mandarin collar. Many of the men wore the looser, and shorter, male equivalent, but others had opted for Western clothing.

Turning onto Le-Loi Street, the Executioner walked on slowly, getting a feel for the strange city that he had once known so well and giving his mind time to construct a plan.

He had to find Mr. Vu, and he had no idea where to begin.

Moving onto Nguyen-Hue Street, Bolan saw that the flower market still remained. He walked past the long rows of booths, stopping suddenly in his tracks when a flash of something familiar—yet much out of place—caught his eye.

He moved behind a booth selling rhododendrons and peered through the petals and leaves. On the other side of the vegetation, he saw two males in their late teens. Both took a quick look around, their faces nervous.

Bolan knew what was about to go down, and it was no wonder the youths were nervous.

In the U.S. a first-time bust for illegal-drug possession, or even distribution, usually brought no more than a stern look and a slap on the wrist.

In Vietnam either violation could lead to the death penalty.

Bolan watched the taller of the two reach inside his faded field jacket and pull out a small plastic film canister. He stuffed it quickly into the pocket of the shorter man, who handed him a fistful of bills. The bills disappeared where the canister had been, then without another word both youths turned and walked away in opposite directions.

Bolan gave the kid in the field jacket a twenty-foot head start before stepping away from the rhododendrons and falling in behind him. People never failed to amaze him, particularly kids. They could be executed for what they had just done.

He shook his head as he followed the boy. He was young; death to him was nothing more than a distant reality that happened to other people.

The young man relaxed his gait as Bolan followed him farther away from the scene of his crime. Soon the soft notes of whistling drifted back to Bolan on the wind, indicating that the kid had entirely forgotten the chance he'd just taken.

Bolan had learned over the years that a criminal's fear of punishment, regardless of how severe, was a short-term fear. Where there were human beings, experience had taught him, there would be a certain percentage of them who wanted drugs. Another portion of the population would be willing to provide those drugs, regardless of the risk. The fact was, stiff penalties simply drove up the price, resulting in an even higher profit margin for anyone willing to risk the consequences. Those people always bonded together into tight-knit organizations that stuck together and eliminated any small-time competition.

All of which meant the young street dealer Bolan was following was likely to have connections that went higher than his American counterpart would possess. And that in turn meant he might even know Vu himself. If not, he would know thugs who did.

Staying back, he watched the teenager strut along like a peacock on the make, doing his best to give the kid as much lead as he could without losing him in the crowd. But the teenage drug dealer was no rookie, and by the time they had reached the botanical gardens, the young man had looked over his shoulder twice. Bolan knew he'd been made, and prepared himself for the chase he thought was about to occur.

He was wrong. The kid didn't run. Not by a long shot.

Swaggering on past the first tall greenhouse he

came to, the boy turned off the sidewalk as if he'd decided to visit the exhibits.

Bolan slowed his pace, at least half-knowing what was about to happen. The kid was big for an Oriental, nearly as tall as the Executioner. But he wasn't as big as he thought he was. He thought he was big enough to wait around the corner and jump the Westerner he'd caught following him.

Bolan's instincts assured him that this was what was about to go down. The only part he wasn't sure of was what weapon the young man planned to use.

He found out as he turned the corner.

The knife came around in a fast arc toward Bolan's chest as he stepped behind the greenhouse. Instinctively his arm shot up, blocking his adversary's wrist with his own.

Shock shot from the young man's eyes like bullets as Bolan wrapped his fingers around the wrist he had just blocked, then he pulled sharply.

The drug dealer jerked forward, and the elbow of Bolan's other arm stopped him cold.

The Executioner looked both ways but saw no witnesses. A quick glance inside the greenhouse told him it was empty, and five seconds after the kid had slumped to the ground Bolan had dragged him inside.

Laying him face up on the concrete in the humid greenhouse, he knelt next to the unconscious form and slapped his face. When four slaps didn't bring the youth around, Bolan rose and found a potted plant brimming with water. He dumped the muddy concoction over the kid's face and stood back as the teenager sputtered himself awake.

He opened his eyes and tried to get up.

Bolan knelt again, wrapping a wrist around the kid's arm. The arm bar held him in place.

"We need to talk," the warrior whispered in Vietnamese. "I want you to take me to Mr. Vu."

The youth didn't answer. His face turned surly.

Bolan dropped the young man's arm and reached under his raincoat with both hands. The Desert Eagle came out in his right, the lock-back knife in his left.

He never knew whether it was the size of the pistol or the smooth flash of the opening blade, but one or the other convinced the youth to talk. The surly expression vanished and his eyes flashed nervously back and forth between the weapons. "I don't know Mr. Vu," he finally said in a hoarse, trembling voice, "but I can take you to someone who does."

THE CAFÉ CROWD had thinned considerably from what McCarter had seen earlier when they passed Tiananmen Square. The patrons who remained were a mixture of foreigners unused to restrictions like curfews and government escorts anxiously trying to coax their charges home without dropping the false smiles and phony cordiality.

Leo Turrin sat alone at the table facing the window as McCarter opened the door and walked in. Stony

Man's top undercover man and Washington lobbyist wore a lightweight cotton suit, white shirt and banana yellow tie. He had just finished most of a plate of foul-looking black substance. Whatever it had been, Turrin had left only the heads.

McCarter decided he didn't want to know as he slid onto the chair at Turrin's side. "I assume you didn't bring the toys in here, Santa," McCarter said.

The little Fed chuckled. "There's an old joke about what you do to both you and me when you *assume*, David."

McCarter nodded. "But I've heard it too many times for it to be funny anymore."

"Hungry?"

The Briton looked down at whatever it was Turrin had eaten. "Never again."

Turrin chuckled. "Sure you don't want anything?"

"Just to pick up the package and get back to the hotel before our adolescent escorts find out I'm not there."

"Fair enough," he said as he picked up the check.

McCarter followed Turrin to the cash register and waited quietly as his companion fished into his pockets.

Seconds later the door opened and two Chinese National Police officers walked in.

McCarter avoided eye contact with the two, but studied them hard in his peripheral vision. These were no cadets. Both men were at least forty, and had that burned-in expression of perception that experienced cops get on their faces regardless of race or nationality.

Turrin, McCarter knew, had seen them, too. But the undercover specialist handed the money to the old woman and took his change with the same nonchalance McCarter would have expected of an American paying for lunch in his hometown.

The cops stared at them as they walked out the door, waiting until both were on the sidewalk before following.

The cop who spoke was a burly sort with a wide face and heavy shoulders. Turrin turned toward him, and shrugged his shoulders. "English?" he said. "Hope so. That's all I know."

The stocky man recognized the language and switched to halting English. "You do what out here by selfs at nighttime?" he asked.

"What?" Turrin asked, frowning.

"You do what?" the other man, shorter and looking more like a marathon runner, asked. "Where you escorts?"

McCarter watched the change come over Turrin's face as he decided what persona to project. When he spoke next, he had become an arrogant diplomat used to asking the questions rather than answering them. "We go eat, that what," he said haughtily. Taking McCarter's arm, he spun the Phoenix Force leader and they started away from the officers.

They got four steps.

Strong fingers gripped the sleeve of McCarter's field jacket and swung him back in time to see the other cop do the same to Turrin. There was a ripping sound as the sleeve of Turrin's jacket tore from elbow to cuff.

"You give passport!" the burly cop ordered. "You give now!"

Turrin's face had turned cherry red with anger. "I'll do better than that," he said, reaching into his jacket and pulling out a sheaf of papers.

The stocky cop ripped them from his hand. But not before McCarter had the chance to see the seals of both the United States Senate and the People's Republic of China stamped on the first page.

The wide face stared down at the papers angrily. Slowly the anger faded. The face took on a look of surprise, then shock, then regret, then fear. Finally it turned to subservience.

The cop handed the papers back to Turrin. "Please accept most sincere apology of me," he said. "Not know who you were."

He paused, said something in Mandarin out of the side of his mouth to his partner, then turned to McCarter. "You are—" he started to say.

"With *me*," Turrin finished the sentence for him. "And we are both tired of your questions."

The cop's head bobbed up and down in agreement.

"We take you both back to hotel," he said. "Not safe you go by selfs."

Turrin continued to play up the diplomatic immunity. "Not safe," he said sarcastically. "Not safe? In the crime-free People's Republic? The land of plenty where all are equal and nobody has to steal?" He shook his head. "No, we'll go on by our 'selfs' if you don't mind, Officer. You've helped us quite enough for one night." Without another word, the undercover specialist turned on his heel and stormed away.

McCarter followed.

"They still watching?" Turrin asked out of the side of his mouth a block later.

McCarter glanced over his shoulder. The two men had vanished. "No, Senator," he said. "I think you scared them off."

Turrin let out a deep breath. "Good. Because they sure as hell scared me." He walked with McCarter for three blocks, then turned down a side street before entering an alley.

"I'm spending a good portion of my time in alleys these days," McCarter said.

"Good for you," Turrin replied. "Get back to your roots." He headed for a large white trash container with McCarter at his heels. "Let's just hope this wasn't garbage-pickup night in the People's Republic."

McCarter checked both ends of the alley and the darkened windows overhead as Turrin opened the lid and produced two briefcases. He set them on the ground and said, "Can you find your way back to the Plaza, or should I take you by the hand?"

"Just shake the hand, tell me how much you love me, then go back to bed, old boy," McCarter replied. "And thanks."

Turrin nodded. "Be careful out there, David," he said, his voice turning serious. "Whoever is behind the politburo assassinations is good."

"Point taken." McCarter lifted the briefcases, and the two men started toward opposite ends of the alley.

Thirty minutes later the Phoenix Force leader was back on the warehouse roof and staring across the alley at the Plaza. He had returned the lock and clasp to the rickety door and was wondering how he'd get back to the roof ten feet away and another floor higher. Jumping the gap from a story above where he now stood hadn't been that hard. But now he faced the problem of how to get across the alley and *up* a floor to the roof. As he stood contemplating the dilemma, fate stepped in to hurry his decision.

Police sirens sounded somewhere behind him. As the vehicles neared, the Briton tried to tell himself that there could be thousands of reasons they were coming his way. But his instinct told him that someone had seen him go up the wall of the warehouse and reported the mysterious behavior.

McCarter jogged across the roof toward the side street where the flashing lights could now be seen streaking above the retaining wall. He heard tires squeal as he reached the edge, and looked over the wall in time to see two marked units screech around the corner and come to a stop at the front of the hotel.

The Phoenix Force leader knew he had to be back in his room before the cops reached it, and he saw only one chance of getting that done. He would have to vault the same alley he had earlier that evening.

McCarter wasn't sure it could be done, but he knew he'd never do it carrying two briefcases filled with guns and ammunition. He'd have to stash the weapons and come back for them later.

Turning back toward the stairs that led down into the warehouse, he looked at the door. He'd never get the lock off again in time. His eyes moved on across the darkened roof, falling on an attic-fan vent to the side of the door. Most of the time, vents like that were screened. If that was the case—and the screen would support the weight of the briefcases—he could stash the guns on top of the screen, and the housing would keep them hidden.

Sprinting to the fan, McCarter dropped to his side and stuck his head through the side hole. Too dark. He reached in, extending his arm down almost to the shoulder, then grinned. His fingers just brushed the screen.

McCarter grabbed the first briefcase and swung it into the housing, carefully setting it down with the handle up. He had been barely able to reach the screen, and if either or both of the cases toppled over, he'd have the devil's own time fishing them out again.

The second case followed the first. Without hesitation the Phoenix Force leader jerked his head and arm back out of the housing and turned back toward the Plaza.

The retaining wall rose above the warehouse roof almost waist high. That would help, cutting roughly three feet off the upward flight he would have to make as he crossed the alley. But it also meant he would have to leap the three feet or so from the roof to the wall at the end of his sprint. If he took the smaller initial jump off his right foot, he would be forced to shove off with his left. And if he led the short wall jump with his left, he stood a good chance of slipping when he hit the narrow retainer. If that happened, he'd end up a bloody memory on the ground in the alley.

No, McCarter thought as he again scanned the roof, he needed a more gradual slope. His gaze landed on what appeared to be several crates on the opposite side of the roof.

Racing to the crates, he looked down in disappointment to see the screened tops. Inside he could see the evidence that someone had recently kept pigeons in the cages.

With time running out, the Phoenix Force leader lifted the nearest cage and hurried back to the retaining wall. Turning, he paced off twelve steps, then turned back.

Maybe the screens would hold and maybe they wouldn't. Maybe he'd make it across and up to the roof of the Plaza, and maybe that wouldn't happen, either. And even if he did, he hadn't thought about how he'd get back down from the hotel roof to his room again.

The Briton had no more time to wonder about details. With a deep breath, he sprinted forward, silently counting off the steps as he ran. When he hit twelve, he vaulted up onto the pigeon cage, then onto the retaining wall.

A split second later the Phoenix Force leader was in the air.

Oklahoma City, Oklahoma

"AND WHAT THE HELL is this thing?" Carl Lyons asked from the shotgun seat as Blancanales pulled the van into the shopping mall parking lot just off Oklahoma City's Northwest Twenty-third Street. He looked at the three cotton vests Schwarz had just pulled out of his suitcase.

Behind him Gadgets Schwarz laughed. "They're called safari vests." He threw a light brown vest to Lyons.

The Able Team leader caught the garment and looked at it as if Schwarz had just tossed him a sack of dog droppings. The front of the vest had three pockets and a row of what appeared to be shotgun-shell loops. "I'll never get a 12-gauge shell in any of these," Lyons said in disgust. They're too small."

Schwarz and Blancanales exchanged knowing glances. "I didn't pick them up to carry shotgun shells," Gadgets said. "I got them because it's too hot for jackets. The vests are to cover weapons, Ironman, not advertise the fact that we're carrying."

"If that's the case, then why do they have shotgun-shell loops on the front?"

Schwarz and Blancanales looked at each other again.

Blancanales found a parking space and pulled in. "People who wear them don't really put shells in the loops," he said. "They're just for show."

Schwarz nodded, then looked back at Lyons. "It's a fashion thing you wouldn't understand," he told the Able Team leader with a deadpan expression.

Lyons shook his head in disgust. "Yuppies," he mumbled under his breath.

Blancanales killed the engine and turned in his seat as Schwarz handed him a green vest. Seeing that Lyons was busy making sure the sleeveless garment hid his Colt Gold Cup .45, he winked at Gadgets. "Hey," he said, "the brown one would go better with the pants I'm wearing."

Lyons looked up long enough to give him a dirty look.

"They aren't brown and green," Schwarz said, his face still expressionless. "They're called rust and teal."

"Yuppies," Lyons said again, louder this time. He slid the .357 Magnum Colt Python under his vest.

Carl "Ironman" Lyons checked the rest of his equipment. He loved Schwarz and Blancanales like brothers, but every once in a while they seemed to decide they were Heckle and Jeckle. Neither one of the other Able Team warriors gave any more of a damn about fashion they he did—they were just in the mood to bait him.

Lyons turned in his seat. "Okay, straight time, funny men," he said. "The situation as it stands— both state and city authorities rejected Brognola's offer of Justice Department assistance."

"Why?" Blancanales asked.

"Because they feel like they can handle it themselves," Lyons said. They haven't had a major riot here since the 1920s."

"Then they're overdue," Blancanales commented.

"Okies are an independent bunch," Schwarz said. "Pioneer spirit and all that. And they have a basic distrust for federal authorities."

Blancanales shrugged. "Can't completely blame them there."

"Anyway," Lyons went on, "we're here without sanction to help out if we can." He paused, unbuckling his belt to slide the nylon sheath that would carry his collapsible ASP baton beneath the vest. "So we stay low-profile."

Schwarz slid his own ASP onto his belt. "What we really need, Ironman," he said, "is to figure out who's instigating these demonstrations and how they're turning them violent."

"So keep your eyes and ears open," Lyons said, nodding.

Schwarz handed out a trio of belt-clip two-way radios and wraparound earphones with attached voice-activated face mikes. If anyone paid any attention, they would chalk the electronics up to being TV or radio news equipment.

The three Able Team warriors exited the van, Blancanales sporting a brown wooden cane topped by a round wooden ball. The Able Team commando had studied *bo jujutsu* fighting for years, and would rely on the walking stick instead of one of the collapsible batons.

The men from Stony Man Farm crossed the parking lot to Twenty-third Street and stopped at the curb. Up and down the street, Lyons saw restaurants announcing Chinese, Vietnamese and Thai food.

The parade had already begun and was six blocks away, the roar of the crowd mounting as it neared Able Team. Police had set up barriers to contain the marchers, and officers in riot gear stood behind the wooden barricade. Behind the police line, Lyons led Schwarz and Blancanales through the spectators who had gathered to watch the show. As the trio mingled with the onlookers, they saw signs, placards and banners held above the marchers' heads: U.S. Out Of Southeast Asia, Mind Your Own Business, Washington, and Remember Last Time? A chant started: "U.S. always makes a mess! Stay out of Southeast Asia, it's not a game of chess!"

"Clever," Schwarz said behind Lyons.

When they had drawn within a block of the oncoming crowd, Lyons turned to his men. "Let's go to work," he said. "You two mingle in as they go by and see if you can pick up any Intel. There's enough pale skin among the Orientals to make it work."

Both Schwarz and Blancanales nodded. "You aren't coming with us?" Pol asked.

Lyons shook his head. "I'll follow along but stay outside the ranks. I want to watch and get a feel for the overall demonstration."

Gadgets and Pol waited until the marchers had drawn abreast, then hopped over the barriers and disappeared into the mass.

Lyons moved along the margins of the demonstration, tuning out the chants and catcalls and concentrating on the details of what he saw. Most of the marchers were Oriental, probably a representative mixture of the various Oriental residents of that section of Oklahoma City.

Who, or what, looked out of place? the Able Team leader asked himself as he eyed the crowd. The muscular black man with dreadlocks, his deltoids, pecs and biceps bulging through the tight rag-top sweatshirt? No, as the man walked by, Lyons saw that he was holding the hand of a pretty Oriental woman who was almost invisible behind his bulk.

How about the gray-haired Caucasian woman dressed in faded Levi's jeans and a T-shirt? The former L.A. detective fought a smile. Hardly. She'd probably been waiting to do this again since the sixties and jumped at the chance.

The Able Team leader walked along, gradually letting the crowd pass by. He saw other men and women who didn't fit the profile but also found a logical explanation for each. A third of the way back, he caught a glimpse of Gadgets's frowning face before the Able Team's electronics expert disappeared in the throng again.

"Able One to Two," Lyons said into his face mike. "You read me, Gadgets?"

"Affirmative, Ironman."

"You got something?" Lyons asked. "I just saw a flash of your sour puss through all the armpits."

"Don't know, Ironman. Maybe." He paused. "Look about ten feet ahead of where you saw me. Two guys—one's got a beard, the other has a red bandanna tied around his forehead as a sweatband. Samurai-style topknot sticking out above it. You see him?"

Lyons squinted in the direction Schwarz had advised, but saw nothing.

"Just in front of the fat woman in the cutoff jeans," Schwarz said. "Next to another Oriental wearing a red T-shirt."

"I see him." Pol's voice came from somewhere within the crowd. "Looks like Kurtzman's main man, Akira."

Lyons finally spotted the topknot bouncing above the red bandanna. The man sporting the semisamurai garb was of medium height and build and wore a cutoff denim jacket. His face was harder and the features sharper, and he was older, but at least in general dress and appearance he did resemble Akira Tokaido, Kurtzman's assistant in the Stony Man computer room.

He walked next to a shorter man who was built like a gymnast and wore a heavier beard than most Orientals could sprout.

"What about him?" Lyons asked into the mike.

"They aren't chanting along with the rest," Schwarz said. "That caught my attention almost as soon as I stepped over the barriers. They just whisper back and forth every so often and glance at their watches." Able Team's electronics man paused, and the microphone deactivated for a moment. Then Schwarz said, "And several other hard-looking cases have made their way up to them, spoken for a second, then taken off in different directions."

Lyons moved along, keeping his eye on the man in the topknot as best he could. The Able Team leader had been a cop too long not to accept the fact that a trained operative's subconscious could pick up suspicious behavior that didn't register consciously. And Schwarz was as good at it as anyone. If Gadgets thought there was something mysterious about the two men, then there was.

Three blocks later Lyons saw what Schwarz had been talking about. A slightly built Oriental with a flattop and wearing a white T-shirt elbowed his way through the marchers to Topknot's side. He whispered something and the man nodded.

The flattop went scurrying away as if he had just gotten an assignment directly from God.

A block after that, Lyons watched Topknot start casually working toward the edge of the marchers as the man with the beard made his way toward the other side of the parade. Police had cordoned off the intersections, and at the next cross street the pseudo-samurai suddenly leaped over the barrier and started down the street in the opposite direction.

Lyons lost sight of the man with the beard in the crowd. But he had to step back as Topknot walked directly in front of him.

"You see Mr. Topknot jump the fence, Ironman?" Schwarz asked.

"That's affirmative, Gadgets," Lyons said. "He

just passed by going the other way within arm's reach of me.''

Blancanales cut in. ''Beard Face just went over the wall on the other side,'' he said. ''He's heading south right now.''

''Go after him, Pol, but don't let him see you,'' Lyons ordered. ''Gadgets, stay here. Check in with the Farm and advise Barbara what's happening.''

''What *is* happening?'' Schwarz asked.

''I don't know,'' Lyons said. ''But something. I'm going after Topknot. We'll all stay on the air unless we're afraid it'll burn us. If you have to kill the radios, get back on as soon as you can.''

''Affirmative,'' both Schwarz and Blancanales said.

Lyons pivoted on the balls of his feet and took off down Twenty-third Street after the man in the topknot. He shook his head in disbelief. The guy *did* look like Akira Tokaido.

BOLAN TOOK ANOTHER quick look around the greenhouse. Still clear. But it might not be for long. He leaned in close to the teenager on the ground. ''You got a name, kid?'' he asked.

The young man's eyes kept shifting back and forth from the Desert Eagle to the knife folder. ''Bui Vien,'' he whispered.

''Listen close, Bui,'' the Executioner said. ''I'm going to stick this gun and knife back under my coat, then help you to your feet. Then you're going to take me to someone who knows Mr. Vu." He stopped momentarily and let his eyes narrow. "How old are you?"

"Nineteen."

Bolan nodded. "If you ever expect to see twenty, don't forget what's under the coat."

The Executioner stuck the Desert Eagle back in its holster and clipped the knife into his right front pocket before reaching down and pulling the kid to his feet.

Bolan fell in next to him as they walked along under the well-lit sidewalk. By now there were few people on the streets, and for a moment the Executioner was surprised Bui was keeping to a path so easy to spot. Then the kid's plan dawned on him, and he looked over at his new charge. "Did I forget to mention that if the police stop us I'm going to cut your throat from ear to ear?" he asked.

Bui didn't answer. He just led the way off the lit path down a dark side street at the next corner.

They left the downtown area and entered a run-down neighborhood of government-built, multifamily housing. Men, women and children sat outside the apartment houses on steps and splintering chairs. The men smoked quietly. The women talked among themselves almost as quietly. The children wrestled, laughed and played games, too young to realize yet that the squalor around them was all for which they could ever hope.

The Vietnamese youth led Bolan between two buildings and opened the door to a crumbling shed. Inside, Bolan saw a thirty-year-old Honda 350 cc motorcycle that looked as if it had been held together over the years with baling wire and paste. Bui turned to him, and in the kid's eyes the big American still saw fear. But now he also saw a pathetic pride in the dilapidated bike.

"It is mine," Bui said. "We will have to take it. The man who will know Mr. Vu will be too far away to walk."

Bolan nodded.

Bui looked at him curiously.

"You drive," Bolan instructed. "I'll be right behind you." He tapped the Desert Eagle through his raincoat significantly.

Bui wheeled out the motorcycle, kicked the starter several times, then got off and adjusted the carburetor. The next kick brought the battered motorcycle coughing to life.

Bolan slid on behind the youth and gripped the strap across the seat in front of him. A moment later they were traveling through the deserted streets.

Few cars were on the road at this time of night, but here and there a bicycle puttered slowly along. Every few minutes the Honda choked and threatened to die. Each time Bui downshifted, twisted the throttle and brought the machine back to life with a jerk.

Two miles from where they'd picked up the Honda,

they took an overpass and saw a marked police unit cruising slowly along in front of them. "What do I do?" Bui shouted into the wind over his shoulder.

"Try prayer," Bolan said.

It was too late to turn, as they'd have already been seen in the rearview mirror. Bui kept the Honda moving, easing their speed slightly.

The police car slowed to a crawl. Bolan saw the officer in the passenger seat turn and stare at them through the rear window.

"What should I do?" Bui asked frantically.

"Just keep going," Bolan said. "Make sure you're under the speed limit, and act like everything's cool."

Bui slowed a little more, then steadied the speed.

Bolan hunched lower behind the young man, grateful now that the kid was as big as he was. When he judged they were nearing a distance at which the cops might recognize his Caucasian features, he turned slightly away from the car.

The Executioner felt two sets of eyes on the Honda as the motorcycle passed the police car.

Bui drove on, keeping his pace moderate. Neither of them turned around, but in the mirror mounted on the handlebars Bolan saw that the unit hadn't increased pace. Gradually they began to leave the car behind them until finally it became nothing more than a tiny blue-and-white speck.

Two turns later Bui guided the Honda off the thoroughfare into the commercial area of the city. They

began to pass steel mills and related operations, and
the stench of iron grew thick in Bolan's nostrils. A
few more turns and several blocks later, Bui twisted
the bike into a narrow passageway behind a dark storage building. Killing the lights, he drove on, then
twisted the key and let the motor die, as well. The
Honda rolled silently between the buildings, the silent
experience eerie in the darkness.

They came to a halt, and both men got off. "Mr.
Son will be in here," the frightened young man whis-
pered. "Just press the button by the side of the door."
He started to turn the Honda around.

"Where do you think you're going?" Bolan asked.

"Home," Bui said. "You will not need me. Just
tell him—"

The Executioner drew the Desert Eagle and
jammed it into Bui's gut.

"I don't think so," Bolan said. "Come on."

The Honda had no kickstand, and Bui laid it carefully over on its side, then led the way to the door.
Bolan holstered the big .44 pistol, leaving his raincoat
unbuttoned. Drawing the Benchmade knife, he
dropped it into the side pocket of the coat.

The weight in the pocket would act as a ballast,
making it easier to sweep the coat back and away
from the weapon should he have to draw quickly.

And a little voice in the back of his head told him
a fast draw was a distinct possibility.

Bui reached up with a shaking hand and hit the buzzer.

A small window in the top of the door slid open. A voice spoke rapidly in Vietnamese, but from where he stood to the side of the window, Bolan couldn't make out what it said. Bui spoke back and got another fast answer. Finally the young man turned to Bolan. "He does not know you."

"That's why I brought you, Bui." Bolan moved closer to the youth and shoved the .44 into his ribs beneath the sight line of the window. "Convince him to let us in."

Bui spoke in a pleading tone. A few more exchanges took place. Bui told the eyes and nose in the window that the big man next to him had urgent business with Mr. Son. Closer to the window now, Bolan heard the man in the window finally agree.

The door opened.

Bolan pushed Bui in ahead of him and followed. They found themselves in a short entryway, and the rest of the doorman's face and body appeared. The man was of medium height and build, bald on top, and had a six-inch knife scar running down the left side of his face. He eyed Bolan suspiciously but turned and opened another door behind him.

The Executioner followed the others through the door into a casino that would have rivaled some of the smaller gambling houses in Las Vegas. Blackjack and poker tables, roulette wheels and other gaming tables spread across the middle of the room, and slot machines lined the walls.

The doorman turned back to them and said, "Wait here." He disappeared into the crowd.

Bolan took the opportunity to survey the establishment. The players were all men, but at least a third of the people inside the casino were women: Orientals, Caucasians, Arabs and Africans. All wore seductive and revealing attire and were heavily made-up. Some moved though the room with trays of food and drink. Others sat sullenly next to men at the tables. As Bolan watched, a beautiful black woman in a skintight miniskirt took the hand of a drunken man and began leading him up a staircase at the side of the room.

So Son ran prostitutes, Bolan thought. Then the women had to have come from Mr. Vu.

The doorman appeared again suddenly at their side. "Mr. Son wishes to know who you have brought to see him, Bui Vien, and what the gentleman wants."

"Tell him I've got a business deal for him," Bolan said.

"What kind of business deal?" the man with the scarred face asked.

"One that I'll tell *him* about."

The doorman stared at Bolan, and his forced smile told the Executioner he'd like nothing better than to give the American a scar to match his own. Finally he turned sideways and held out his hand.

Bolan and Bui followed him through the crowd. They left the main room and walked along a dimly lit hallway with soft Oriental music playing from speakers over their heads.

The man with the scar stopped halfway down the hall and knocked on a door, then opened it. He stepped back and waved them inside.

Bolan shoved Bui gently ahead of him. He didn't think this was a setup on the young Vietnamese's part, but if it was, the kid was going to get it first.

The office was furnished in European decor, with a heavy French influence. The mahogany furniture— end tables, chairs and two love seats—were all French Provincial. Framed prints of Monet and Manet, some vulgarly enlarged until they reached from ceiling to floor, lined the walls between Japanese watercolors, Korean sculpture and other works of art.

Mr. Son sat behind a mammoth oak desk. From what Bolan could see of him, he was a frail man in his late fifties. Son wore a bad gray toupee. The sides of his hair were cut short and *almost* matched. A long, wispy mustache flowed from the corners of his upper lip like something out of a B-grade kung-fu movie.

Son steepled his hands under his chin, and the mustache fell over his knuckles like a tiny waterfall. "Would you care for tea?" he asked after waving Bolan and Bui into chairs in front of his desk. "Or perhaps a drink?"

Bolan shook his head; Bui sat and turned to stone.

"Then we shall get right to business," Son said. "Which means you will have to begin the conversation, Mr...."

"'Smith' will do," Bolan said. "I'm looking for Mr. Vu."

Son placed his hands flat on the desk and smiled. "I do not know a Mr. Vu," he said. "And that does not sound like business to me. At least not *my* business."

"I'll make it worth your while to lead me to him," the Executioner said.

"Oh? In what way?"

In what looked like one smooth motion, Bolan stood, swung back his raincoat, and drew the Desert Eagle. "I won't kill you," he said quietly.

Son seemed unimpressed. He reached up casually and twisted one end of his mustache. "No, I know you won't." With the other hand he tapped the desk in front of him.

Suddenly four of the large wall paintings swung away out to reveal hidden doors. Two men stepped into the room from each door, all eight leveling sawed-off 12-gauge shotguns at Bui and the Executioner.

CHAPTER FOUR

Stony Man Farm, Virginia

It was a short flight from Washington, D.C., to the Shenandoah Valley, roughly eighty air miles. But it always seemed to Hal Brognola that it took forever to get there. He supposed the impatience he felt whenever he flew out to the Farm came from the fact that the journey was always prompted by an international emergency.

This time it was three international emergencies.

Brognola bit down on the stub of unlit cigar between his teeth, reviewing the three missions Stony Man currently had going. First Bolan was trying to find out who was financing the Confederation of Southeast Asia. The poor Communist countries didn't have the finances to do it themselves, and the Golden Triangle warlords appeared on first glance to be the most likely culprits. But Bolan wasn't convinced; there were holes in the theory.

Mission number two had come about because of the CSA. Many Americans, particularly those of

Oriental descent, were concerned about America getting involved. They were demonstrating against such involvement, which was all fine and good. But those demonstrations were turning violent, and Able Team had taken on the dual assignment of stopping the violence and finding out who was behind it.

Brognola sighed wearily. Either task would have been plenty to keep him awake at night. But just for good measure, fate had thrown the Farm yet another task. While all of this was going on someone, some group or some country had been assassinating Chinese politburo members and leaving a trail that made it look as if the U.S. were responsible. That had Phoenix Force in Beijing and up to its ears in the situation.

Brognola came out of his mental summary of the Farm's current missions as Jack Grimaldi, Stony Man's top pilot, set the helicopter down on the landing pad.

Grimaldi turned to Brognola and held out a hand. "That'll be ten seventy-five, plus tip, sir," the ace flyboy said, smiling. "Thank you for flying with us."

Brognola grunted. His mind was too full at the moment for jokes. "Bill my office," was the best rejoinder he could come up with at the moment.

A lone "farmhand," really a crack commando rotated in to serve as Farm security, pulled up in a Jeep Cherokee as Brognola stepped out and ducked under the slowing blades. He got into the front seat next to the man, then turned back to Grimaldi. "You coming, Jack?" he asked.

Grimaldi shook his head. "Not unless you need me," he said. "Thought I heard something in the engine on the way down. This thing is due for a maintenance check anyway." He waved the director on. "I'll walk on up when I'm finished."

Brognola nodded. "Let's go," he told the driver.

The two men rode in silence, the hum of the Jeep the only sound. The man from Justice stared out past the outbuildings just beyond the main house, his mind thousands of miles away and in three spots at the same time.

Three teams, Brognola thought, three different missions. Sometimes it was hard to keep them all straight.

The head Fed waxed nostalgic for a moment as the vehicle pulled up in front of the main house. Sometimes it felt as if he'd been born on Stony Man Farm and never left the grounds. Other times it didn't feel as if much time had passed since he'd been a young U.S. Department of Justice agent chasing what he thought at the time was a whacked-out Vietnam-vet vigilante who the press called the Executioner.

The memory brought a thin smile to Brognola's lips as he got out of the Cherokee and started toward the front door. That was when he'd first met Carl Lyons, who was then an LAPD detective looking for the same wacko. Before long he'd finally met Mack

Bolan and learned that the man wasn't as crazy as he'd first believed.

Time had crept by, Brognola mused as he stepped up onto the porch and walked toward the door. Stony Man Farm had come about when guys like him and Lyons had realized that they were fighting the same war as the Executioner and joined forces. Gradually, utilizing the skills of men Grimaldi, Bolan and Lyons had worked with before, and picking up other talent where they found it along the way, the Farm had grown into the most effective clandestine strike force the world had ever known.

Brognola entered the access code into the steel front door and heard the buzz. Pushing the door open, he let it close behind him and nodded at the man on duty at the security window. Turning right into the seldom-used den, he entered the communications room to see Barbara Price sitting at her desk. The mission controller looked up from the papers she was studying as Brognola walked in.

"Switch your lines and come on in with me," Brognola said. Without breaking stride, he hurried through the office and into the computer room.

Aaron Kurtzman sat in front of a long bank of computers at the top of his wheelchair ramp, busy at a keyboard. Brognola felt the regret that always filled him for a brief second every time he saw Kurtzman. The Bear had been Big Ten heavyweight wrestling champion as an undergraduate student at Michigan.

A big, powerful "bear" of a man, he had given his legs in the line of duty for Stony Man Farm. Brognola pushed the emotion from his soul as he mounted the ramp.

Kurtzman continued to type as Brognola stopped just behind his chair. "Hal," he said by way of greeting.

Price's lighter footsteps came tapping up the ramp, and Brognola glanced over his shoulder in time to see the slim honey blond reach the top of the platform.

The computer man sat back and straightened his rumpled white lab coat. He ran the thick fingers of both hands through his hair, then twirled his chair to face Brognola and Price as the computer screeched, squealed and groaned, trying to digest the information that had just been fed into it. "We just intercepted an indirect communiqué from Chinese Intelligence to the CIA," he said. "One of those deals where they want our spooks to know its from them but don't want to come right out and say it." He took a deep breath. "Want to know how that's done?"

"Sometime," Brognola said. "For now just tell us what they said."

"Basically, in layman terms, 'We know you're killing our people and we're about ready to kill a few of yours.' Of course, it was phrased more diplomatically."

"Of course," Price said.

Brognola felt the acid burn in his stomach. If the

Chinese sent hit teams to kill Americans in retaliation for the assassinations they thought the U.S. was engineering, he'd either have to send a team of blacksuits from the security force or pull Able Team off the riots to provide protection. The blacksuits were good, but they weren't Able Team.

"When did this come in, Aaron?" Brognola asked.

"Just a few minutes ago."

Brognola sighed. "Got one of your probability programs up and running?" he asked.

"Three of them. I'm trying to find out if the Golden Triangle warlords are really the money behind the Confederation. Akira's been narrowing down who the next politburo member to bite the dust is most likely to be, and Hunt has a program going to find out who it actually is behind the assassinations."

At the sound of his name, Akira Tokaido rose from his chair between the tall, dignified black man, Huntington Wethers, and a vivacious redhead named Carmen Delahunt. The trio made up Kurtzman's crack cybernetics team, and as Tokaido came walking toward Kurtzman and Price, the Stony Man computer genius couldn't help the surge of pride that flooded through him.

There were no better computer people in the world than his staff. Nowhere. Ever.

The topknot on Tokaido's head had bounced with every step. Now it settled as the young Japanese man in the sleeveless black leather jacket said, "You rang, boss man?"

Brognola had started to speak when one of the lights on Kurtzman's phone lit up.

"That's me," Price said. She leaned forward and tapped on the speakerphone. "Price."

"Able Two, here," Gadgets Schwarz's voice said over his cellular phone. "Ironman wanted me to check in with you."

"Affirmative, Two," Price said. "Hal's here. What do you have?"

"We're in Oklahoma City," Schwarz said. "So far so good. But there's electricity in the air. It's a powder keg that could go off any minute."

Brognola could hear the crowd in the background. "Why didn't Carl call in himself?" he asked Schwarz.

"He's tailing a guy who might be just who we're looking for. Japanese, I think. Wears a topknot and cutoff jean jacket." The electronics expert chuckled over the phone. "Is Akira with you?"

"I'm here, Gadgets," he replied, smiling, "and I have witnesses."

"Yeah, but are they reliable?" Schwarz asked. "Seriously, though, this guy looks suspicious. He may be involved. At least, he's the best bet we've seen so far. Anything new?"

"Nothing on your mission. But there's a chance the Chinese will send hitters to the U.S. in retaliation for the assassinations Phoenix Force is working on. Be ready to pull off this riot assignment for bodyguard duty."

Schwarz groaned. "Another baby-sitting job?"

"Could be," Brognola said. "But not yet. Get back to us if Carl finds out anything."

"You got it," Schwarz said, and killed the line.

Brognola turned his attention back to Kurtzman. "So where do we stand on the Chinese hit parade?" he asked.

Kurtzman whirled halfway back around, tapped several keys, and the laser printer to his side began to purr. A few seconds later a hard copy came rolling out into the tray.

Brognola reached past him and picked it up.

"The program came up with three politburo members of almost equal probability for the next hit," he said. "The first, Guang, comes out of the chute at ninety-four percent. Lee scored ninety-three percent, and Yang barely makes the cut at ninety-one percent." He clasped both hands behind his head and laced his fingers together. "There's a margin of error of five percent, plus or minus. So you could call them pretty much all equal."

Brognola studied the brief biographies of the politburo members on the sheet he held. "No way to pinpoint one man?" he asked.

Kurtzman stared at him. "My program is good, Hal," he said dryly. "It's not perfect."

Brognola handed the page to Price. "Get this to McCarter as soon as you can," he said.

Price nodded and hurried back down the ramp.

The Justice man turned back to Kurtzman. "How long will it take you to get another of these probability programs functioning?" he asked.

Kurtzman frowned. "Fifteen, twenty minutes maybe. But this is a very complex program, Hal. I've never tried to program in four at the same time before. It'll take—"

Brognola held up a hand. "Aaron," he said, "don't waste our time trying to explain to me how it works. I'm from a different age—the clock on my VCR is still blinking 12:00." He paused, waiting for Kurtzman to smile at the exaggeration. "Just tell me, can you do it or not?"

"Oh, it can be done," the man in the wheelchair said. "Just don't ask *me* to pay the electric bill this month."

"I won't," Brognola said. "Check you later." He started back down the ramp. Halfway down he heard Kurtzman's fingers flying across the keys again.

ROSARIO BLANCANALES cared about people, what they did and what happened to them. He didn't like seeing them get hurt, and even when forced to use violence against the guilty to protect the innocent, he didn't enjoy it.

"The Politician" had gotten his nickname due to

an almost uncanny ability to defuse potentially volatile situations. As a gifted student of psychological warfare, the knowledge of more-general psychology had come as a natural byproduct. Pol had watched, listened and analyzed the intentions and goals of both friend and foe alike for so many years that it had become as natural to him as breathing. Rarely did he even realize what he was doing anymore.

The Oklahoma City marchers continued their chant. Occasionally the cadence was broken by a cat-call or threat, or the accusation that the U.S. wouldn't be trying to interfere if the people of Southeast Asia weren't "of color." Blancanales clutched his walking stick under his arm as he politely made his way through the crowd.

He tried to keep the bearded man in sight as he moved through the marchers, but it wasn't easy. The man might be built like a block, but he was several inches shorter than the average Oriental and kept disappearing and then reappearing as he made his way toward the edge of the throng. He looked almost like a fireplug with hair, but as Pol watched he saw that the man moved fluidly with a grace that came only from long practice of martial arts or dance.

Pol's guess, all things considered, wasn't dance.

Finally the bearded man vanished behind three portly marchers and didn't reappear. Blancanales fought his way through the crowd more aggressively now, knowing that he had to reach the edge before

Mr. Beard Face disappeared. He made it to the wooden barriers with only a few dozen curses in various languages, one punch to the abdomen and two elbows in the ribs. None of the blows was serious, and he skipped over the blockade just in time to see the bearded man do the same two hundred feet ahead of him.

Blancanales lowered the walking stick to the ground in his left hand to keep his right free for the Beretta 92-FS or the other weapons under his safari vest. Not that the cane couldn't kill—Able Team's psych-op expert had made a lifetime study of stick fighting.

Beard Face walked along next to the marchers. He turned south at the next corner they came to.

Blancanales hurried forward, then slowed before rounding the corner. Pulling a pair of sunglasses from the pocket of his vest, he wrapped them around his head. The cane tapped exploringly in front of him, and by the time he had turned after the man in the beard, he could have convinced anyone that he was blind.

Beard Face was still approximately a hundred feet ahead. Halfway down the side street he'd chosen, he cut to the other side of the block, glanced over his shoulder and walked to the other end. He passed a small fish market and stopped briefly outside a liquor store, looking up and down the street, then turned the corner of Twenty-second Street and vanished again.

Pol dropped the blind-man act and sprinted across the street to the corner. Pressing his back against the wall, he peered down the street to see Beard Face walking swiftly in front of a smattering of houses and stores. Able Team's psych-op expert turned the corner, the cane tapping along again as if acting as his eyes.

The man with the beard walked two blocks farther, then entered a small white concrete-block building that looked like a neighborhood tavern. A neon Tsing-Tao beer sign in the window by the door was the only clue, but said it all.

Blancanales moved closer, glancing around quickly for cover. Something was about to take place in this tavern in the Oriental section of Oklahoma City, and he needed to be able to alert the other members of the team as soon as it broke. He scanned the street. Except for the neighborhood bar, fifty-year-old houses in various states of disrepair were all that met his eyes. A cracked sidewalk ran in front of the houses on both sides of the street, and tall pines and a few towering oaks separated the sidewalks from the street itself.

The Able Team warrior continued on, drawing little attention from the few people out on the street. Directly across from the bar, he could see two preschool children peddling a rusty tricycle around the driveway of a house. He stopped under a thick pine, glancing across the street at the bar.

The glance told him nothing new. Beard Face was

inside, but what was he doing there? The only way to find out was to wait, and if he waited too long in the open, his lighter skin would soon draw the curiosity of the Orientals who populated the area.

A screen door opened behind him. Pol fought the urge to turn around. A blind man, at least a blind man who had been blind any length of time, wouldn't bother. He'd just listen.

A female voice screamed in Cambodian for the children to get into the house. A halfhearted protest came from the little boy on the tricycle, then Blancanales heard two tiny feet padding up the steps. The screen door closed again.

Pol didn't waste any time. As he saw it, there was only one place where he could remain unseen while he watched the bar, and that place was straight up.

With a quick glance up and down the street, Blancanales stuck the cane under his arm and reached for the lowest branch of the pine tree. Pulling himself up, he climbed higher through the branches until they grew too thin to support his weight. Lowering himself to a sitting position, he felt the sticky sap on his fingers and palms. He jammed the cane into the fork of two limbs, looked around quickly to satisfy himself that he couldn't be seen from the street, then parted a bough and looked down at the white concrete building.

Blancanales had a good view of the door where Beard Face had entered and could see most of the parking lot to one side of the building. An alley ran to the rear, and unless someone left the back door or approached at a ninety-degree angle, he'd be able to see that, too.

The Able Team warrior took a breath of relief and silently thanked the mother in the house behind him for watching over her kids. He reached under his vest and drew the Beretta, double-checked both chamber and magazine and reholstered the weapon under his arm. His backup gun came next—a Smith & Wesson 640. The stainless-steel revolver chambered .357 Magnums rather than .38 Specials.

Finally Blancanales reached to his belt at the small of his back and unclipped the Spyderco Civilian knife. Both Bolan and Phoenix Force's knife expert, Calvin James, had carried the hook-bladed weapon on several occasions and swore by its devastating potential. The opinions of two warriors of their stature were enough to convince Blancanales to give it a try. So far, he hadn't been disappointed.

He reclipped the knife to his belt, adjusted his face-mike, then tapped it. "Able Three to Two," he said softly. "Come in, Two."

"Able Two to Three?" Schwarz came back uncertainly. "Pol, that you?"

"Affirmative," Blancanales said.

There was a pause, then Schwarz said, "Pol, I'm getting a lot of static. There's some kind of interference."

Blancanales glanced over his head and saw the power and telephone wires. The proximity to either could cause radio interference, and he'd had the bad luck to climb a tree right under both.

"Three to Two," he said. "Sit tight. I'll get out of the area if there's anything important to report." He paused. "You copy that?"

"You'll move if you need to talk," Schwarz said.

"Affirmative." Blancanales settled in on his limb, looked back across the street at the bar and hoped the man in the beard didn't plan to just drink beer all night and waste his time.

KOSUKE YAMAGUCHI had trained most emotions out of his heart many years ago. The *ninja* knew that emotion was superfluous. It did nothing but get in the way of one's goals.

Hating an enemy didn't help. It just clouded your thinking and tempted the warrior to dehumanize that enemy by thinking of him as stupid, incompetent and less capable than he really was. Such was rarely the case.

And that kind of thinking could get a man killed.

Even anger was destructive. Anger in battle made the fighter lose control. Fear, of course, was devastating, and jealousy served no constructive purpose in any circumstances.

But of all the emotions, Yamaguchi knew, love was the most catastrophic. Any kind of love. Falling in love with a woman took one's attention away from other aspirations. Brotherly love made it too painful to lose a comrade in battle, and a general love of humankind could cause a warrior to question his actions and hesitate before the kill. Hesitation at the wrong moment meant you got killed instead of your target. And love of God was the worst aspect of the worst emotion. It could send the warrior into a frenzy of speculation on the universe and promoted self-doubt.

So Yamaguchi had worked hard over the years to first dull, then eliminate most emotion. But the *ninja* knew that to completely kill his feelings was impossible; he needed some emotional outlet or the repressed passions were likely to surface suddenly and at inopportune times. With this in mind, he had picked what he considered the least destructive emotion to the warrior and concentrated on it.

Lust. Lust was short-term and manageable.

And besides, Yamaguchi liked lust the best of all the emotions. So, very simply, he had spent his life having sex and murdering without regrets.

Next to him, driving the hatchback Mitsubishi Mirage, Takaka twisted the wheel under a streetlight and turned the corner. Ahead Yamaguchi saw Tiananmen Square.

The politburo had called an emergency night meeting to discuss the fact that they were quickly decreasing in number. For security reasons they had decided to meet secretly in a room at the Great Hall of the People rather than at their usual offices.

Yamaguchi pulled down the visor in front of him and looked up into the mirror attached to the back. He wore purple eye shadow, a light rouge and mascara on his eyelashes. Over his short flattop hair, he had pinned a long black wig. The makeup looked good, so he lowered the visor farther. The tight tube top accented the false sponge-rubber breasts, and his short black leather miniskirt went well with the black fishnet panty hose.

Yamaguchi giggled girlishly. "How do I look, Takaka?" he asked the driver.

Takaka laughed. "*I* would not make love to you."

"No, but that is only because you know that I am really a man," Yamaguchi said, still practicing the feminine voice and flirtatious delivery. "But suppose you didn't?"

Takaka glanced over at him nervously. "I suppose you would be attractive," he said. "In a slutty sort of way."

Yamaguchi had gotten completely into character—a necessity if one wanted to be effective in dangerous undercover roles—and he replied as the whore he had dressed to be. "You're cute, Takaka," he said. "Want me to make you happy before I go in?"

Takaka's normally sallow skin darkened. "I know you are rehearsing your role, boss," he said, "but you are, nevertheless, disgusting."

Yamaguchi threw his head back, the long black hair of his wig flipping over his shoulder. He giggled again. "Lighten up, big boy," he said. "Who knows? You might really like it."

Takaka pulled the car to the curb in front of a café that catered to tourists a block from Tiananmen Square. "Have fun," he said.

"Oh, Takaka," Yamaguchi said, batting his eyes at the driver. "I will." He slung his purse over his shoulder, opened the door and stepped out onto the sidewalk. Then, turning back to the open window, he leaned in. "Do you know why I am the greatest *ninja* in the world, and you are simply average, Takaka?" he asked, breaking character for a moment and speaking as a man.

Takaka didn't answer.

"Because I am willing to do whatever it takes to achieve my goals. I do anything necessary to complete a mission successfully." Turning swiftly, he stepped back up on the curb and clicked away on his four-inch stiletto heels.

Fully aware of the lustful looks he drew from men, the *ninja* moved on along the sidewalk. For a moment he enjoyed the stares in a vain way, but as soon as he recognized that emotion he banished it from his soul. Narcissism was destructive. It clouded judgment like all emotions.

Yamaguchi walked on. As he neared Tiananmen Square, he saw Comrade Kwon Lee's Mercedes 500E in the middle of the parking lot adjacent to the Great Hall of the People. The man had parked far enough away from the streetlight that the *ninja* should be able to work unseen. He smiled as he neared the lot. Four times more uniformed guards than usual ringed the perimeter, emphasizing the lot's importance rather than playing down the meeting as the politburo members had hoped.

Yamaguchi wiggled his hips as he strutted up to the nearest gate. As the uniformed sentry stepped down from the guard shack, Yamaguchi leaned over, hiking up the black leather miniskirt and adjusting the seams in his stockings. When he looked up and smiled, he saw that the guard's eyes were glued to his legs.

"Papers and permit," the man said in a hoarse, throaty voice.

Yamaguchi glanced down and saw the bulge in the man's uniform pants. "I am to meet someone," he said, again using the seductive, girlish voice. "At his car." He pulled the skirt back down, straightened and batted his eyes.

The guard's gaze stayed on the *ninja*'s legs. "I will still need to see your papers," he whispered huskily. "And I will need to know who it is you are meeting."

Yamaguchi arched his back, throwing his false breasts out in front of him. "I have no papers, of course," he crooned. "And surely you must realize I cannot tell you who it is I am meeting."

The guard's face had turned red by now. He shook

his head. "I must account for everyone who enters," he said. "I am obligated—"

Yamaguchi let his feminine voice turn bitchy. "I cannot tell you who I am meeting, and you look smart enough to understand why." His tone turning suddenly seductive again, he added, "But I see no reason you should miss out. I can give you a preview, and if you like, I'll be by later." He gave the man a sultry glance again, then nodded toward the guard shack.

The man in the uniform visibly gulped, his throat expanding with the effort. He looked at the guard shack, then back to Yamaguchi. After another glance over his shoulder, he nodded.

Yamaguchi followed the guard up into the small booth, closed the door behind him and took out a packet of photographs from his purse. He pulled the guard closer, then let him view the beautifully executed color closeups.

The guard's breathing grew heavier and he wanted to press his lips against the *ninja*'s. With a graceful motion and a light laugh, Yamaguchi eluded him, then smiled into his eyes. "No, not yet. But keep these photos and I'll be back. Just be ready for me. If you like my downy nest, keep looking and it will keep you in prime form, you naughty man."

With a wink and a wave of the hand, Yamaguchi slung his purse over his shoulder and waltzed out of the guardhouse.

With the four-hundred-gram block of Trialene, pro-

duced by the Belgian firm PRB and labeled the NR
416 demolition charge, in his purse, the *ninja* walked
toward the Mercedes under the light of the moon.

MCCARTER LEFT THE ROOF on his right foot, launching up and out into the darkness, the top of the retaining wall that ran the circumference of the Beijing
Plaza's roof a dim shadow against the night sky.

The Phoenix Force leader's shoulders strained to
extend his arms forward. His fingers stretched until
the webbing between them felt as if it would split.

Then, suddenly, the Briton's chest was crashing
against the side of the hotel. Air rushed from his
mouth as his hands caught the top of the wall. For a
moment he hung suspended in the air, gasping for
breath.

The former SAS officer glanced down once, then
slowly hauled himself up and over the retaining wall.

McCarter hit the roof on his side and rolled to his
back, still trying to catch his breath. He closed his
eyes, then opened them again to a heaven of twinkling
stars. As his breathing returned to normal, he rolled
back to his feet.

He had no time to waste. By now the cops would
be on their way inside the hotel.

The Phoenix Force leader sprinted to the front of
the roof and saw the two police cars parked across
the street, the drivers still behind the wheels. He
looked directly down and caught a quick glimpse of

four dark green uniforms as they entered the lobby, then turned and sprinted for the door leading down into the hotel.

A padlock similar to the one on the roof across the alley held the door, but McCarter had no time to unscrew the clasp. Grasping the lock with fingers of steel, he ripped both lock and latch from the splintering wood and dropped it to his side.

The Phoenix Force leader bounded down the stairs three at a time, wondering what he would do when he reached the fourth floor. He remembered passing the staircase when they'd first arrived at the hotel—the entrance-exit door stood directly behind the hall monitor's desk.

McCarter reached the fifth floor and grabbed the banister as he whirled the corner toward the next flight of steps. He could vaguely hear speech just outside the door below, and as his feet finally hit the landing, he recognized Calvin James's voice.

The Briton peered out into the hall through the triangular window at the top of the door. James was standing in front of the old woman's desk, a *People's Republic of China* travel guide open in his hands. He was speaking rapidly to the old woman.

McCarter could see only the old woman's back, but her shoulders kept shrugging and her hands were outstretched, palms up.

Still speaking a mile a minute, James glanced up at the stairwell window and gave McCarter a slight nod. A second later the guide book fell from his hands to the floor.

McCarter had slipped out of the stairwell by the time the book hit the floor. He paused for a moment behind the hall monitor's chair and saw James take a step toward the fallen book. His foot "accidentally" kicked the book on down the hall a few feet.

The Phoenix Force leader didn't wait to see James move after the elusive guide book. As the old woman stared at the clumsy American, McCarter flew silently down the hallway toward the suite.

Encizo had the door already open. He swung it back as McCarter barreled into the living room.

Manning stood in the center of the living room wearing a pair of plain tan pajamas and holding a similar pair in blue. He followed McCarter down the hall as the Phoenix Force leader began ripping off his jacket, shirt and pants.

By the time they reached the bedroom, McCarter was nude. He stuffed his clothes under the bed and caught the pajamas Manning threw him as Hawkins— also dressed in night clothes—ripped the covers back on the bed.

McCarter tossed the pajama top onto the chair next to the bed and jumped into the pants. By the time he hit the bed, Manning and Hawkins had disappeared into their bedrooms.

The Phoenix Force leader reached out, killed the lamp on the table next to his bed and pulled the covers to his chin as the loud knock sounded on the door.

Under the covers McCarter rolled over the sheets to crumple them. He heard the door open. Irritated voices spoke in broken English. A moment later the footsteps of several men sounded as they made their way through the suite.

McCarter closed his eyes as the footsteps neared. Then the door opened, and the overhead light switched on.

McCarter sat up sleepily in bed. He squinted at Hong in his light green cadet uniform, rubbed his eyes, then squinted at two other men in darker green.

Hong was obviously embarrassed when he spoke. "Special Agent Green," he said, "I am sorry we have had to disturb your sleep." He paused, glanced down at the floor, then looked back up. "But there are questions I must ask."

McCarter yawned. "Fire away, Hong," he said in his Kentucky accent.

"Er, Special Agent Green, have you or any of your party left the suite since my departure earlier?"

McCarter shrugged. "I haven't," he said. "But then the jet lag had gotten to me and I hit the sack almost as soon as you left. I can't speak for the others."

Voices sounded in the hall, and James appeared in the doorway. He stood in front of Manning and Encizo, and behind them McCarter could see parts of two more dark green uniforms. "I went out into the hall just a few minutes ago," James said. "Couldn't sleep and wanted to ask the woman a few questions about the friendship stores." He smiled pleasantly.

A man wearing lieutenant's bars pushed into the room. The others followed, until the tiny bedroom was crammed with men in pajamas and green uniforms. The lieutenant was short, squat, and if the expression on his face was any indication, also surly. He stared at McCarter with the dead black eyes of a deep-water fish as he spoke rapidly to Hong in Mandarin. Hong answered and the man replied angrily.

The cadet turned to McCarter, obviously reluctant to translate what the lieutenant had said. "Special Agent Green," he said, "the lieutenant wishes me to inform you that an elderly gentleman who lives in an upstairs apartment across the street saw a man climb from your window to the roof of the hotel earlier this evening."

"What?"

The lieutenant spoke again, and Hong sighed. "Special Agent Green," he said, "I am sorry but I must ask you directly. Did you or any of the others climb out of the window this evening?"

McCarter chuckled and threw back the covers. Hong stepped back as the Phoenix Force leader stood and walked to the window, looked down, then turned. "That's four stories out there," he said.

"Yes." Hong nodded.

"I'm a U.S. special agent, Hong, not the amazing

Spider-Man," McCarter said. He paused for a moment but, seeing no recognition of the comic-book crime fighter on Hong's face, went on. "The thought of falling half that far is enough to keep me in this room." He paused, forced a shudder, then said, "But I think I can figure out what happened."

Hong translated. The lieutenant and the other officers continued to stare.

"Right before I turned in for the night," McCarter drawled, "I opened the window for a few minutes to get some fresh air. I stood there for a while looking out. That's what your man across the street must have seen. You said he's elderly?"

Hong nodded. "Yes. He is a retired widower. He lives alone and is in a wheelchair."

McCarter shrugged knowingly. "There's your answer, then. The man's old, lonely and bored. He let his imagination run away with him. Happens a lot in the States. Local officers are always getting calls from elderly people who live by themselves. Their minds don't function like they once did, and most of the time they actually believe they saw what their imaginations tell them they saw." He moved back to the bed, took a seat on the edge and scratched his neck. "You'll find that out for yourself after you graduate. Tell your lieutenant what I just said. He'll already know."

Hong translated. The lieutenant might have bought the story, but his glare didn't indicate it. He spoke again to Hong, then turned and led his men out of the room.

"The lieutenant wishes for me to express his regret that we disturbed you," he said. He bowed slightly, then followed the other men.

The Briton's teammates grinned, then retired for the night to their own rooms. James was the last to leave and flipped off the light before closing the door behind him.

McCarter lay on his back looking up at the ceiling. The excitement of the evening would make it difficult to sleep. But he knew he'd better try. He closed his eyes.

There was no telling when he'd get the opportunity for sleep again.

CHAPTER FIVE

The samurai topknot skipped with every step as the man who looked like Akira Tokaido hurried away from the protest march.

Lyons stayed a half block back. The man with the topknot had walked directly past him, and couldn't have helped seeing the Able Team leader. Whether he had noticed Lyons was another question, but if they ended up someplace where Mr. Topknot saw him again, he'd need to change his appearance somewhat.

Two blocks in the distance, Lyons could see a huge milk bottle on stilts. Painted on the side of the over-size container was a cow in a frilly white dress. She smiled down at the Able Team leader as he and the man with the topknot neared.

Topknot ducked under the milk sign and stepped into the parking lot of a small shopping center. Lyons scanned the strip. An upscale Chinese restaurant sat at one end, a sign above the door proclaiming it the Lido. The rest of the buildings appeared to be a mixture of small Oriental-related retail outlets and offices.

Next to the shopping center, the big ex-cop saw a large sign announcing the Oriental Market. He slowed as Topknot walked up the steps and inside. A quick glance around him told Lyons there were as many Caucasians as Orientals shopping inside. He shouldn't draw any attention.

On the chance that Topknot had noticed him earlier, Lyons ducked behind a small storage building on the lot, pulled the headset off his ears and drew both the Government Model .45 and Colt Python. Quickly he stuffed the weapons in his belt and pulled out his shirt tail to cover them. Shrugging out of the shoulder rig along with the vest, the Able Team leader threaded the hip holster off his belt and rolled both rigs up in the sleeveless garment.

Lyons entered the store to find an Oriental delicatessen just to his right. The smell of spicy egg rolls, crab rolls and pastry combined to make his stomach growl. The store evidently catered to the restaurant business, as well as to home shoppers, because beyond the deli stood row after row of twenty-pound bags of MSG. To his left the Able Team leader saw ornately painted dishes, cases of plastic and wooden chopsticks, pots, pans and cooking utensils.

At the rear of the store, the topknot barely visible above a row of cans, Lyons saw the man he'd been following. Another head, older and balding, was visible next to him. The Able Team leader made his way casually down an aisle between cans of exotic fish and other imported delicacies until he stood on the other side of the two men.

Picking up a can of octopus, Lyons pretended to read the label. The two men were conversing in low tones. The big ex-cop couldn't understand a word they said, but he recognized the language as Japanese.

A moment later the man with the topknot turned and walked through a door at the rear of the store.

The Able Team leader glanced quickly around. He had remained anonymous enough by pretending to shop, but entering the back room would immediately draw attention. Maybe he could casually work his way toward the door, get as close as possible...

The sound of a door opening and closing changed Lyons's plans.

Setting the can back on the shelf, Lyons walked back out of the front entrance as quickly as he could without drawing attention. Once outside, he broke into a jog around the corner of the building and down the shopping strip. He reached the back of the property in time to see Topknot climb over a short wooden fence, then cut down an alley to the next block.

Lyons wrapped the headset around his head and followed, staying out of sight. He felt his jaw set firmly as all doubt that he was following the wrong man washed away. You didn't go in a store and out the back door unless you were trying to shake anyone who might be following you. Had Mr. Topknot made him? He didn't think so. The stopover at the grocery store had looked more like just a standard precautionary tactic.

The big ex-cop emerged from the alley on a low-income residential street and continued pursuit. Topknot finally turned back onto Twenty-third, followed it to May Avenue, then another mile to Pennsylvania. Cutting back north on Penn, he turned into a small Italian restaurant. The hand-painted sign read Tony's.

The Able Team leader proceeded slowly now. If he went into the café, there was every chance the Japanese would remember him. Topknot had to have seen Lyons immediately upon leaving the demonstration, and probably noticed him again in the grocery store without the vest. He might have realized he had seen the same man both times. But Lyons's gut instinct said no.

Still, the Able Team leader knew that going into the small café was taking too big a chance. He might spook the Japanese before he found out what the man was up to. No, he had to change his appearance, if ever so slightly.

The answer to the Able Team leader's dilemma came walking down the street ten seconds later. Tall, gangly and smelling as though he'd just climbed out of a vat of beer, the man in the cowboy hat and boots fairly reeled down the pavement.

Lyons didn't have time for formalities. He stepped into the man's path. "I'd like to buy your clothes," he said.

The cowboy's red eyes focused suspiciously. "You want to what?" he slurred.

"I'm going to a costume party," Lyons said. "I'll give you a hundred bucks for your hat and boots." He glanced down at the scuffed leather on the cowboy's feet. They'd be tight, but they looked big enough to get on.

The cowboy scratched his unshaved chin and breathed a toxic wave of stale beer Lyons's way. "Throw that there belt radio in and you got yourself a deal," he said. "That thing get FM and play tapes, too?"

Lyons shook his head. "Can't do it," he said. "Present from the wife."

"Oh, hell, then," the drunk said, nodding. "Better not get the old lady's tail caught on the fence by givin' it away. But you got to at least throw in them tennie boots you're wearin'. I don't aim to walk around bare-tootsied all day."

Lyons was out of his athletic shoes before the man could get the dusty black hat off his head. The Able Team leader placed it over his hair, had a brief thought about lice, then reached for the boots with one hand as he shoved five twenty-dollar bills into the cowboy's hand with the other.

The boots were tighter than he'd imagined, but he got them on his feet.

Lyons pulled the headset from his ears again and entered the café. Except for Topknot, in a booth against the wall on the far side of the room, it was deserted. The Able Team leader pulled the brim of his hat lower over his eyes, glanced at the sign that said, Please Seat Yourself and ambled over toward the opposite wall. He wasn't going to understand Japanese, so there was little point in risking a closer booth.

The waitress came over, got a whiff of the hat and wrinkled her nose. Lyons had just ordered coffee and a meatball sandwich when he heard the front door open again.

Two men who looked to have just stepped out of a Fourth Reich training manual entered Tony's. The one in the lead was at least six-four and weighed a good two hundred and fifty pounds. Both fat and muscle strained against the tight gray sweatshirt he wore above tattered denim jeans tucked into black paratrooper boots. His head had been shaved recently, but he sported a few days' stubble.

The second man had longer hair that was pulled straight back from his broad, meaty face. A good six inches shorter than his friend, he looked every bit as sturdy. He wore a white T-shirt beneath an artificially aged brown leather bomber jacket, and camouflage fatigue pants tucked into his boots just like his partner's. He shrugged out of the leather jacket, and Lyons's suspicions about white supremacists were confirmed.

The Aryan Brotherhood tattoo stood out boldly on his left arm.

Both men surveyed the room, their eyes falling on the man with the topknot. A moment later they slid into the booth with him.

Lyons kicked himself mentally for not getting closer. The conversation was going to be in English. The Able Team leader doubted that the two goons who'd just entered even did very well in their native language, let alone foreign tongues.

The waitress brought Lyons's coffee and sandwich and walked over to take the other men's orders. Lyons sipped his coffee and started in on the sandwich, watching the other booth out of the corner of his eye. As soon as the waitress left, the men bent low over the table, whispering to one another.

The waitress returned, and all three men sat back up straight. She placed a carafe in the center of the table and poured a small glass of red wine for each man, then left again.

As soon as she was gone, the conversation resumed.

Lyons drank his coffee. The two men across from Topknot guzzled their wine, but the Japanese didn't touch his glass. All three continued to speak in hushed tones that couldn't be overheard.

Who was this guy? Lyons wondered. He studied the man with the bouncing hair, searching his memory for anything he'd seen in Stony Man files, or anywhere else, that would flag the Japanese. The only thing he could think of was that, with the samurai hairstyle and punk-rock mode of dress, the guy looked a little like Akira Tokaido.

The wine in the carafe dwindled, and Lyons saw that the amount the men were drinking had registered with the Japanese. Finally Topknot lifted his glass, drained it, then poured what remained in the carafe and set the glass back down in front of him.

Lyons caught himself smiling. Topknot had finally drank his wine not because he wanted it but because he wanted the other men to quit drinking. That meant they were getting ready to do something for him.

But that wasn't what had brought the smile to the Able Team leader's face. He watched the Japanese toy with the stemmed wineglass. There would be prints on the glass when Topknot was finished. And if the guy had a record, Carl Lyons would know who he was before the day was out.

The waitress brought out three steaming plates of spaghetti and set them on the table, then lifted the carafe and looked at them questioningly. Before either of the other men could respond, Lyons saw Topknot shake his head and wave her away.

The other two men looked disappointed but began to eat. They shoveled massive forkfuls of rolled spaghetti into their mouths while the Japanese picked at his plate, occasionally glancing up at them in disgust. When they'd finished, the waitress brought the check.

Topknot leaned in, said a few final words, then reached inside his cutoff jean jacket.

He passed the white envelope under the table to the big man.

All three men stood, with Topknot leaving the money on the table. They exited the café together, then the Japanese took off one way with the two men going the opposite direction.

As soon as they were out the door, Lyons was on his feet. He left a twenty-dollar bill on the table, glanced around to make sure the waitress was still in the back, then hurried across the room to the booth the men had shared. Lifting Topknot's wineglass, he held it up to the light and his smile returned. He could see the prints on the glass without even dusting for them.

Taking pains not to smudge the prints, Lyons rolled the glass into the vest next to his holsters.

By the time he got to the sidewalk, Topknot was a block south, crossing an intersection with the light. The two men with whom he'd met had headed north and were roughly the same distance away, which meant Lyons had to make a decision. He couldn't be two places at once.

Gut-level instincts had guided the Able Team leader all of his life, and he saw no reason to change tactics at this point. Right now his gut was telling him to follow the neo-Nazis.

Taking off the soiled cowboy hat, Lyons wrapped

the headset around his ears, flipped the On switch and spoke. "Able One to Two and Three."

"We hear you, Ironman," Schwarz said.

"You're coming through," Blancanales added. "But barely." Lyons could barely hear him, as well. There was a lot of interference.

"Three, you still on your man?" Lyons asked.

"...much," Pol came back weakly. "I'm in... Beard Face...inside..."

"Pol, you're cutting out. Repeat. You still with the Beard?"

This time Pol kept his answer short and it came through. "Affirmative."

"Stay with him, Pol," Lyons said. "Gadgets, Topknot's headed back your way. Try to pick him up but don't let him see you."

"Affirmative," Schwarz answered. "You going to be behind him?"

"Negative," Lyons said. "I'm following two neo-Nazis he just met with. They're up to something."

"Affirmative, Ironman," Schwarz said.

Lyons started after the two men. The tight boots hurt his feet, and he knew his punishment for wearing them would be blisters. But there was nothing he could do.

As he drew even with the edge of Tony's Café, he saw a trash can against the side of the building. Grasping the dirty cowboy hat by the brim, he threw it backhanded.

The hat sailed through the air and disappeared over the edge of the container.

THE SHOTGUNS HAD LEFT the Rossi factory as that company's normal double-barreled Coach Model. But Son's men had cut the stocks at the pistol grips, and the barrels had been chopped even with the forends. Fairly useless now at distances of any length, they were nonetheless devastating at close range.

Any one of the 12-gauge barrels could shred a man with the shot it would expel. And sixteen of them were aimed at the Executioner's head and chest.

Son smiled and twisted the end of his mustache again. "Raise your hands," he ordered Bolan and Bui.

Both men complied.

"I am very disappointed in you, Bui Vien," Son said, dropping the mustache and standing up behind his desk.

The nineteen-year-old drug dealer's eyes were as frightened now as they'd been when Bolan held the Desert Eagle on him. "I had no choice, Mr. Son!" he cried. "He told me he would kill me if I did not bring him to you!"

"So now it will be me who must kill you." Son's eyes narrowed. "Who are you and what do you want?" he asked as he walked around the desk, shifting his attention back to the big American.

Bolan noted that Son was even shorter than he'd

looked sitting down. He also noted the fury in the little man's eyes when he didn't answer.

Son's hand returned to the hair on his upper lip. He nodded to the man closest to Bolan. "Check him for weapons."

The gunman handed his shotgun to the man next to him and stepped forward, opening Bolan's raincoat. He drew the Beretta from under Bolan's arm, his eyes widening slightly when he saw the sound suppressor. Handing it back over his shoulder, he pulled the Desert Eagle from Bolan's hip holster.

A patdown revealed the Benchmade knife. He continued the frisk until he was satisfied that Bolan held no further weapons. Stepping back, he turned to Son and shook his head.

Son had leaned back against his desk and folded his arms. "I will ask you again," he said. "Who are you and what do you want?"

"Like I told you, I'm looking for Mr. Vu," Bolan said. "We have business."

Son's face darkened again with anger. "That tells me what you want but not who you are," he said. He nodded to his flunky again.

The man stepped forward and, putting his entire body into the blow, backhanded Bolan across the face.

The Executioner felt the sting and tasted blood in his mouth. But the man couldn't have weighed more than one hundred and fifty pounds, and there had been no real power behind the blow.

"Who are you!" Son roared. "It is obvious you are American. CIA?"

"Just an American guy who wants to meet Mr. Vu," Bolan said calmly.

Son's anger boiled over. He launched off the desk and took two steps toward Bolan, caught himself, then looked to his underling again.

This time Bolan got three slaps.

As he cuffed the warrior the third time, an idea burst into Bolan's mind.

He noticed that Son had taken another step toward him. The little Vietnamese gangster was chomping at the bit, wanting to get his hands on his prisoner himself.

That might be the only chance the big American had against the eight 12-gauges.

Son was breathing heavily when he said, "This will be the last time I ask you. Who do you represent and why have you come to see me?" He leaned forward slightly, obviously on the verge of moving in to tear Bolan apart with his bare hands. "If you do not answer now, I will order my men to continue beating you. To death."

Bolan looked him in the eye and smiled. "Go ahead and give those orders," he said. "If none of your men can hit any harder than this goon, I'll live a long and pain-free life."

Son rushed forward, murder in his eyes.

The Executioner waited until the little man raised his fist, then reached up and grabbed Son's arm and spun him. Pulling the short, frail form in tight against his chest, he wrapped his left arm around the man and reached for Son's throat with the right. His fingers dug deep behind the trachea on one side of Son's neck, his thumb circling behind it on the other.

Son squirmed, coughed and made other unidentifiable sounds.

The shotguns that had been unconsciously lowered rose suddenly as the men readjusted their aim at the Executioner.

"All right, listen!" Bolan yelled to the men with the shotguns. "You want to shoot, go ahead! You'll get me, but you'll blow his head off, too!"

For a moment no one moved except Son, who continued to wiggle like a fish being removed from the hook. Then Bolan said, "Put the shotguns on the floor and back up against the walls!" When the men still didn't move, he gripped Son's windpipe tighter.

Son's violent movement began to lessen. Finally he slumped forward over Bolan's arm like a rag doll, unconscious.

"You don't have much time," Bolan said in a lower voice now. "In a few more seconds, your boss is going to quit breathing."

The man who had assaulted him turned to the others and spoke rapidly in Vietnamese. Quickly the men leaned forward and placed their guns on the carpet.

Bolan glanced over at Bui. The young drug dealer appeared to be in total shock. "Gather the guns and put them in a pile over here," he ordered, indicating the corner of the room behind him with a nod.

Bui didn't move. "Do it!" Bolan shouted.

The teenager moved swiftly around the room, gathering the sawed-off weapons. The Executioner snatched one from his hands as he walked past with the first armload and let go of Son's throat.

By now Son had lost consciousness, and Bolan had to hold him erect with a forearm around the neck. He jammed the barrels of the shotgun against the man's temple and waited as Bui retrieved the rest of the scatterguns.

"Now go get my pistols and knife," Bolan ordered.

Operating somewhat like a robot in a trance, Bui obeyed. A moment later the Desert Eagle, Beretta and Benchmade folding knife were back in place under Bolan's raincoat.

"I need a vehicle. Which one of you boys wants to loan Bui and me a car?"

None of the men answered.

Bolan didn't hesitate. Aiming the shotgun at a spot just to the side of the nearest man's feet, he pulled one of the triggers. The scattergun erupted like an atomic bomb against the walls of Son's office, an echo of the blast fading down the halls behind the paintings. A huge chunk disappeared from the carpet next to the man's shoes while a few pellets took the man in the ankle and foot.

He screamed as he hopped around the room on one leg.

The warrior aimed the shotgun at a man in a pin-striped business suit. "You want to give me *your* keys?" he asked. "Or would you rather walk with crutches for a while, too?"

The man reached into the side pocket of his jacket.

Bolan raised the shotgun slightly. "Be very careful what comes back out with your hand."

The man in the suit paused. Slowly his hand returned to sight. With trembling fingers he reached into his pants pocket and produced a key ring.

Bolan nodded. Still holding Son around the neck with his forearm, he leaned forward and ripped the keys from the quivering fingers. "Now," he ordered, "show me what you had in the other pocket."

The hand at the end of the suit coat looked as if it had palsy now as it returned to the side pocket. Slowly, holding the tiny weapon's grips with his thumb and index finger, the would-be trickster pulled out a minirevolver and dropped it on the floor.

"Okay," Bolan said. "Everyone on the floor, face-down, hands behind your heads. Now!"

The eight men fell forward to their faces and clasped their hands behind their necks.

Bolan turned to Bui. "You know which car is his and where it's parked?"

Bui nodded.

Bolan jerked his head toward one of the hallways behind the paintings. "And do you know how to get there?"

"Yes. But...I work for Mr. Son."

"Not anymore," Bolan said. "You heard him say he was going to kill you for bringing me here." He paused to let the information sink in. "But if you'd rather stick around and find out if he was kidding, go ahead. It's up to you."

Bui glanced at his unconscious boss, still hanging from Bolan's arm, then to the men on the floor. "Let's go," he said, his voice small and weak.

"Lead the way. And remember that if you try anything, you'll get the first bullet."

Bui gulped, then started for one of the doors that had been hidden behind the paintings. Bolan backed after him, dragging Son. As he reached the door, one of the men who lay on the ground unclasped his hands and stuck one of them under his jacket.

The pistol came out a microsecond too late. Bolan squeezed a trigger on the shotgun and sent a 12-gauge load into the man's chest. Dropping the empty weapon, the Executioner drew the Desert Eagle. He waited a moment, his eyes moving around the room to the other men. They had frozen, their faces pressed into the carpet. "No one else want to play?" he asked finally in a steady voice.

There were no answers. But Bolan wouldn't have heard them if there had been.

By the time the men's paralyzed lips had unfrozen, the Executioner, his arm still clasped around Son's neck, was following his new, and unwilling ally down the corridor.

KENJI TAKAKA SAT behind the wheel and watched Yamaguchi get out of the car. The *ninja* swung his hips seductively as he strutted down the street under the evening lights.

Takaka turned away, wondering if Yamaguchi had guessed his secret. He knew that lately he hadn't been doing as good a job of hiding it as he once had. The stress and strain of the assassinations was getting to him, and that meant he had let his defenses down in other areas.

Takaka shuddered in the coolness of the night. If he wasn't careful, his secret would be out. Yamaguchi and the other *ninja*s, while owing no particular allegiance to Yuji Tanaka and his brothers other than the money they had contracted for, would realize that Takaka couldn't be trusted. He would be killed.

It was as simple as that.

Yamaguchi sashayed down the street like a thousand-dollar hooker, which was, of course, what he intended to portray. Takaka saw him stop and con-

verse with the guard at the edge of the parking lot
and knew he would find a way to make short work
of the man's interference. The guards used to secure
the parking areas around Tiananmen Square were a
cut below even the average People's Republic soldier,
and certainly no match for the wits of a *ninja*. That,
Takaka should know. For he had been trained as a
ninja himself since birth.

Takaka watched Yamaguchi follow the guard to the
tiny white shack next to the gate. They entered, and
Takaka watched their dark silhouettes embrace. Then
he turned away, his mind traveling back over the
years to his childhood. Born into the famous Togak-
ure camp of "invisible assassins," he had always
known that he was to be a *ninja*. As early as he could
remember, his joints and muscles had been bent,
twisted and manipulated so they would remain pliable
and thus enable him to maneuver in and out of entrances and exits that would have halted the average
warrior in his tracks. He had learned the art of the
knife in all its forms, the short sword and, of course,
the throwing stars known as *shuriken* that the general
public thought of as synonymous with *ninjutsu*. His
senses had been trained through a variety of drills and
exercises until his vision functioned almost as well at
night as it did in the daylight. He could detect the
slightest change in noise. He could walk across broken glass barefoot and not be cut, or mount hundred-
year-old steps without causing the wood to creak.

Yet Kenji Takaka knew he wasn't one of the best *ninja*s in Japan. Good, but not the best. Certainly not like Yamaguchi.

He watched his fellow *ninja* descend the short steps back to ground level, then proceed to the Mercedes. He stopped at the vehicle's passenger door and picked the lock so quickly and skillfully that it would appear to the watching guards that Comrade Kwon Lee had indeed provided his whore with a key. Yamaguchi slid into the seat and out of sight.

Takaka watched the parking lot, knowing that Yamaguchi was busy rigging the Mercedes with the demolition charge. He was doing it in full view of the parking-lot guards, who even now shot curious glances his way. One of the guards had made his way to the guard shack, where he was undoubtedly talking to the man there about his "good luck" with the high-dollar prostitute. They stood laughing just outside the shack.

Would they laugh if they knew that the prostitute was in reality a man? Takaka wondered.

Yamaguchi finally exited the Mercedes and stopped to wave at the guard once more. He then turned away, crossed the street and got back into the car with Takaka. The *ninja* was laughing softly, but his eyes showed a void rather than joy. "I told the guard the meeting had run too late and I had other important men to see." He batted his eyes. "Are you sure *you* are not one of those men, Takaka?"

Takaka felt himself redden in the face as he twisted the key and pulled away from the curb. Yamaguchi clearly felt certain that he knew the secret—that Takaka was a homosexual.

Well, perhaps that was good. Perhaps Yamaguchi's belief that Takaka was gay would keep him from learning the real truth.

Kenji Takaka drove away into the night with Yamaguchi laughing softly at him in the passenger seat. He wasn't gay, as the expert *ninja* next to him believed. Homosexuality was not his secret.

Takaka's secret was the fact that he hadn't been able to drive emotion from his soul as Yamaguchi had. Nor had he been able to become amoral like Yamaguchi. Money had never been, and never would be, sufficient motivation for him to use his *ninja* skills. He needed something more concrete, something more lasting, in which to put his faith.

And for that reason he had taken his skills to the Japanese Defense Force, where he'd been assigned to the Intelligence unit.

Takaka was a *ninja,* all right, but he was also an agent for the Japanese government.

And even as he drove, he was making his case on Yamaguchi, and Yuji Tanaka and his brothers.

He hoped he'd survive long enough to testify.

DAVID MCCARTER LOOKED out over the audience of law-enforcement officers who had assembled from all parts of the world. "So in America we finally find ourselves in the same position that many of you have been in for years," he said in his Southern accent from behind the podium. "We face two enemies, one from without, the other from within. Identification of specific terrorist organizations thus becomes somewhat difficult at times because the two factions often operate in the very same ways. You see, ladies and gentlemen, terrorists also watch the news. They learn from each other's mistakes. They adopt the techniques they see working for other organizations, even if their ideologies are diametrically opposed to the other groups'. Their modus operandi become similar." He paused to clear his throat. "This makes it all too easy to misidentify perpetrators at the initial stages of an investigation."

The Phoenix Force leader looked out over the auditorium at the seventy-odd men and women listening to him. He saw some faces he recognized and others he didn't. But none of the familiar faces recognized him; of that he was certain. He had met many of the world's top counterterrorist officers over the years, but it had always been during times of combat.

And men looked different on the battlefield in combat fatigues than they did behind the podium in conservative gray suits.

"As an example of this phenomenon, we can look at two similar acts of terrorism perpetrated upon American soil in the last few years," McCarter went on. "The World Trade Center bombing and the bombing of the Murrow Federal Building in Oklahoma City." He paused to take a drink from the water glass Hong had left on the shelf beneath the top of the rostrum. "The World Trade Center came first, and we soon discovered it had been perpetrated by fundamentalist Muslims. There were many similarities between it and the subsequent explosion in Oklahoma City. Because of these similarities, many of the investigators in Oklahoma went about with blinders on during the first few hours after the bombing. They looked for anyone who might have ever even heard of the Koran. A neo-Nazi could have walked by with ten tons of TNT strapped to his back and he'd never have been noticed."

There were a few guarded chuckles from the audience. But the Oklahoma City bombing was still fresh in the memories of most, and to laugh even remotely made them all feel uncomfortable. It had been the worst act of terrorism ever recorded in the U.S., but there had been an even darker side to the mass murder than the deaths of the DEA, Secret Service, IRS and other federal employees, and that aspect of the disaster was almost too much to bear for the most hardened law-enforcement officials.

The second floor of the Alfred P. Murrow Building had contained a day-care center for the children of those government employees.

"And as you all now know, the act was perpetrated

by radical fringe elements of the right wing," McCarter went on. "These were not foreign terrorists— these were home-grown domestic crazies." He took another sip of water, then adjusted the knot in his tie. "What I am saying, ladies and gentlemen, is that the Oklahoma City bombing had so many similarities to the World Trade Center incident that our initial reaction was that it had to be perpetrated by the same group. It appeared that they had learned from their experience in New York and come back with a better bomb the second time."

The Phoenix Force leader glanced out over his notes to the third row where T. J. Hawkins sat between Gary Manning and Calvin James. He saw Hawkins jerk slightly as if he'd just been bitten by a small bug. Then Phoenix Force's newest man looked directly at the podium, nodded and tapped the bridge of his nose.

The gesture had been arranged with McCarter before the Phoenix Force leader began his presentation. It meant that Hawkins had just received a call and the cellular phone was vibrating against his skin beneath his shirt.

McCarter went on as Hawkins rose, shuffled past the other seated people in his row, then started up the aisle. "But there were things that didn't add up," the Briton said, speaking by memory now, his mind following Hawkins up the aisle. "First it was soon learned that the bomb used was a low-level explosive composed of fertilizer and diesel fuel. While this didn't rule out terrorists of Mideastern groups, it wasn't consistent with their standard operating procedures in the past.''

He glanced up to see Hawkins disappear out the door. ''Then we got lucky. The surveillance camera outside a bank down the block had panned past the federal building and caught two male Caucasians getting out of the rental truck that was later determined to have housed the explosive. Luck stayed with us. An Oklahoma highway patrolman had stopped a man driving through Perry, Oklahoma, in a car without a license tag and subsequently arrested him for carrying a concealed weapon. When the artist's composite sketch went out over the wires, journalists in Canada recognized him as a white supremacist who'd nearly beaten an old man to death in their country.'' He paused for effect. ''The matchup was made only minutes before the perpetrator was about to bond out of jail on the weapons charge.''

The Phoenix Force leader watched Hawkins enter the auditorium again and walk back down the aisle to his seat. The young commando's stride wasn't fast, and anyone who didn't know him as well as McCarter and the other members of Phoenix Force would believe exactly what Hawkins had wanted them to believe—that he had simply felt the call of nature at an inopportune time and was now returning for the rest of the speech.

"The point is, ladies and gentlemen, that it is entirely too easy to focus on one element of terrorist activity at the expense of another. Terrorists, whether foreign or domestic, have their own peculiar MOs, but they learn from each other, as well, and what appears to be a tactic unique to the Japanese Red Army today may be picked up and added to the standard operating techniques of the Irish Republican Army tomorrow." He paused for another drink of water. "Or, as in our case, the procedures used by the Muslim fundamentalists at the World Trade Center were adopted by white supremacists."

Hawkins sat down and looked at the podium. This time he tapped his nose three times in succession.

McCarter looked down at the index cards in front of him. He had perhaps another fifteen minutes prepared. But what Hawkins had just done told him not only that Stony Man had called, but there was urgent business for Phoenix Force.

"Ladies and gentlemen," McCarter said in his Southern drawl, "that concludes my presentation and I thank you." He turned and quickly walked offstage.

Hong sat in a straight-backed wooden chair in the wings. The man in the light green cadet uniform leaped to his feet, his face confused, as McCarter hurried up. "Special Agent McCarter?" Hong said, his voice reflecting concern. "Your time was not up. Is anything wrong?"

The Phoenix Force leader grasped his abdomen

with both hands. "I should have listened to your advice about breakfast, Hong," he said with a grimace on his face. "Whatever that was, I...just point me toward the nearest rest room, will you?"

Hong nodded, spun on his heel and led McCarter toward a door against the wall. The Phoenix Force leader hurried into the room, shut and locked the door behind him and waited. A minute later he flushed the toilet. Waiting again, he repeated the flushing procedure, then turned on the water in the sink and washed his hands.

McCarter opened the door and stepped out. He had dampened his face with water and appeared to be sweating. "Take me back to the room, Hong," he said weakly. "I'll get someone else to cover my speech this afternoon. I'm afraid I'm through for the day."

The young cadet was genuinely concerned as he led the Phoenix Force leader out the door toward the van.

Ten minutes later Encizo opened the door for McCarter and Hong. He, Hawkins, Manning and James had already been dropped off.

Hong walked McCarter all the way to the bedroom and began pulling back the bed covers. "Special Agent McCarter," he said, his voice worried again, "is there anything I can get you? Any medicine?" He paused and now his face grew even more worried. "It is natural sometimes to react adversely to a strange diet," he said, "but our breakfast was mild. You do not have any food allergies, do you?"

McCarter looked into the worried face and almost felt guilty for deceiving the kid. Hong was a sincere young man intent on helping them. "No, Hong," he said. "No allergies. Just a touchy intestinal tract sometimes." He lay on the bed without removing his clothes and said, "You go on, Hong, you've done everything you could. I'll be all right by tomorrow. I just need to get it out of my system."

His face still troubled, Hong bowed and left the suite.

No sooner had he left than the men of Phoenix Force gathered around McCarter's bed. "I think I brought some antacids," Manning chided.

"Too much roughage in this diet," James stated.

McCarter sat up and looked at Hawkins. "What have you got, Hawk?" he asked.

"Kurtzman's come up with a couple of things Hal wanted us aware of. First the Chinese no longer 'suspect' the CIA is behind the assassinations. They're convinced, and they're ready to start retaliating by killing Americans."

Manning nodded. "Whoever's doing this is making sure it looks like our fault," he said. "It was only a matter of time before the Reds bought it."

Hawkins went on. "Bear has also run what's happened so far through his magic machine and come up with a list of the three politburo members most likely to get hit next. Their names are Guang, Lee and Yang.''

James let out a low groan. "How are we supposed to cover all three?" he said. "It's hard enough getting away from our junior G-man baby-sitter, and—"

Hawkins held up a hand. "It gets better. Just before the call, Bear had Carmen tap into an emergency memo sent out to all of the politburo members. They pulled an all-night special at the Great Hall of the People trying to figure out how to keep from getting offed.''

McCarter leaned forward. "That'll help some. At least it gets all three candidates in one place."

Hawkins grinned. "Better than that," he said. "Kurtzman found out that Guang is currently out of the country on a diplomatic trip to India, and Yang's with his family on vacation in Bermuda. Neither could be contacted in time to make the meeting."

"Then that leaves only Lee?" Encizo asked.

"Yeah," Hawkins confirmed.

McCarter shot up off the bed and began to change into his jeans and field jacket. "The meeting still going on?" he asked.

"It was when Barbara called. But there's no telling when it'll break up. As scared as the politburo may be, it's almost noon and they aren't machines. They'll have to call a halt to it soon."

McCarter looked at the men around him as he pulled on his athletic shoes. Of all the Phoenix Force commandos, Encizo would draw the least attention on the streets of Beijing. Manning was big enough to be noticeable, and James would attract extra scrutiny— McCarter hadn't seen a black man on the street since they'd arrived.

"Rafe," McCarter said, "get ready, you're coming with me." He turned to Manning. "Gary, you're already scheduled for a panel discussion this afternoon, right?"

"Affirmative, Chief." Manning grinned. "'The Controlled Use of Explosive Devices as an Entry Team Technique,'" he said, quoting the brochure.

"Good." McCarter nodded. "I know it's a pain in the arse, but we need to keep this Police Institute cover going as long as possible. Eventually it'll blow. But until then it's useful."

The Briton turned to James. "Calvin," he said, "you'll have to step in and cover my lecture on the AFIS fingerprint system this afternoon. Give my apologies and make a few polite jokes about my dysentery."

He turned to the newest member of Phoenix Force. "Hawk, figure a way to distract the hall lady again. They'll be watching the roof, and Rafe and I will have to take the stairs. After we're gone, you and the others hang loose and be ready if we call."

He paused to draw a deep breath. "Gentlemen, I've got a feeling things are going to break loose fast. When they do, and our cover is blown, you know who the cops are going to suspect of being CIA assassins first, don't you?''

The men of Phoenix Force nodded. None of them had to be told. As soon as the five "Police Institute delegates" disappeared, they'd be the first to be suspected.

McCarter turned back to Encizo. "Rafe, get ready."

Encizo spread his arms and looked down at his shoes. "What's wrong?" he asked. "My shoes don't match my bag or what? I'm ready."

For the first time McCarter noticed that while he'd been talking, the Cuban had changed into faded blue jeans, an OD green field jacket similar to his own, a black T-shirt and cheap black athletic shoes like the ones they'd seen on the feet of the Chinese.

McCarter smiled as he led Encizo to the door. That's what he liked about leading the men of Phoenix Force.

When you were the leader of leaders, your men were *always* ready.

CHAPTER SIX

Carl Lyons followed the men of the Aryan Brotherhood down the street to where they cut across the corner lot of a shoe store. The Able Team leader lagged back out of sight as they crossed the street at an angle toward a one-story frame shack, two houses from the corner. Stepping over broken bicycles, toys and other assorted garbage as they went, they passed between a Dodge Ram pickup in the gravel driveway and an aged Ford Thunderbird on concrete blocks in the front yard, then made their way up three rotting wooden steps and past a broken washing machine sitting on the front porch.

The big ex-cop shook his head in disgust at the slatternly appearance of the house's exterior. White *supremacists?* He would be more inclined to call them white trash.

Lyons slowed his pace, sauntering along until the men had opened the front door. He caught a brief glimpse of a flag on the wall inside. Unless his eyes were playing tricks on him, the flag bore a swastika.

The Able Team leader squinted after the closing door. At first glance, Oriental activists teaming up with white neo-Nazis didn't seem likely. But he had seen Topknot pass these guys an envelope, and that envelope more than likely contained money.

If so, this wouldn't be the first time the old "long green" had turned natural enemies into strange bedfellows.

Lyons reached the shoe store and looked inside the broad picture-window front. He needed a place to wait and watch until something else broke. The tight boots on his feet made the decision easy. The shoe store meant he could kill two birds with one stone.

He jerked the face mike from his headset and dropped it into his pocket. With only the earphones in place, he looked like any of the hundreds of thousands of other people one encountered these days going about their lives with a personal stereo leading the way.

Entering the self-serve store, Lyons scanned the signs above the racks for his size. A silent prayer escaped his lips when he saw the number 11 near the front. Benches were scattered along the aisles, so he could sit down, try on shoes and watch the ramshackle house across the street at the same time.

Quickly selecting a pair of gray-and-white nylon street hikers, Lyons watched the window as he tugged off the cowboy boots and put them on. Piling the cracked leather boots in the box, he stood and headed for the checkout counter.

A pretty young woman smiled at him from behind the counter. "Will this be all, sir?" she asked as she ran the box across the price scanner.

Lyons glanced over his shoulder. The door to the house across the street was still closed. "You know," he said, "I don't know. I think I'll try on a few others. The prices are right. But let me go ahead and pay you for these now. I've got a ride coming, and I might have to leave while you're busy."

The woman smiled again. "Okay." She took the fifty-dollar bill he handed her and made change.

"Mind throwing these away for me?" the Able Team leader asked, handing her the cowboy boots.

She tried to keep from wrinkling her nose as she took the smelly leather. She wasn't quite successful. "Gladly," she replied, and dropped them into the trash can behind her.

Lyons returned to the bench where he'd found the hiking boots, pulled a pair of athletic shoes from the rack and sat back down. The salesgirl disappeared to the back of the store, so he didn't bother to try them on.

Satisfied that there was no one within hearing distance, Lyons reattached the face mike. "Able One to Two," he whispered. "Gadgets, you there?"

"Affirmative, Ironman. But Topknot isn't." Schwarz paused. "Guy must have turned off somewhere. I don't think he's even come back to the demonstration."

Lyons frowned. Something was beginning to gnaw at his subconscious, but he couldn't put his finger on it. "Okay," he said. "You heard from Pol?"

"He's coming in now and then, but there's bad interference. Must be too close to some high lines. Hey, wait a minute." Lyons heard Able Two call to Three. Scratches and a screech sounded over the airwaves, then Schwarz came back. "He's still outside the bar, Ironman. You pick him up at all?"

"Just a few snaps, crackles and pops. I'll have to go through you if I need him." The Able Team leader went on to explain his position. "I don't know exactly what our goose-steppers here are up to, but I'm beginning to get a bad feeling. What's the crowd doing?"

"Still as peaceful as a backyard barbecue at the Dalai Lama's," Schwarz said. "They've made the turn north on Meridian. Their permit states they plan to head back east when they reach Thirty-sixth Street. Wait a minute. I'm getting something from Pol...." His voice trailed off.

As Lyons waited, he suddenly saw the front door across the street open. The Nazi flag appeared on the wall inside again, then a head he hadn't seen before peered out. A moment later five men, including the two who had met with Topknot, came down the steps.

Each carried a suitcase in one hand, a can of Coors beer in the other.

The big ex-cop squinted at the luggage. The cases had been made for clothing, and that's exactly what they might contain. They looked harmless. On the other hand, they were large enough to hide short-barreled carbines, shotguns or a multitude of pistols.

The suitcases could also be filled with enough explosives to blow up another structure like the Murrow Federal Building.

Lyons drew in a deep breath. The people of Oklahoma City had seen enough explosions from the kind of subhumans he saw before him now to last several lifetimes. They didn't need another.

The Able Team leader stood up quickly as the two men who'd met with Topknot slid into the Dodge Ram pickup. One of the Aryan Brotherhood men broke from the group and hurried around the side of the house. A moment later an old Plymouth station wagon suddenly emerged, stopping long enough to load the remaining two men and their suitcases. Then the pickup backed out of the gravel driveway and turned toward Pennsylvania Avenue with the Plymouth following.

Lyons had made it to the door of the shoe store by the time the two vehicles turned north on Penn toward Thirty-sixth Street. "Gadgets!" he shouted into the microphone. "Gadgets! They're moving! North toward where the marchers will be!"

"I'm not surprised," Schwarz came back on the airwaves. "Able Three just told me that ten of the meanest-looking Orientals he's ever seen just left the bar." He paused for a moment, and Lyons heard him take a deep breath. "They loaded what looked like rifle cases from where Pol was sitting."

THE TUNNEL OUTSIDE Son's office was roughly twenty yards long. What appeared to be a gray steel door stood directly ahead at the end. Bolan couldn't be sure. Discerning detail was impossible. The bare bulbs of dimly glowing overhead lights cast eerie, graveyardlike shadows over the concrete walls and dirty tile floor and distorted the images.

Bui led the way, his shoes clicking rapidly across the tile. Bolan's rubber-soled boots followed more quietly. Son, still unconscious, was still in the big American's headlock, but the little man was so light Bolan had lifted the Vietnamese pimp almost completely off the ground. Only the heels of Son's shoes dragged along the tile.

The Executioner had slammed the tunnel door behind him after firing the shotgun shell into the chest of the man who had drawn the gun. If the other flunkies came unglued from the floor where he'd left them and decided to pursue, he'd hear it open.

They did.

And he did.

The door creaked before Bolan and Bui had made

it halfway down the hall. The Executioner whirled, spinning Son with him. A man wearing an electric blue double-knit polyester suit stood framed in the doorway, his eyes trying to adjust to the dimmer light inside the tunnel. The barrels of his sawed-off Rossi moved back and forth across the hall.

Bolan wished momentarily that he had the sound-suppressed Beretta in his hand rather than the ear-popping .44 handcannon, then pushed the useless desire from his mind. There was no time to holster the Desert Eagle and draw the 9 mm pistol, and he couldn't go for the Beretta with his left hand without dropping Son.

Squeezing the Desert Eagle's trigger, he sent a massive .44 bullet streaking down the hallway into the man's throat. The noise threatened to deafen him in the narrow confines of the tunnel, but the 240-grain hollowpoint did its job at the other end.

The momentum knocked the man in the leisure suit back out of the doorway as a flood of crimson washed down to stain the electric blue.

Bolan's ears still rang with the explosion as another foolish gunner stepped in to take the first man's place. Bolan fired again. His next 240-grain hollowpoint hit the middle of the man's chest.

The Executioner backpedaled, with the Desert Eagle still covering the door. No one else stuck his head into the tunnel, and suddenly Bolan felt his back slam into Bui. The sound of Bui, in turn, ramming into the metal door rang dully through the .44-caliber roar still in Bolan's ears.

"Open the door," Bolan ordered.

Bui twisted the knob, pushed the steel forward and stepped to the side to allow the American through.

Bolan started to step through the opening, then caught a glimpse of Bui out of the corner of his eye. The teenager's eyes were wide and he was holding his breath.

Shoving the Desert Eagle's barrel into the young man's face, Bolan said, "You first."

Bui's eyes flickered with horror. He started to speak, but Bolan prodded him with the Desert Eagle. *"Now,"* he said through clenched teeth.

The Vietnamese turned toward the door. "Do not shoot!" he screamed. "It is Bui!"

Bolan stepped in behind the young man and shoved him through the doorway. He followed, crouching.

Two men with pistols stood at the edge of a parking lot. The one on Bolan's right wore an open-collared white shirt and gripped a 9 mm Cao Dai NATO copy of the U.S. Government Model .45.

Bolan swung the Desert Eagle his way, hammering out two rounds that took the man in the upper chest. Pulling the pistol back behind Bui, he turned to the man on his left.

This gunner wore a black shirt and slacks, and held a Cambodian 9 mm pistol. He fired once, his jittery hands sending the round high over both Bui and the American.

Bolan heard the round hit the concrete building behind him and go singing off a second before he triggered the Desert Eagle. His first round struck the pistol in the man's outstretched hand and glanced off into his arm. The man in black threw back his head and screamed. But his wail of agony didn't last long.

The soldier's next round took him squarely between the eyes and sent him flipping backward to the pavement.

The Desert Eagle's slide locked open, empty. Bolan jammed it back into his hip holster and tore the Beretta from shoulder leather. Jamming the sound suppressor into Bui's back, he prodded the teenager forward. "Find the car that fits these keys and do it fast."

Bui glanced over his shoulder, swallowed hard, then moved forward through the parking lot. Bolan followed with Son still in tow. They came to a halt next to a Chevy Suburban, and Bui looked at the warrior for further orders.

Bolan shoved the keys into the youth's hand. "You drive." Opening the back door, he threw Son inside, then held the gun on Bui as he circled for the passenger door.

As soon as Bolan was inside the vehicle, Bui twisted the key and the Suburban fired to life. Bolan waved him out of the parking lot with the barrel of the Beretta.

They were just about to turn into the street when the remaining hardmen raced around the side of the building. Seeing what had happened to the gunners who attempted to follow the intruders down the tunnel, they had evidently opted to exit the building through the front door and approach from the side.

Bolan hit the button to lower the window. He flipped down the front grip below the Beretta's barrel and held it in his left hand. Aiming the machine pistol through the window, he thumbed the fire-selector switch to 3-round burst.

The gunner in the lead spotted the Suburban and fired. The short-barreled scattergun sent a load of buckshot toward the vehicle, but by the time it had reached its target most of the pellets had spread to the sides. A few bounced harmlessly off the windshield as Bui turned the corner into the street.

Bolan held the Beretta's trigger back, sending a 3-round burst splattering into the shotgunner's chest and abdomen. As the man fell, Bolan let up on the trigger, then waited for the Suburban to carry the sights to the next gunner in line. Bolan squeezed again.

The first two rounds cut through the second gunman's midsection, causing him to drop his shotgun. The third round of the burst carried on to the third man in the procession.

The soldier let up on the trigger once more, then

squeezed again as the fourth man fell in line with the barrel. Bui had increased the Suburban's speed now, and only the first 9 mm jacketed hollowpoint struck home. But it was more than enough, drilling through one of the gunner's ears and out the other.

The second round of the burst bore into the arm of the last man in line. He spun recklessly. The third round flew wild as the Suburban continued to increase speed.

Bolan flipped the selector back to semiauto. As they raced past the spinning man, he twisted out the window and lined up the sights.

A lone 9 mm round struck Son's gunner squarely between the shoulder blades as he whirled. His spin stopped suddenly, and he fell forward to his knees, then on his face.

Bolan pulled the Beretta back inside the Suburban and turned it toward Bui. Behind him he heard Son begin to stir. "So you knew there would be men waiting outside the tunnel?" he asked.

Bui looked like a boa swallowing a pig as the lump went down his throat. Staring straight ahead at the road, he nodded slowly. "There are always men at the exits," he almost whispered. "I wasn't trying to get you killed...I just didn't want them to shoot me."

Bolan nodded. "I understand," he said. "Bui?"

"What?"

"Look at me."

The youth turned to face the soldier as the Suburban took a corner.

Bolan raised the Beretta and fired.

The lone round passed a micrometer under the tip of Bui's earlobe.

The teenager screamed.

"Relax," Bolan said as the Suburban moved on through the night. "It barely left a scratch. What you're feeling is the burn." He waited while the teenager reached up to reassure himself his ear was still there, then said, "But you try anything like that again, and it won't just be your ear that gets shot off."

McCARTER SWUNG the suite door open and stepped back to let Hawkins into the hall. As soon as the Phoenix Force commando had passed, he let the door swing back, catching it an inch away from the frame. Encizo moved in at his side.

McCarter watched Hawkins walk down the hall until he was out of sight, then listened to the man's footsteps, estimating when he would reach the woman at the desk.

"Well, howdy, ma'am," Hawkins said. "Just thought I'd step out for a breath of fresh air."

A machine-gun burst of rapidly spoken Mandarin came from the old woman at the desk.

"Yeah, right, whatever you say there, ma'am," Hawkins said as he walked away. "I'll be back to see you soon."

A moment later McCarter heard the door to the stairs swing open. The old woman's voice grew louder and more shrill. He heard her chair scoot back against the tile, then her own footsteps pattered through the door.

The Phoenix Force leader waited until he heard the sound of the door closing, then peered around the door frame down the hall. A smile crossed his face. Just as he hoped, the hall monitor had followed Hawkins onto the stairs. Without turning to Encizo, he said, "Let's go."

The two Phoenix Force warriors hurried down the hall to the stairs behind the vacant desk. McCarter peered through the window in the door and saw that the landing was empty. He cracked the door and heard the sound of footsteps on the floor above him. The woman's voice rattled on.

"Awful nice of you to escort me," Hawkins said, his voice coming down the steps. "But it ain't really necessary. Just goin' up to the roof for some fresh air." Both sets of footsteps continued to ascend the steps.

McCarter opened the door the rest of the way and stepped on the landing. Encizo followed, and they hurried down the steps away from both Hawkins and the old lady.

Through the window to the third floor, McCarter saw another hall monitor at her desk. From the back, she could have been cloned from the one on their floor. He led the way on down to the second floor, cast a brief glance through the window to make sure the monitor wasn't watching, then continued down the steps to the ground floor.

The Phoenix Force leader stopped to peer carefully out the window. From where he stood, he could see the lobby and part of the front desk. The clerk behind the counter appeared to be reading a magazine.

Encizo glanced at his watch. "Ten, nine, eight..." he whispered. He continued counting. A second after he said, "One," the phone on the shelf behind the front desk rang shrilly.

The man abandoned his magazine and turned around. "Right on time," Encizo said. "Anyone else in the lobby?"

McCarter shook his head. "No one I can see. But my view is restricted. Come on. We'll have to chance it." He opened the door, stepped through and held it for Encizo.

The Briton breathed a sigh of relief as soon as he could see the whole lobby. It was empty except for the clerk, who stood facing away from them, the phone pressed to his ear. Encizo took the lead, hurrying silently across the lobby toward the front door. McCarter fell in behind, his gaze locked to the back of the clerk's head.

"Ice?" the clerk said into the phone. "I very sorry, hotel not have ice." He paused for either Calvin James or Gary Manning to speak, then said, "No, you no understand. It not that hotel have no room service. Hotel have no ice. No ice—even you come yourself."

Encizo reached the steps that led down to the front door, descended them and cut quickly around the corner out of sight.

McCarter turned toward the door. He was halfway down the same steps when he heard the voice yell, "Hey, you. Where you go?"

The Briton turned back to see the clerk still holding the receiver in his hand but looking squarely at him. "Who, me?" he said.

"You, guy, you," the clerk said. "Where you go? You no have escort. Must have Hong."

"That's okay," McCarter said. "Just thought I'd run down to the corner for a pack of cigarettes. I know where it is." He started to turn again.

"No!" the clerk yelled again. "You no go! You wait. I call nice escort."

McCarter sighed. He forced a smile and a shrug, then nodded and started back up the steps. It was still too early to break cover, and he'd already drawn enough suspicion with his escapade the night before. Besides, Encizo had made it without being seen. The Cuban knew where he had stashed the FEG .380s and would get them, then go on to recon the politburo meeting.

The Phoenix Force leader walked to the desk and stopped. It was worth at least one more try. "Really," he drawled, "I'm just going a block down. I can find it and be back in five minutes."

The desk clerk just shook his head and dialed the phone.

Fifteen minutes later McCarter and Hong were buying cigarettes at the kiosk a block from the hotel, and five minutes after that the Phoenix Force leader was back in the suite. He took a seat on the couch in the living room and looked at the Chinese cigarettes.

Things could be worse, he reasoned as Hawkins, James and Manning entered the room to find out what had gone wrong. He'd had to buy the cigarettes as part of the cover for getting caught.

But he might have had to smoke them, too.

ENCIZO HEARD THE VOICE a split second after he'd ducked around the corner. A moment later he heard McCarter answer, then the Phoenix Force leader's boots padded back up the steps.

The Cuban waited, hidden by the wall between the doorway and a picture window. From inside the lobby came the voices of both McCarter and the clerk, but their words were indistinguishable. Moving carefully to the window, Encizo cupped a hand against the glass and peered around the edge.

McCarter had been busted—that was clear. And he wouldn't be getting out of it unless he wanted to break cover.

Encizo waited until the clerk turned to dial the

phone, then produced a pair of black plastic sunglasses from a pocket of his fatigue jacket and
wrapped them around his face. He had purchased the
shades at the airport after seeing half the men and
women sporting similar eye wear. From another
pocket he pulled a rumpled navy blue baseball cap.
They, too, were popular with Chinese men, and with
his eyes and hair now hidden, he hoped his light
brown skin and five-eight frame would be regarded
as that of a slightly tall Chinese.

The Cuban scurried away from the window and
down the block. At the corner he turned toward the
warehouse where McCarter had stashed the guns and
slowed his pace.

Encizo frowned as he walked along, passing other
men similarly dressed in the fatigue jackets and jeans.
At that time of day, the warehouse would be inhabited. Somehow he had to get to the roof, then back
down again. He couldn't do that without some kind
of subterfuge or a diversion, and how he could im-
plement either without speaking was beyond him. He
knew no Mandarin.

Turning the corner again, Encizo walked past the
warehouse with his gaze straight ahead. As he drew
abreast of the door, he saw what he'd feared. Just
beyond the doorway was a man wearing some kind
of police-military uniform.

The Cuban didn't recognize the uniform or insig-
nia, but the clipboard on the desk in front of the man

made his purpose all too clear. He made sure everyone who entered signed his or her name and noted their purpose for entering. They probably had to sign out, as well.

Encizo walked on, still wondering how he could get past the man without speaking. At the alley he took a quick 360-degree glance around him, then ducked in. Following the rough brick surface to the alley that ran between the warehouse and hotel, he turned and looked overhead.

Four stories above he could see the roof of the warehouse. Another story higher, on the other side of the alley, stood the top of the Beijing Plaza. Encizo shook his head as he walked along. McCarter had made one hell of a jump the previous night. The Briton was lucky the rest of the team hadn't had to come out to mop him up off the ground.

The back door to the warehouse stood open, but through the opening Encizo could see a half-dozen men loading crates with a forklift. He walked by. He had seen no guard at the rear entry, but the men inside were sure to notice him if he just walked in. Even if he made it past them, he had to get up four flights of stairs and onto the roof without being challenged. Then he had to get back down again. The answer to his quandary suddenly came to him.

There wasn't an answer. At least not now. He'd have to go to the politburo meeting, scout it out, then come back for the .380s after the warehouse was closed for the night.

His mind made up, Encizo hurried from the alley to the street and saw a cab passing. He decided to risk it, holding out his hand and waiting as the car came to a halt. He jumped into the back and leaned forward across the seat, making no attempt to pass as Chinese at this close distance. "Tiananmen Square," he said.

The driver, an elderly man with a long, wispy mustache, eyed him suspiciously.

"You speak any English?" Encizo asked.

The man looked at him blankly.

"Spanish?"

He drew another blank.

"French?"

The old man's face lit up. *"Oui."*

Encizo nodded. His own French left something to be desired, but it was better than playing charades at this point. "I want to go see Tiananmen Square," he said in French, grinning. "Had a meeting back at the People's Security Institute—you know, the symposium going on?" He hoped his broken French was getting through.

The driver continued to stare.

Encizo laughed to break the ice. "Had to lose my escort," he said. "Kid wanted to take me to the Temple of Confucius."

The driver didn't return the laugh until Encizo

reached into his pocket and pulled out a roll of yuan bills. He finally smiled and nodded as the Cuban pressed several into his hand, obviously delighted both at the money and that the Communist system had been diverted. He threw the car into gear and took off.

Encizo and the man rode in silence through the streets of Beijing. The Cuban watched through the windows, seeing noodle shops and other street vendors on the sidewalks. Finally they turned a corner, and Tiananmen Square appeared in the distance.

Encizo had opened his mouth to direct the driver to the curb when a blast erupted. The taxi shook with the force, shimmying back and forth as did all the cars on the street. To their sides the windows in storefronts shattered. Ahead, on the other side of a guarded parking lot, Encizo saw what looked to have once been an automobile.

The Cuban stared ahead. He didn't have to be told what had happened or to whom.

Or what it meant to the men of Phoenix Force and the United States of America.

LYONS'S NEW GRAY STREET hikers got their baptism by fire as he sprinted down Pennsylvania Avenue. Six blocks ahead he could still see the Dodge Ram and Plymouth. Traffic on Penn wasn't heavy but it wasn't light, either, and while the other cars slowed the pickup and car somewhat, the big ex-cop knew they wouldn't slow the Aryan Brotherhood men enough. Gradually the two vehicles began to increase their lead.

The former LAPD detective raced down the sidewalk. "Pol, you there?" he shouted into his face mike.

"Barely picking you up now, Ironman," Blancanales came back weakly. "I'm in some kind of dead zone...but I've commandeered some wheels and I ought to be out of it—" his voice suddenly rose several decibels and became more clear "—soon."

"You just did get out of it," Lyons panted as he sprinted on. "You still got your people in sight?"

"Affirmative, Ironman. They're heading north. My guess is that they're going to cut off the march."

Lyons nodded as he ran, watching the Dodge and Plymouth become tiny specks in the distance. Two blocks farther up the street he saw a short shopping strip. "Gadgets, you with me?" he huffed into the mike.

"Heading north on Meridian," Gadgets replied. "I'm pulling the caboose for the march right now."

"Stay there and keep your eyes peeled," Lyons said. "Something's going down, and I'd guess it'll be from both ends."

A half block from the shopping strip now, Lyons saw several Harley-Davidson motorcycles parked along the sidewalk. Three men in denim, leather and biker colors stood around the bikes. On the backs of their sleeveless jackets Lyons could see patches the shape of the state of Oklahoma. As he drew closer, the Able Team leader was able to read the letters on the patches: Naysayers M.C.

Lyons slowed as he neared the bikes, focusing on a tall man who weighed at least three hundred pounds. The biker faced him, leaning against the saddle of a freshly painted black-and-orange Harley. He had shoulder-length hair tied back in a ponytail, a black bandanna wrapped over his skull, and rings in both ears. The other two Naysayers were smaller but no less gaudy in dress.

All three turned to Lyons as he ground to a halt.

The Able Team leader looked the big man in the eyes. "I'd like to borrow your bike," he said.

"Right, dude."

"Let me put it another way," Lyons said. "I *need* to borrow your bike."

The three men laughed. "You sure are one crazy mother," the fat man said.

Lyons glanced down the street. The Dodge and Plymouth were out of sight now. He knew where they were headed and could figure out their route but if he got there too late...

The Able Team leader looked back to the big biker. "You sell dope?" he asked.

"You a cop?" the biker asked.

"No. You've got my word on it."

"Then yeah, I got a little crank if you want it. But you don't look like the type."

"I'm not," Lyons said.

The bearded biker grinned. "Want it for your old lady?" he asked. "Get her high and get off?"

"No," Lyons said. "I just wanted to know if you sold dope. That way I won't feel so bad when I do this." His right fist suddenly shot forward into the bridge of the bearded biker's nose. A sharp crack sounded as both bone and cartilage snapped. Blood spurted from the biker's nose as he somersaulted backward over his motorcycle.

The big ex-cop didn't give the other Naysayers time to react. Without turning, he threw a back-fist that caught the man to his right squarely in the Adam's apple.

The third biker, taller than the first but half as heavy, shot a hand inside the pocket of his dirty, frayed jeans.

Lyons wondered briefly what he was going for, then resigned himself to the fact that he'd never know. His foot lashed out, giving the new gray street hikers their second field test of the day as the lug sole of the left shoe made contact with the groin of the skinny man.

With all three Naysayers on the ground, Lyons jumped on the orange-and-black Harley and kicked the starter.

The Dodge Ram and Plymouth were nowhere to be

seen as Lyons weaved in and out of traffic, ignoring the horns of protest his actions prompted. "Able One to Two," he shouted into the wind. "Position, Gadgets?"

"Still on Meridian but getting ready to turn back east," Schwarz came back. "Everything still looks peaceful."

"Pol?"

"Coming up fast on Meridian." Blancanales's voice came in strong now. "I can see the front of the marchers turning the corner now. They're... Wait a minute...yeah...my guys have suddenly slowed down."

Lyons cut between a slow-moving Chevy and an oncoming Isuzu. "They don't want to catch them on Meridian," he reasoned out loud. "They're waiting for them to turn into the Nazis. They're going to catch them in a cross fire."

"Looks like it to me," Pol agreed. "The press will blame it on the Aryans, and it'll look like the Orientals were just defending themselves."

An older-model Cadillac suddenly pulled onto Penn from a side street in front of Lyons. The big ex-cop had time to see the startled faces of an old man in a hat and his wife in her scarf before he had to lay the bike on its side.

Sparks flew from the motorbike as it slid across the pavement toward the Cadillac. Lyons skidded after it, feeling the concrete rip through his jeans and then his skin. A thud like a distant bomb sounded, and a huge dent appeared in the driver's door as the bike struck the Caddie. The car jerked to a halt.

Lyons bounded back to his feet. He glanced down as he ran toward the overturned motorcycle and saw blood streaming down the leg on which he'd slid. Almost the entire left pant leg was gone.

One look inside the Caddie told Lyons that the old couple were shaken up but not hurt. He righted the Harley, jumped astride and kicked it to life once more.

Nearing Thirty-sixth Street, Lyons saw that the street had been blocked off to traffic. His eyes scanned the roadside where cars had parked bumper to bumper. Neither the Plymouth nor the Dodge was anywhere in sight.

Between Thirty-fourth and Thirty-fifth, the Able Team leader shot past an alley and caught a glimpse of steel out of the corner of his eye. Leaning hard to his left, he skidded through a U-turn and headed back.

Parked twenty yards into the alley, in front of a row of corrugated trash cans, Lyons saw both the Plymouth and pickup.

Cutting the handlebars low again, the big ex-cop twisted the throttle and roared back toward Thirty-sixth. Ignoring the protests of several cops stationed behind the barricades, he gunned the engine again and crashed through the nearest sawhorse. Turning left toward the oncoming march, he raced down the middle of the street.

The crowd of onlookers who had come to watch the show cheered Lyons on as he raced by, his eyes canvassing the sides of the street for the Aryan Brotherhood men and their suitcases. Topknot's plan was all too clear in Lyons's brain now.

A few well-placed shots by the Aryans would give the Orientals the excuse they needed to fire back. Or maybe the Orientals would start the firing. It didn't really matter, because killing each other wasn't what the men he had followed, or those Pol was trailing, had in mind.

Their real objective was to kill the innocent people marching down the street.

And any of the demonstrators who didn't catch a bullet would stand a good chance of being trampled in the panic that resulted.

Lyons roared on, seeing the oncoming demonstrators less than a block away now.

"Ironman!" Blancanales's voice suddenly said in Lyons's ear. "My subjects just cut down Thirty-fifth and parked two blocks ahead of the protestors. They're getting out now—they're uncasing the rifles."

Lyons had started to answer when a flicker of movement ahead and to the side caught his eye. He let up on the throttle and tapped the brake to slow the

Harley as his eyes focused on a row of bushes outside a small church.

Two of the men he had seen come out of the house knelt within the branches and leaves. Their suitcases lay open before them, and as Lyons watched, one of them pulled out an M-16. The other produced a scoped Mauser SP-66.

Lyons squeezed the brake harder and the Harley fishtailed, threatening to overturn as he guided it into the parking lot to one side of the church. The men in the bushes had all the bases covered. The M-16 would cast a deadly, all-encompassing spray over the marchers. The scoped sniper rifle would pinpoint specific targets.

That was bad enough. What was worse was that there were still three of the Aryans unaccounted for. They had to be hiding somewhere else with who-knew-what kind of weapons.

Lyons didn't have to wonder where they were for long.

As he guided the motorcycle across the parking lot toward the men in the bushes, the first rounds rang out across the street. Drawing the Colt Python, the Able Team leader twisted the throttle back again.

CHAPTER SEVEN

Small, weak, pitiful little sounds came from the seat behind the Executioner.

Twisting, Bolan reached into the back, grasped Son by the scruff of the neck and jerked the little man's face up. "Welcome back to the world of the living, Son."

For a moment the Vietnamese gangster's eyes refused to focus. Then the fury Bolan had seen earlier returned. His lips clamped tight in a snarl.

"Tell Bui how to get to Mr. Vu's."

Son still didn't speak.

Bolan sighed. Pulling Son closer, he pushed the man's frail chest against the seat. With his other hand he drew the Benchmade knife, stuck the tip of his index finger into the bottom of the opening hole and flipped the blade open.

Son stared at the smooth steel shining in the moonlight that drifted in through the windows. The snarl vanished.

Bolan held the knife to the man's throat. "Son,"

he said quietly, "I don't have the time or desire to make this a long process." Twisting further in his seat, he reached up and grabbed one end of the wispy mustache with his free hand.

Son winced as the hairs pulled the tender skin between his nose and upper lip.

Slowly, methodically Bolan cut the mustache from the left side of the gangster's face. When he'd finished, he rubbed his fingers back and forth, letting the feathery hair fall in front of Son's face.

The man looked at him with the almost uncontrollable anger again. Almost uncontrollable, for the same hate-filled eyes had room for terror, and the terror held his temper in check.

The Executioner looked into the fearful face and said, "Direct us to Mr. Vu. I won't ask you again. If you don't answer, more-painful parts of your anatomy are going to start dropping off just like your mustache."

Son took a deep breath. His upper lip began to quiver, and he raised his hand nervously to curl his mustache. Finding only a stubble of hair, he changed hands, furiously twisting the side that still remained. "Bien Hoa," he whispered.

Bolan dropped Son and turned to Bui. "Let's go," he said.

The village of Bien Hoa lay twenty miles from Ho Chi Minh City on the banks of the Dong-Nai River. The center of the country's sculpture-and-pottery trade, it bordered Vietnam's famous hunting grounds of Cum Tien and the Lagna plain. Years earlier the American aid program had built a four-lane highway from Ho Chi Minh City to this nucleus of Vietnamese art, and it was onto this road that Bui turned as Bolan settled in for the drive.

The big American glanced into the back seat at his captive. Much of the little man's courage had been lost with his gunmen, and the rest had floated away with the wispy hairs Bolan had cut off. The gangster seemed to have accepted his fate.

But it wouldn't hurt to keep an eye on him just the same. Bolan pulled down the sun shade in front of him and saw a mirror fixed to the back. He positioned it so he could look at the man, and made sure Son saw him do so.

According to Bui, Mr. Vu was the top underworld figure in Ho Chi Minh City. He dealt in gambling, narcotics and the sale of information both political and criminal, but his real money maker was white slavery. All of that boiled down to the fact that he'd be holed up in an office or house somewhere and have even tighter security than Son had had.

The Executioner had no intention of wasting valuable time as he had with Son. He suspected more than ever now that it wasn't the warlords of the Golden Triangle who were financing the Confederation of Southeast Asia. But before he went after the real money behind the CSA, he needed that suspicion confirmed. And if anyone knew who actually was backing the CSA, it would be Vu.

Bolan concentrated on his breathing, taking the air in through his nose before letting it escape from his mouth. He needed sleep, but he wasn't likely to get any for a while. The next-best thing was relaxation.

He continued thinking while he rested. He had to talk to Vu; there was no way around it. And unless he wanted to get tied up again as he had with Son, he'd have to somehow get to the man and still keep the upper hand. The way he saw it, there were two possible approaches.

Son knew Vu, and Bolan might be able to order the gangster to take him through Vu's security as a confederate. But any new face coming in would sound a double security alert, regardless of who was providing the introduction.

In short, Bolan knew he could find himself in a trap similar to the one Bui had led him into at Son's casino.

The direct approach was a better choice this time. Hit hard, hit fast and don't give the enemy time to react. A hard strike would be made more difficult by the fact that he had two unfriendlies in his custody, but it was still the better of the two plans.

The village of Bien Hoa appeared in the distance as the sun began to rise. Bolan turned in the seat once more. "Okay, Son," he said. "Does Vu work out of an office or house?"

Son looked up from the floor. "Both," he said. "He has an office in his house."

"Where is it?"

Son looked down at his hands in his lap. "On a hill overlooking the river, not far from the School of Applied Arts."

Bolan turned to Bui. "You know where it is?"

"The school, yes," he said. "Not Mr. Vu's house."

"I will direct you once we reach the school," Son said from the back seat.

Bui pulled off the highway and entered Bien Hoa. They drove down a shady lane as the birds of morning awakened and began their first songs of the day. Bolan watched out the window as they passed the Buu-Son Temple where he remembered seeing a fifteenth-century granite statue of Cham origin years ago when he'd been on R&R during the war. Prior to its discovery, the statue had been hidden for several centuries in a tree trunk if he remembered correctly, and he wondered briefly if it was still there or if the Communists had ruled it "subversive" as they had so much Vietnamese art.

Bolan looked down the road, forgetting about the statue. He wasn't in the village to study art. He was here to find out what Vu knew about the Confederation.

Any way he had to.

They left the center of town and drove toward the Dong-Nai, passing the School of Applied Arts and then taking a side road. Son directed them through several more turns, then suddenly a house appeared in the distance atop a hill.

Bolan guessed they called it a house. It looked more like a palace. A long, winding driveway led off the road and up the hill.

"Pull over," Bolan ordered.

The teenager didn't hesitate.

The soldier turned in his seat once more. "How many guards does Vu have?"

The gangster shrugged.

Bolan's arm shot over the seat, his thumb and index finger grasping what remained of Son's mustache. He tugged sharply forward.

Son screamed and slammed against the back of the seat again. "I don't know! Twenty? Thirty? Maybe more if he's expecting trouble. Maybe less if he isn't."

"Tell me about the layout."

"I don't know—"

The Benchmade knife leaped out of Bolan's pocket, and the blade flashed open.

"Wait!" Son said.

Bolan lowered the knife but kept it open. He released the gangster's mustache and shoved the man back against the seat. "Go on."

Son's hand shot up to rub his sore mouth. "There is a front gate by which all must enter," he said weakly. "There will be two guards there."

"How about back or side gates?"

"Four gates in all. But the other three are kept locked."

"Guards?"

"Yes, there are guards at all entries. But they will not open the other gates, just point you toward the front."

Bolan nodded. "What about after you get on the grounds?"

Son stopped rubbing his half mustache and began to twist it. "There is a curving drive to the front door. More guards will be stationed on the porch. Others in the house." He paused and took a deep breath. "I do not know exactly where."

"You've been in the house before," Bolan said. It was a statement rather than a question.

"Of course. But the guards move around inside. It is impossible to predict where they'll be when you arrive."

Bolan glanced out at the rising sun. "Is Vu an early riser?" he asked.

"What do you mean?"

"Will he still be in bed or will he already be in his office?"

"I do not know what time of day he begins work. My guess would be that he is still asleep. I have often been here, and seen him out, well after midnight."

Bolan turned back to Bui. "Get in the back seat next to Son."

Bui had given up resisting the American even before Son did so. The door opened, and a second later he was sitting next to the gangster.

"Give me your right hand," Bolan ordered.

The young man's arm shot out.

The soldier pulled a set of plastic handcuffs out of his coat and looped one cuff around the young man's wrist.

"Now," he said, looking to Son. "I want your left."

Son raised his hand.

The soldier looped the flat plastic cord around the little man's wrist and secured the ends. He moved over behind the wheel, then turned back. "We're going in hard and fast," he said. "I'll be shooting with one hand, and I'll have you two in the other. That won't be easy if I don't have your cooperation." He paused. "The guards aren't going to have time to make out little details like the fact that you're my prisoners, and they won't care if they do. Vu and his men are drug-dealing pimps and murderers, and they won't care if they kill you, too. So I suggest that you *do* cooperate. It's your only chance of getting out of here alive."

Son cursed under his breath in Vietnamese; Bui began to pray in the same language.

Bolan threw the Suburban in gear and pulled back onto the road. A few moments later he turned onto the winding driveway that led up to Vu's palace. The road twisted around the hill, both to keep the grade to a minimum and to give Vu's people plenty of time to spot anyone approaching the house, Bolan suspected.

He rounded a final curve and saw the front gate ahead. He slowed, his eyes scanning the entryway. The iron fence was a good twelve feet high and topped by concertina wire. The gate was closed, and two men stood next to it on either side. Both gripped Vietnamese Model K-50M submachine guns.

Bolan drew the sound-suppressed Beretta and placed it in his lap. He studied the gate guards' weapons as he drove slowly forward. Sort of a cross between the Chinese Type 50 and the French MAT 38, they were state-issued, hardly available to private citizens of Communist Vietnam.

That meant Mr. Vu was connected. Not just to the underworld but to the government itself.

The iron gate opened far enough to let one of the guards step out. The gate swung back toward the house, and neither of the guards bothered to refasten the clasp.

The man in the white shirt walked forward, his subgun slung over his shoulder, muzzle forward in assault fashion. Bolan saw him trying to look into the Suburban, past the driver to the men in the back seat.

By putting both of the Orientals in the back seat, he had hoped to accomplish two things. First they'd be easier to jerk out of the Chevy and drag with him once the battle had begun. But secondly, and of equal importance, it would appear at first glance that they were important men being chauffeured to see Mr. Vu by some Caucasian flunky.

Bolan didn't move until the guard had circled the Suburban and stepped in to the driver's window. Then in one smooth movement he raised the Beretta and put two near-silent rounds into the man's face. He collapsed to the ground without a word.

Leveling the Beretta on the Suburban's hood, the Executioner sent two more rounds drilling into the chest and nose of the other guard.

A moment later the Chevy Suburban was crashing through the gate and racing toward the front of Mr. Vu's palace.

"THAT'S WORSE LUCK than the hen stumbling into the fox house," Hawkins said. He leaned in toward McCarter from the love seat across from the couch in the living room of the suite. "At least Rafe got away."

"That's right," Manning said. The big Canadian sat on a straight-backed wooden chair he'd pulled in from the kitchen. "He'll get the job done."

James half sat, half reclined on the couch next to McCarter. "It was a twist of bad luck," he said. "But it could happen to anybody. Nobody's perfect. We wouldn't be able to stand you if you were. Hey, David, no use kicking yourself over it."

The Briton nodded, but inside he was doing exactly what James had warned him not to—kicking himself for letting the clerk see him leave.

Every mission, the Phoenix Force leader knew, was a long series of smaller missions. Getting out of the hotel under the scrutiny of the staff was one of those smaller missions. He had failed, and failure didn't sit well with the former SAS officer.

McCarter forced his self-recriminations out of his mind. They were, he knew, a form of self-indulgence and served no practical purpose. In fact they were detrimental to achieving a goal. Once a mistake, rotten luck, a calculated risk gone bad or whatever you wanted to call it occurred, the best thing to do was assess the damage and rectify the situation as best you could. Then move on.

And in this case, the Briton had to admit, little, if any, damage had been done. As Hawkins had said, Encizo had gotten away, and the Cuban could pick up the guns and recon the politburo meeting at Tiananmen Square as well as he could. When he returned, they would all put their heads together and set up a plan to protect Lee and any other politburo members who stood to be assassinated.

James broke back into McCarter's thoughts. "Rafe knows where the guns are stashed, right?"

"I told him, but I don't know what the situation is like at the warehouse during the day. He might have to wait until the place closes to go get them."

Manning snorted. "Just as well. Those .380 mouse guns don't add much to my sense of well-being." He paused. "I'd just as soon have an ax handle."

Hawkins grinned. "If I shot like you, I would, too."

The wisecrack broke the tension that had formed, and the men from Stony Man Farm began to chuckle. What was really bothering them, from McCarter on down, was not the fact that the Phoenix Force leader had gotten caught leaving the hotel—that was, in reality, of little consequence. What was really bothering them was the waiting. There was little they could do until Encizo got back.

If Hawkins's humor had relieved the tension, the door to the hallway suddenly being kicked in refocused their attention on the gravity of their situation.

The Phoenix Force commandos rose instinctively as a flood of green flowed into the room. The Chinese regulars in their dark green uniforms came first, carrying Type 85 submachine guns and Chinese Type 51 Tokarev-style pistols. They fanned out, forming a circle around McCarter and his men, screaming orders in Mandarin that fell on deaf ears.

At the door McCarter saw Hong in his lighter green uniform.

The same surly lieutenant McCarter remembered from the night before stepped out of the cluster of green. Leveling his weapon on the Briton's chest, he glared at McCarter with gleaming black eyes. "Hong!" he yelled over his shoulder.

The cadet trotted forward like a whipped puppy.

The lieutenant spoke.

The only word, or letters rather, that McCarter picked up were "CIA."

Hong translated. "Special Agent McCarter," he said, "it seems there has been some confusion. Lieutenant Chang thinks there is a chance that you and your men are not actually police officers but rather U.S. government agents."

A tall, slender officer with a subgun aimed at Manning stepped forward and whispered into the lieutenant's ear. Chang turned immediately and slapped Hong across the face. The blow was hard enough to send the cadet to the floor.

McCarter fought the urge to step in and return the blow on Hong's behalf. The kid had been good to them. He didn't deserve treatment like that even if he was softening his translation of what the lieutenant had said.

Now the slender officer with the Type 85 became the interpreter. "You men are CIA agents!" he accused, translating Chang's words more directly, McCarter guessed. "And you are under arrest for the bombing of Comrade Lee's car!"

McCarter shook his head. "We are not CIA agents," he said emphatically. "We are U.S. Justice Department agents. The two agencies are completely

separate. We work domestically. The CIA is foreign."
He paused and nodded toward Chang. "Tell him
that."

The officer translated. Chang spit on the floor, then
rattled off another string of Mandarin.

"Lieutenant Chang says there is no better cover
than the one that looks natural," the officer said.
"You portray Justice Department agents here in Beijing. But in reality you are the CIA."

The lieutenant looked around the room, then uttered more angry words.

"Where is the fifth member of your party?" the
slender officer asked.

McCarter felt his temper flaring and fought to control it. "Went out for a walk or for cigarettes or just
left because he was sick of being a prisoner, would
be my guess. I don't know. I don't watch my men
twenty-four hours a day like you do. I trust them."

The officer translated. Chang's shark eyes continued to stare.

McCarter started to speak again, but Chang held up
a hand and screamed. The Phoenix Force leader
couldn't understand the words, but he got their drift
and closed his mouth.

Chang barked at his men, and they began to tear
the suite apart.

McCarter and the others were ordered to sit back
down. The Briton knew they'd be looking for components for whatever type of explosive had been used

in the bomb they were talking about. Well, the team was safe there. Chang would find no fuses, timers, blasting caps or any other ingredients for making explosives. But what he would find, either sooner or later, was the modified cellular phone that connected them to Stony Man Farm. And when they got their hands on that, they'd be convinced beyond a shadow of a doubt that the Justice agents were actually CIA assassins.

The Briton wondered if Hawkins was wearing the phone or if he'd stashed it somewhere in his room. Chang hadn't ordered a body search yet, and if Hawkins had the phone on him, it would buy them some time. The Phoenix Force leader glanced over to the young man, caught his attention, then dropped his eyes to his teammate's shirt.

Hawkins caught the movement and its meaning. He nodded.

He was wearing the phone.

McCarter breathed a sigh of relief. At this point he didn't know whether they were really about to be arrested or the threat was a bluff on Chang's part. If the Chinese cops didn't find the phone, there was a chance Phoenix Force wouldn't be taken in. And even if they were, the trip might give Hawkins a chance to ditch the piece of high-tech equipment.

The Briton's hopes began to grow as, one by one, the searching cops returned from their designated areas and shook their heads. But when the last man had informed the lieutenant that he'd come up with no incriminating evidence, Chang barked more orders that dashed McCarter's hopes for good.

"Take off your clothing," the tall, slender officer ordered.

Five minutes later Chang held the cellular phone as the other officers handcuffed McCarter, James, Manning and Hawkins, then marched them out the door into the hall. Chang spoke a final time, and the interpreter stepped up to McCarter.

"Lieutenant Chang says he will find the fifth man from your group," he said. "Then, when he does, you will all be executed together."

WINDOWS AND WINDSHIELDS in the other cars around the Mercedes shattered. Glass in the nearby buildings cracked. Shards of metal, plastic and glass mixed with ragged pieces of upholstery and matted clumps of car-seat wadding rained over the parking lot. Flames from the burning Mercedes shot up to meet the falling rubble, and smoke, as black and thick as a moonless night, clouded the air.

A uniformed guard, his shirt afire, ran madly through the lot until two other guards tackled him and rolled his smoking form across the pavement.

Traffic outside the square ground to a halt.

Rafael Encizo knew better than to get out of the cab. In a few minutes the entire area would be crawling with Chinese cops. Everyone on the streets would be suspect, and subject to detainment and interview.

If officials found an American in the vicinity, it wouldn't matter if he was a certified public accountant from Poughkeepsie or a Southern Baptist evangelist. Considering the suspicions the Chinese already had as to the assassinations, he might just as well have CIA tattooed on his forehead.

The cabdriver had frozen behind the wheel, his mouth gaping like an imbecile at the burning vehicle ahead of them. Encizo leaned forward and placed a hand on the man's shoulder. "I'm out of the sightseeing mood," he said softly in French. "Let's go back."

The man flinched as he came out of his shock. He turned toward the Phoenix Force commando, his eyes still wide. Finally he nodded, cut an illegal U-turn in the middle of the street and started back toward the hotel.

Encizo directed the man to the curb three blocks from the Plaza and shoved a handful of money over the seat. "Let's keep this trip between the two of us," he said. "I don't want any trouble for sneaking out."

When he saw the bills in the Cuban's hand, the cabdriver's eyes got almost as wide as they had when the bomb had exploded. He nodded, glanced around as if someone might be just outside the cab and ready to rob him, then took the money and stuffed it down the front of his shirt.

Encizo got out of the vehicle. The tip he had given the driver probably amounted to a month's take-home salary, and he suspected it would keep the man from reporting the strange American he'd taken to Tiananmen Square. On the other hand, it didn't hurt to be careful, so he waited until the cab had disappeared around a corner before proceeding toward the hotel.

Keeping his head down again, Encizo sauntered along the sidewalk, passing other pedestrians and people on broken-down one-speed bicycles that had seen better days. When he reached the warehouse, he found that activity had slowed. But the place was still a long way from shutting down for the night.

Encizo cursed in Spanish under his breath. Again he would have to wait before retrieving the weapons. And waiting was beginning to get on his nerves.

Encizo walked down the street. This mission was a strange one for Phoenix Force. They weren't used to the downtime that the Southern Police Institute cover was forcing them to endure. The Cuban, like the rest of the people from Stony Man Farm, was a man of action. The inactivity was making him restless, and he had seen the same restlessness in the eyes of the other men.

The Cuban stopped dead in his tracks as soon as he turned the corner. Ahead, double-parked in front of the hotel lobby, he saw the same police vans that had brought them from the airport. McCarter, Manning, James and Hawkins were being escorted into the vehicles just as they had been as soon as their plane had touched down.

But Encizo saw two major differences from the way they had boarded the vans at the airport.

Now their escorts weren't police cadets in light green uniforms. This time only Hong wore the light green tunic. The other five men, their submachine guns slung over their shoulders, wore the darker green of police regulars.

And this time Phoenix Force was handcuffed.

CHAPTER EIGHT

The Executioner knew well that normally the key to victory in armed confrontations was twofold: superior manpower and superior firepower.

As he guided the Suburban away from the clanging iron gate toward Vu's front door, he had neither.

Which meant all he could rely on were surprise and speed.

Bolan leaned hard on the accelerator as he steered the vehicle toward the house fifty yards away. Meticulously tended flower beds paralleled the pavement, which looped around several carefully planted groves of sycamore trees. The Suburban's tires squealed in protest as they curved past the landscaping.

Twenty yards from the front door, Bolan made his decision. It was impossible to tell if the door was reinforced, but a man cautious enough to surround his property with concertina-topped fences and armed guards seemed likely to install more than just a simple dead bolt.

That meant Bolan could waste valuable time trying

to kick in the door, time during which the armed men inside would be organizing their defense.

Flooring the accelerator, he steered the Suburban straight toward the front door. The hood of the vehicle bounced high into air as the front tires hit the steps leading up to the porch, then the big four-wheel-drive settled as it drove into the face of the house.

Bolan slammed forward against the steering wheel as the bumper crunched against the door and frame. As the Suburban choked and stalled, he looked through the windshield to see an eight-foot opening in the middle of the house. A loud buzzer pierced the air, and as he drew the Desert Eagle and leaped from the driver's side, it was joined by an ear-piercing bell alarm.

Ripping the back door open, Bolan had reached inside for Bui and Son when the first of Mr. Vu's house-security staff stepped out of the cavernous hole onto the front porch. This man wore the same white shirt and khaki slacks as the men at the gate, but his clothes were soaking wet.

Bolan looked past him into the house. Inside, it looked as if it was raining.

The house guard gaped at the Suburban in awe, then narrowed his eyes as he spotted Bolan. He held an AK-47 by the forend and pistol grip, the wooden stock hooked under his armpit. He raised it to belt level and fired.

With the fingers of his left hand clenching the plastic cuffs that bound Bui and Son at the wrists, Bolan jerked both men out of the car.

The guard's careless round flew high over their heads.

Twisting at the waist, the Executioner caught a quick flash picture of the Desert Eagle's front sight and squeezed the trigger. The .44 Magnum pistol bucked in his hand, exploding over the noise of the humming buzzer and clanging bell.

A 240-grain hollowpoint drilled into the white shirt, turning it instantly crimson. The AK-47 went flying from the gunner's hands. The force of the round drove him back inside the house, and it was then that Bolan finally saw the source of the "rain."

The fire alarm and security system were somehow linked. When the Suburban had crashed through the door, it had set off not only the burglar alarm but an overhead-sprinkler system, as well.

Bui gasped and Son whimpered as Bolan yanked them both toward the yawning hole that led to the living room. As the big American started to enter the cavity, a face appeared around the corner.

Bolan shot at it, scoring a hit.

Pulling on the plastic-cuffs, Bolan stepped inside the living room and was immediately drenched by the sprinklers. He scanned the immediate area. To his right stood an archway that led to an elaborately decorated dining room. A swing door on the other side of that room probably led to the kitchen.

To his left Bolan saw a hallway just past a spiral staircase that led to the second story. Vu would be there, he knew, either still in his bedroom or already in his office. Both would be on the second floor and at the rear of the house. Bolan was sure of it; a man who'd go to the trouble of setting up a security package like Vu had would put his private spaces as far from the front door as possible.

The Executioner stepped over the body of the man who had peeked around the corner and glanced down at the gunner who'd come out on the porch. Both men had carried AK-47 assault rifles. For a moment Bolan considered commandeering one of them, then discarded the idea.

The long guns would be harder to wield down the halls inside the house. He glanced at Bui and Son. Especially with one hand.

Water continued to pelt the soldier's head and shoulders from the overhead-sprinkler system. He had started toward the spiral staircase with his captives in tow when he heard footsteps to his right. Turning the Desert Eagle that way, he saw a bald guard with what appeared to be a French MAT 49 submachine gun with an unusually long barrel. The door to the kitchen was still swinging on its hinges behind him.

The Desert Eagle boomed. Two massive hollow-points sailed through the archway and struck the bald man in the chest and head. He collapsed soundlessly to the floor.

Bolan turned back toward the staircase in time to see two more of the white-shirted staff blunder into the living room from the hallway. Two more times the Eagle leaped in his hand. Two more times, men fell.

Moving to the bodies next to the staircase, the Executioner looked down to see that they, too, had carried the long-barreled French MATs. Leaning down, he snatched one of the weapons from the water-soaked carpet and raised it to his eyes.

The long barrel was a replacement. The 9 mm subgun had been rebarreled for the Soviet 7.62 mm Type P pistol cartridge. But even with the added length, it was considerably shorter than the AK-47s.

Bolan reached down and grabbed the magazine from the other converted MAT. Holstering the big .44 pistol, he pulled Bui and Son past the stairs and into the hallway. He saw no signs of other guards, but fired a quick burst down the hall anyway. His purpose was twofold: to test the function of the MAT and discourage anyone who might even be considering coming out one of the doors along the hall.

Moving back across the saturated carpet, Bolan started up the stairs, stopping abruptly when he saw a flicker of movement above. Raising the modified French subgun he fired up through the twisting steps and heard a grunt. A moment later a body tumbled down the stairs.

Bolan stepped to the side and pushed the body past

him, Bui and Son. He caught a quick glance of his prisoners' faces. Both looked like wet dogs. Bui's black hair was drenched, and Son's equally wet toupee had begun to curl up on the sides. The wispy hair of his new half mustache was matted over his lip and chin on one side.

Sprinting up the steps, Bolan crouched low as his boots hit the second floor. The light was dimmer here than below, and he waited for his eyes to adjust.

The man in the white shirt didn't give them time.

Stepping around the corner of one of the two hallways, the security man appeared as a blur to Bolan's contracted pupils. But the white shirt reflected what light there was on the second floor, and the shape of the object in the man's hands was unmistakable—another of the long-barreled MAT 49s.

Bolan squeezed the trigger of his own subgun, beating the man to the punch by a microsecond. He couldn't see where the rounds struck, but wherever it was, they did their job.

The indistinct shape flew back against the wall, his own MAT pointed skyward. His trigger finger contracted in death, and a long burst exploded from the subgun into the ceiling before the magazine ran dry.

His eyes adjusted now, Bolan dragged his prisoners behind him as he passed the dead man and peered down the hall past several closed doors to the second hallway on the other side of the stairs. Bolan walked swiftly to the opening, the MAT ready in front of him.

The other hall looked similar to the first, with doors along the wall, all closed.

Suddenly he realized that the second floor was dry. Evidently the sprinkler system activated only in the zone affected. The alarms, however, both buzzer and bell, continued to sound as loud as ever.

The Executioner hesitated. Vu would be in a room at the end of one of the halls. The two rooms were equally remote from likely entrances and exits to the house, and that would be where a paranoid like Vu would feel safest. One of the rooms would be his office, the other his sleeping quarters.

But which was which? And which one was he in?

Bolan glanced at the luminous hands on his watch. It was still fairly early, and he couldn't see a man who ran hookers, gambling facilities and other night-related activities getting up at the crack of dawn. Vu would still be in bed.

But which was the bedroom?

Tugging Bui and Son behind him, Bolan started down the hall he stood in. There was only one way to find out where Vu was, and that was to go look.

Halfway to the closed door at the end of the hallway, a door on the right opened and a man tucking his shirt into his trousers stepped out. Looking up, he saw Bolan, and his right hand dropped to the Cao Dai 9 mm pistol holstered on his hip.

Bolan didn't break stride, firing a 3-round burst into the man's chest.

The Executioner stopped at the end of the hall. Without dropping the plastic cuffs, he jammed the MAT under his arm and pulled out the nearly spent magazine. Reloading with the fresh clip in his pocket, he stepped back and kicked the door.

The big American went in low, tugging Bui and Son behind him and assuming they'd have the good sense to duck, too. But the caution was wasted. Bolan found himself in Vu's empty office.

Turning quickly, he hurried back down the hall to the staircase, circled the rail and moved down the other hall. This time none of the doors opened to invite death, but as he neared the final door he sensed— rather than heard or saw—movement behind him.

The big American whirled, sweeping the MAT around in front of him. Bui and Son dropped to their knees as he tapped the trigger and sent a burst into a man with rotten brown teeth. The man fell face forward onto the carpet.

Turning back to the door, Bolan kicked again. The hinges broke, and the door sailed a good three feet into the bedroom before falling onto the floor.

Yanking Bui and Son behind him, Bolan stepped inside. The room was large and, like the rest of the house, expensively—if decadently—decorated.

Torture devices such as thumbscrews, branding irons, nipple clips and other sadomasochistic paraphernalia lined the shelves against one wall. From another hung chains with padded wrist and ankle cuffs. In one corner stood a medieval rack.

The Executioner knew that a certain segment of people played at such odd erotic games, living out their fantasies without ever hurting anyone. But others took such activities seriously, and he had no doubt that Ong Vu fell into the latter category. No doubt whatsoever.

Dried blood stained the carpets in several places.

In the center of the room, and obviously the main attraction, was a huge round water bed. Held in place by a wooden frame, the frame had been mounted on a platform that slowly revolved on some hidden axis.

Vu lay in the center of the bed. To his right was a black woman in white hose and garters. On his left was a white woman whose matching costume was black. Both women had their hands tied behind their backs. Ball gags were stuffed into their mouths, and they were blindfolded.

But the women could still hear, and the gunshots that had blasted throughout the house had them struggling wildly against their restraints.

Vu himself wore a black sleep mask. Bolan could see the stubs of earplugs sticking out of the sides of his head. He had slept through the entire assault.

The Executioner's eyes narrowed as he stared down at the man in the water bed. It was time his sleep came to an end.

Bolan raised the MAT and fired a burst into the

foot of the mattress. The bed seemed to explode as the pressure ripped the space between the 7.62 mm holes to create one large, gaping perforation. Water rushed out through the puncture, and Vu and his playmates washed forward over the frame and onto the carpet.

Vu ripped the mask off his face. "What—?" he screamed in Vietnamese. Then he saw Bolan and the MAT.

The big American twisted the plastic cuffs tight in his left hand and threw Bui and Son against the wall. The two men slumped to sitting positions facing him. Slowly Bolan reached down and pulled the earplugs from Vu's ears.

"Time to wake up and smell the coffee, Vu," he said. "You and I need to have a little talk."

LYONS HELD THE THROTTLE back as the Harley jumped the parking-lot curb to the grass next to the bushes.

Across the street, from atop a three-story building, came the roar of high-powered rifles. As he neared the bushes, the Able Team leader saw three tiny heads.

All had short-cropped hair.

The first of the demonstrators had drawn even with the men in the bushes when the gunfire froze them in their tracks. From the rear of the assembly came the sound of more shots, AK-47s, unless Lyons missed his guess.

As he drew nearer the bushes, the Able Team leader could see that the man with the Mauser was the big man who had met with Topknot at the café. Both of the Aryans faced away from the oncoming Harley, the noise of the crowd and the gunfire masking the machine's approach.

As he drew the Colt Python from under his shirt, Lyons watched the big man press his eye to the scope and sight in on some unseen target through the bush.

The big ex-cop double-actioned a 125-grain semijacketed hollowpoint from the barrel of the revolver. The round entered the loose skin hanging from the big man's nape and blew out his face, spraying the bushes in front of him with blood, bone fragments and what little gray matter the Aryan possessed. The force of the round threw him forward into the mess. The Mauser dropped to the ground.

The Aryan readying the M-16 whirled with the weapon. Lyons recognized him as one of the men who had followed the pickup in the car. Aiming at the oncoming motorcycle, the man pulled the assault rifle's trigger.

Lyons laid the Harley on its side, skidding along the grass under a steady stream of 5.56 mm rounds. Both motorcycle and man slid along the ground and into the Aryan.

The bike struck the man in the knees and sent him

somersaulting over Lyons and the Harley. Finally catching in the bushes, the bike stopped.

Lyons rolled from his side to his belly to face the man with the assault rifle. Somehow the white supremacist had held on to the M-16 as he rolled across the grass. Now he turned in a sitting position to face the big ex-cop.

The former LAPD detective fired another .357 Magnum round that struck the man square in the chest. His eyes and mouth opened wide in surprise, then a stream of blood shot from the open mouth before he fell to the ground, dead.

Bounding to his feet, Lyons heard more high-powered fire from the roof across the street. The automatic rounds continued at the other end of the demonstration. Mixed with the long-gun explosions were 9 mm blasts—9 mm Beretta 92s. That meant Schwarz and Blancanales were on the job.

The Able Team leader moved deeper into the bushes to where he could see the crowd. Most were running now, some taking a few steps one way, then reversing their direction when a round struck near them.

Two Orientals stood back to back ten yards from the bushes, both firing what appeared to be Government Model .45s.

Lyons loosed two rounds at each man, then grasped the revolver with both hands. His right thumb flipped the cylinder latch as the fingers of his left hand swung the wheel out and away from the frame. His right hand shot to the speedloaders on his belt as his left inverted the Python, dumping the empty brass. Six fresh rounds entered the holes, and the cylinder went back into the frame.

The entire operation took a little over one second.

Lyons moved to the edge of the bushes, trying to spot the men on the roof again. Seeing a man with a crew cut firing a bolt-action rifle into the crowd, the Able Team leader cocked the Colt and brought it to eye level. Lining up the sights, he squeezed the light, single-action trigger.

The revolver jumped in his hand. Lyons saw the dust as the Magnum round struck the concrete retaining wall just below the man. The distance was well out of pistol range.

Remembering the Mauser, Lyons hurried back through the bushes to where it had fallen. A moment later he was back at the edge of the bushes. Raising the weapon, he stared through the scope and centered the cross hairs on the man with the crew cut.

The Able Team leader began to lightly press the trigger. Like all good long-distance shooters, he was a little surprised when the round finally ignited.

So was the man with the crew cut. The round cored into his brain, effectively taking him out of the play.

Lyons worked the bolt as he swung the Mauser toward another of the neo-Nazis on the roof. He recognized the man now as the smaller of the two who had met with Topknot. Still, he was big, his broad shoulders leaning over the retaining wall as he worked the bolt on his own rifle.

Lyons centered the cross hairs on the man's nose and squeezed off another round. The Able Team leader's second bullet carved out a third nostril. Death was instantaneous.

The man who had worn the Aryan Brotherhood tattoo fell over the side of the building, hit the ground three stories below and bounced twice before settling in a twisted clump.

Lyons swung the Mauser toward the third man on the roof, but the Aryan had made the Able Team leader's position. Before the ex-cop could work the Mauser's bolt, he saw the man's rifle barrel swing his way.

He dived to the ground a split second before the round whizzed over his head at chest height. Rolling to a prone position, he raised the Mauser and looked through the scope.

The spot on the roof where the man had stood was empty.

The Able Team leader scanned the crowd quickly. By now most of the marchers had run away. A few lay wounded in the street, but the quick return fire from Lyons at the front of the demonstration, and Schwarz and Blancanales at the rear, had forced both the Aryans and Topknot's Orientals to focus their attention on Able Team.

Half a block away Lyons could see Schwarz and

Blancanales. They had taken refuge behind parked cars and were returning fire from some of Topknot's men who hid behind other vehicles on the other side of the street. Both Able Team commandos had seized AK-47s from the fallen Orientals and holstered their Berettas.

Lyons dropped the Mauser and drew the Python again as he sprinted across the street. The man on the roof of the building had only one way to go—down.

And the Able Team leader intended to give him his own brand of welcome reception.

The first floor of the building was a takeout Chinese restaurant, and Lyons burst through the door to the odor of egg rolls, pork and hot mustard. The workers had taken refuge behind the counter during the gunfight, and were only beginning to stick their heads back up over the barrier. They dropped back out of sight as the Able Team leader burst through the door, gun in hand.

"Stay down!" Lyons ordered as he raced through a gate next to the cash register. "Where are the stairs?" He looked down to see three men and two women huddled together on the floor.

One of the women pointed him through another set of doors to the kitchen. "A...hallway...behind kitchen," one of the men whispered.

Lyons started through two swing doors and heard someone ask, "Are you an officer?"

He was already in the kitchen and out of earshot by the time he said, "Not exactly."

The big ex-cop saw the open door to the back hallway on the opposite wall. Moving more carefully now, he transferred the .357 pistol to his left hand and drew the .45 with his right. His thumb on the Gold Cup's extended safety, he kept both weapons pointed ahead of him as he slid across the tile to the hall.

The hall was clear, which meant the white supremacist who'd been on the roof was still on one of the upstairs floors. He hadn't had time to descend to ground level and get away.

Lyons stopped at the stairs, looking up, both guns following his gaze. Normal police procedure in such a case would be to call for backup and wait. Ascending the steps to search for the suspect meant giving away the high-ground advantage. The enemy could lie in wait, watching and listening, then put a bullet in Lyons's head before the Able Team leader had time to react.

No, going up alone after the man would be regarded as foolish in the departmental manual of any police agency in the world. But there was one problem.

Lyons didn't have any backup to call on; both were still on the street getting shot at. And if he didn't take out this last Aryan Brotherhood gunner and get out there to help them, one of the Oriental gunman's bullets might well find its target.

Taking a deep breath, the big ex-cop kept his eyes up as he started to take the steps. The staircase was at least fifty years old, and every step he took, regardless of how light his footfall, brought a groan of protest from the aged wood.

Halfway up the first flight he heard the floor creak overhead and behind him.

The man was there, waiting.

Slowly the Able Team leader pivoted on the balls of his feet and faced the floor above him. On the landing he saw a rail running around the open stairwell. Nothing else.

Lyons's eyes narrowed as the killer instinct that had gotten him through so many gunfights in the past kicked in. His senses heightened, and his mind grew more alert.

Joining the waiting game, Lyons breathed quietly, calm and steady. The adrenaline that pumped through him, strengthening both his muscles and resolve, was powerful but controlled. The absence of such adrenaline, he knew, brought on lethargy in such life-or-death confrontations. But to yield completely to the desire to fight prompted foolish bravado.

And neither extreme was what he needed at the moment.

The floor creaked quietly again. Slowly Lyons shoved the Gold Cup back in his belt and gripped the Colt Python in both hands. The .45 rounds would probably penetrate the wooden floor, all right, but with the .357 Magnum bullets there would be no "probably" to contend with. Just before switching to the Mauser, he had shoved his last speedloader into the wheel gun—six rounds of armor-piercing bullets designed to go through an elephant and the rhino standing behind him.

Lining the red insert in the front sight between the adjustable posts at the rear of the revolver, Lyons aimed at a spot half a foot in front of where the creak had come from. Again he waited.

The gunshots outside sounded dull inside the building, but they reminded the Able Team leader that Gadgets and Pol were engaged in battle. Every second he delayed was one in which he couldn't help his men.

And Carl Lyons had never been accused of being a patient man when he didn't have to be.

Redrawing the .45 with his left hand this time, Lyons's thumb moved over the back strap to disengage the manual safety. With another deep breath, he said, "Well, asshole, who's going to move first? You or me?"

The white supremacist above him heard the words and had to have flinched involuntarily. The floor creaked again.

Lyons fired.

Six rounds of armor-piercing ammo shot from the Python in under two seconds. Tiny holes appeared in the ceiling, and Lyons heard the white supremacist curse as he moved toward the stairwell. His head, shoulders and arms appeared over the rail. He held a Browning Hi-Power in one hand, trying to aim down.

The big ex-cop raised the Gold Cup and cut loose with two more rounds that took the man in the upper chest and under the chin. The top of his head blew up to strike the ceiling above him, then his body toppled forward over the rail.

Lyons stepped to the side and let the body fall to the stairs, then roll down to the ground floor. Slowly, the .45 still aimed at the man on the floor, he moved down the steps himself.

The white supremacist lay on his back, his cold, dead eyes staring up at the ceiling.

Lyons leaned over the man. Three of the .357 rounds had struck him in the legs. A fourth had pierced his groin, and the fifth had entered his rib cage just above the belt line.

The Able Team leader didn't know where the sixth bullet had gone, and he didn't much care.

Standing erect, Lyons hurried back through the kitchen and out through the Chinese takeout's front door. He was on the street, his .45 pistol aimed toward where he'd last seen Schwarz and Blancanales, when he suddenly realized the firing had stopped.

Gadgets and Pol walked toward him, their AK-47s held at port arms.

The big ex-cop scoured the street for any sign of Topknot. There wasn't any. The mysterious Japanese had fled the scene, if indeed he had even been there after leaving the Italian restaurant. Some of his men were still on the street, but they weren't firing weapons anymore.

Lyons looked at the Orientals littering the pavement along the street. They would never fire weapons again.

RAFAEL ENCIZO KNEW he had to act fast.

Getting the other members of Phoenix Force away from the police wouldn't be easy, particularly unarmed. But if he allowed McCarter, Manning, James and Hawkins to be taken to headquarters, freeing them would become impossible.

Encizo watched the men in the dark green uniforms grab McCarter and lift him into the van. The other three members of Phoenix Force stood waiting their turn. Each one had the barrel of a Type 85 poking in his back.

Hong stood off to the side, looking as though he wished he could be anywhere but where he was at the moment.

Encizo knew what had happened. Word of the bombing at Tiananmen Square had reached the police, and the ones who had been keeping tabs on them had added that knowledge to the discrepancies in Phoenix Force's behavior since arriving. The conclusion they had come to was that the men calling themselves U.S.

Justice agents were in reality CIA agents who were behind the assassinations of the politburo members.

Slowly Encizo moved down the block. His only chance was to get close enough to the van to take one of the cops hostage and force the other men's release. He looked down at his jeans and fatigue jacket as he walked. Would the semidisguise hold up long enough for him to get within arm's reach? He didn't know, but he was about to find out.

Moving more swiftly as he neared the van, Encizo watched the officers throw Hawkins through the vehicle's sliding door. His eyes scanned the men outside the van. He would reach the one with the lieutenant bars on his shoulder first, the same man who had been in charge the night before. Good. His plan would work better with the ranking officer as hostage.

Ten feet from the assembled group, Encizo saw a police sergeant turn and look his way. The man frowned and started to speak, but before the words could escape his lips, Encizo had kicked into high gear.

Sliding forward behind the lieutenant, Encizo cupped a hand around the man's mouth. He drove a fist into the lieutenant's right kidney and felt the muffled grunt against his fingers. The Type 85 in the man's hands fell to the end of the sling as the lieutenant's arms went limp.

Taking advantage of the momentary paralysis brought on by the blow, Encizo reached around the man, grabbed the subgun and twisted the sling around to the back. Jamming the barrel into the lieutenant's spine, he yelled, "Freeze! Everybody! Now!"

Encizo didn't know if the Chinese cops understood his words, but they got the drift. All activity around the van suddenly stopped.

The Cuban looked over to the young man in the lighter green uniform. "Hong," he said, "tell these men I don't want to hurt anyone. Then tell them if they lay down their weapons, I won't have to."

Before the young cadet could translate, Encizo saw a flash of movement to his side. He turned to see a man wearing sergeant's stripes reaching for the subgun. Pivoting on the ball of his foot, the Phoenix Force warrior shot a front kick into the sergeant's knee, drew his foot back as the man screamed, then snapped it forward again, this time striking the cop squarely between the legs.

The sergeant's first scream was nothing compared to his second.

"Hong," Encizo yelled, jamming the subgun barrel into the lieutenant's back until the man was almost bent double, "Tell these men that one more trick like that will mean I riddle this guy with lead." He paused. "Better tell them quick."

Hong rattled off a string of Mandarin.

The Chinese cops stood like statues. Only their eyes moved, darting back and forth from Encizo to their lieutenant as they wondered what to do.

Encizo raised the subgun just over their heads and held the trigger back. A 6-round burst blew from the weapon. The cops ducked.

For another moment it looked as if they would freeze in place again. Then, finally, one of the men leaned slowly forward, pulled the sling over his head and lowered his weapon to the ground.

The others followed like sheep.

"Pistols," Encizo said. "Tell them to set the handguns next to the 85s."

Hong translated again, his voice trembling slightly.

The Chinese regulars set their Tokarev-style side arms on the concrete.

Hands still cuffed behind his back, McCarter jumped down out of the van, followed by Hawkins. The Phoenix Force leader looked at Encizo, grinned and shook his head.

"Tell somebody to get the cuffs off all of them and to do it fast," Encizo said.

A slender officer reached behind his back, and Encizo brought the barrel of the subgun out from behind the lieutenant's back. Aiming at the man, he said, "When your hand comes back into sight, it better be holding a cuff key."

No translation was necessary. The officer's hand came back around in slow motion, the key gripped between his thumb and index finger.

As the shock to the lieutenant's kidney started to

wear off, the man began to move in front of Enzico. "Keep still," the Phoenix Force commando ordered.

The lieutenant stopped moving. A string of what Enzico knew had to be choice Mandarin obscenities escaped his lips.

McCarter rubbed his wrists as soon as the cuffs came off, then reached down, lifting a pistol from the ground and shoving it into his waistband. The Type 85 next to it came next. He checked both chamber and magazine, then turned the weapon toward the standing cops. "The rest of you guys," he said, glancing toward Hawkins, James and Manning, "grab some of the toys. Gary, get the van keys from whoever has them."

Hawkins and James lifted weapons from the ground as Manning began to search the pockets of the standing cops.

Enzico reached around the lieutenant and patted the man's pockets. Feeling a key ring in the front left, he reached in and pulled it out. "Here," he said to Manning, then tossed the keys to the big Canadian.

Manning slid behind the wheel of the van, inserted a key and twisted it. The vehicle roared to life. "Bingo," he said.

McCarter turned to Hong. "We'll be taking the van," he said. "Hong, listen to me."

The cadet stared blankly ahead, his eyes those of a man who has been betrayed.

"Hong, we aren't CIA agents," McCarter said.

"And we've had nothing to do with the assassinations. You have my word on that."

"Are you really Justice Department agents?" Hong asked softly.

McCarter hesitated. "No," he finally said.

"Then you lied to me. So why should I believe you about any of it?"

"Because it's true," the Briton stated. "I can't explain it right now, and some of it I can never explain."

"If you are innocent, you should not escape like this. It only makes one believe that you are guilty."

"We've got a job to do," McCarter said. "A job that benefits both of our countries." He turned back to the other men of Phoenix Force.

By now Encizo had dropped his grip on the lieutenant but still had the subgun in his back. The other members of Phoenix Force stood in front of the men whose guns they'd taken.

"On three," McCarter said. "One…"

Encizo saw Hong's eyes widen in horror. The young cadet feared the men of Phoenix Force were about to kill the other cops, and maybe him.

"Two…" McCarter said.

Hong leaned forward like a dog on a leash, chomping at the bit to help but fearing he'd be shot before he'd taken two steps.

"Three!"

Five right crosses shot out simultaneously.

Five Chinese cops dropped to the pavement in synchronization.

Manning slid over to the passenger side of the van as Hawkins, James and Encizo piled in the back. Encizo slid the door closed as McCarter jumped behind the wheel.

"Hong," he said through the open window.

The young cadet looked to be still in shock.

"Remember what I said, Hong. And remember that it would have been easier for us to kill all of you. We didn't."

Throwing the gearshift into Drive, McCarter took off down the street.

"Well," Manning said as they streaked away from the Beijing Plaza, "I'd say our cover is pretty much blown, wouldn't you?"

"It would appear as such," Hawkins agreed, keeping up the understatement. "We just assaulted five Chinese police officers, effected escape from their custody and stole their van. We're on the streets of Communist China, and the authorities think we've been assassinating their politburo members. None of us speaks the language, and we've got round eyes that stand out like a Klansman in Harlem." He paused, shaking his head. "You suppose it could get much worse?"

James spoke up. "Yes, it could be much worse."

"How?" Hawkins asked.

"We could actually *be* Klansmen in Harlem," Phoenix Force's black commando said with a grin.

CHAPTER NINE

Vu stared up at the Executioner from where he had landed on the wet carpet. The man was as large as Son was small. Roll upon roll of fat covered his nude arms, legs and torso, all dripping wet from the exploded water bed.

Bolan lifted a boot, pressed it against his face and pushed.

Vu's upper body toppled backward over the wooden water-bed frame in a storm of jiggling flesh.

Bolan kept his boot on Vu's face, pinning the man to the bed frame as he drew the Benchmade folder knife. Flipping it open with his thumb, he cut the leather restraints from the black woman who sat blindly at Vu's right. Her hands went immediately to her blindfold as Bolan freed the white woman on Vu's other side. He let the women take care of their own gags and blindfolds as he closed the knife, clipped it back inside his front pocket, then waved the MAT toward a stack of clothes to the side of the bed. "Get dressed and get over against the wall with the two men," he ordered.

Neither woman objected. A moment later they were covered and sitting next to Son and Bui.

Bolan pulled his boot off Vu's face and allowed the man to sit up. Anger shot from the gangster kingpin's eyes, very much like the anger the soldier had seen in both Bui and Son before he had called their bluffs.

Would Vu be as easy to break? Somehow he didn't think so. But breaking him would have to occur if Bolan expected to find out what he needed to know.

The big American stared down at the man. "Vu," he said, "you deal in white slavery, which makes you a pimp and a kidnapper. You deal in drugs, which makes you a pusher. And you have people killed when you don't like what they're doing, and that makes you a murderer." He paused to let it sink in. "I'm not particularly interested in any of that. At least not at the moment. What I want to know is who it is financing the Confederation of Southeast Asia."

Vu's lips looked like two fat summer sausages pressed together. "I do not know who you are," he said in a high, wavery voice, "but you will die very slowly and very painfully for your insolence."

"There's always that possibility," Bolan acknowledged, "but it won't happen today, and it won't happen here." He leaned in and jammed the muzzle of the MAT into Vu's belly. "I have a few questions for you, Vu," he said. "You answer them well, and there's still a chance you'll live."

Vu threw back his head and cackled. "I will live. It will be you who is dead. I do not know how you got in here, but in seconds my men will—"

Bolan shook his head. "I don't think so." He moved back to the door and opened it so Vu could see the bodies in the hall. "The others are downstairs, on the steps and in the other hall." He paused, then said, "Oh, yeah, two at the gate. If I missed any, they don't seem too anxious to come get what the others got." He watched Vu's face for any change. The only one he saw was another smile.

"So you will kill me?" Vu said. Again he threw back his head and laughed. "I am not afraid to die. In fact I would welcome death, embrace it as one would a long-lost lover."

Bolan studied the man's eyes. Vu might just be a good actor, but Bolan's gut instinct said the man was serious. A glance at the chains on the walls just past the bed reminded him of Vu's S&M activities. The Vietnamese gangster might indeed have a perverted longing to explore the ultimate in sadomasochistic experiences. If he did, the threat of death was meaningless as a bargaining tool. But there had to be something the man didn't want to lose, and the Executioner intended to find it.

"Where are you going to play your little games when I burn your house down in about five minutes?"

Vu smiled. "In the new house I build, which will be even bigger."

"Really?" Bolan asked. "What are you going to use for money? I'm going to set all your girls free before I leave, too."

"Most of my girls are not kept here," he said. "But even if you find them, there is the gambling, drugs and other business interests. You can't get them all, and each enterprise could finance a house ten times this size."

"I can get them all," Bolan promised. "Believe me, Vu, if I set my mind to it, I can get them—I've done it before. You'll be left without a penny." He glanced at the women against the wall. "You think you're going to get playmates like that without the money?"

"Go ahead. Set the girls free and destroy my businesses. It will make no difference. I have accounts in Switzerland, the Caymans...a dozen other places. I already have more money than I could ever spend. So take the girls, the drugs, the gambling. It would be a load off my shoulders and allow me to enjoy myself like this—" he nodded toward the frightened women against the wall "—all of the time."

The Executioner stared at the man in silence. He had met his share of decadent humans during his long career, but Vu was as bad as they came.

"So you see, whoever you are," Vu said, "there is nothing you can do to make me talk. I do not fear death. It is unavoidable and, experienced correctly, it is the ultimate thrill. If you beat me, even to death, I will enjoy it." He giggled. "And if you choose to leave me alive, I have more than enough money to replace anything you take." He glanced at the women against the wall. "One way or another I will continue with my delights."

Bolan continued to stare at him. Vu didn't know it yet, but he had just given Bolan the answer he'd been looking for.

"You don't mind dying and you can replace anything I take," Bolan repeated. "Well, maybe not everything." He reached down suddenly, digging his fingers into the fat under Vu's laughing chin. Pulling upward, he jerked the man to his feet and walked him across the room to the wall with the wrist and ankle cuffs.

The Executioner secured the man's feet and hands, then stepped back.

"Beat me," Vu breathed. "Beat me...I deserve it...."

"Yes, you do," Bolan agreed. "But you like that sort of thing." He shook his head. "No, I'm not going to beat you, Vu. I'm just going to perform a little much-needed corrective surgery." He drew the Benchmade knife and flipped it open, letting the overhead light glimmer off the razor-sharp steel blade.

Bolan held out an arm and drew the blade across it, shaving the hair off the back of his wrist. "It occurs to me," he said, holding the blade up for inspection, "that you don't mind dying, and you don't mind living because money can replace everything you think I can take."

Vu wasn't laughing now. Maybe he had guessed what Bolan had in mind. Maybe he simply saw the confidence of victory that Bolan was exhibiting. In any case he stared at the blade.

With one swift motion, Bolan lowered the blade under the fat man's scrotum. He raised the tip slightly, letting it rest against the head of Vu's penis. "I'm not sure how you're going to buy another one of these," he commented, "no matter how much money you have in those Swiss and Cayman accounts."

Vu's eyes had lost much of their confidence, but he still possessed good insight. "It is a bluff," he said.

"You sure?" Bolan asked.

Vu nodded. "I know people. That is why I have been successful both in gathering information and in my other activities." He glanced down at the blade and smiled, the confidence returning. "I can read people. And you are not the kind of man who would do such a thing."

Bolan didn't answer. Vu was right. Torture and maiming had never been part of the Executioner's mental makeup. It had been a bluff on his part, and Vu had called that bluff.

It had also been the only route Bolan could think

of to get Vu to talk, and he had no idea where to go from here.

Son, Bui and the women against the wall had been silent throughout the interchange between Bolan and Vu. But now Bolan heard a voice.

"Give me the knife."

Bolan turned to see the black woman rising from her seat against the wall. She walked forward on unsteady legs, and as she neared, the big American could see the scars on what had to once have been beautifully smooth skin. She looked at the man chained to the wall, and all of the pain she had experienced at his hands seemed to come out all at once.

"Perhaps *you* cannot do such a thing," she said, "But *I* can."

The Executioner reversed his grip on the knife and started to hand it to her.

"No!" Vu shrieked.

Bolan turned back to see Vu's eyes darting back and forth from the woman to the blade. He might have known that Bolan wouldn't castrate him, but he was equally sure that the woman he had tortured would.

"Please!" Vu screamed. "Do not give her the knife! I will tell you whatever it is you want to know!"

THE MOTEL ON SOUTH I-35, in the Oklahoma City suburb of Moore, had once been a Stratford house.

The brown brick, steepled roofing and false English decor of the lobby proved it.

Which meant the Super 8 Motel sign outside looked out of place.

Carl Lyons drew the curtains on the window to let in the afternoon sunlight, looked briefly at the sign, then took a seat at the table. Carefully he unwrapped the wineglass from the safari vest. Holding it by the stem, he raised it to the light, scrutinizing the smudges he could see along the rounded surface. It had been a miracle that the glass had escaped his wild motor-cycle race and the ensuing gunfight. If it had managed to survive that and still retain usable fingerprints, well, that would be another miracle.

The Able Team leader set the glass on the table and lifted his fingerprint kit from the floor. Across the room at the desk, he could see Gadgets Schwarz unzipping the portable fax machine that was rarely out of the Able Team electronics wizard's reach.

Lyons dug through the kit, produced a small bottle of fingerprint powder, then glanced back at the glass. A light film of grease appeared to uniformly cover the surface. More than likely the glasses were stored close to the frying grills in the Italian restaurant's kitchen. He'd need a powder that would build up a heavy ridge body in spite of the grease.

Dropping the bottle back in the box, the big ex-cop chose a powder with a higher mercury content. A soft, rounded, camel-hair brush came out with the new bottle.

Lyons glanced across the room again to see Blancanales standing next to the bed, dialing the motel phone. It would be an unsecured call, but only for a moment. Pol said, "One, four, four, four" into the receiver, and the Able Team leader knew that the code meant that, before she even spoke, Barbara Price would activate the trace-and-tap block, as well as a reverse scrambler, that would feed back through the lines to the motel.

Lyons placed the brush handle between the palms of his hands and rolled it briskly back and forth to separate the hairs and expel any bits of microscopic foreign matter that might have accumulated. He unscrewed the lid of the powder bottle, then dumped a tiny pile onto a clean white piece of paper. Dipping the bristles lightly into the pile, he tapped the handle on the table to shake off the excess, then began running the brush lightly across the surface of the glass.

Several ridges appeared almost immediately. Lyons switched to a smaller brush and reversed the direction of his strokes, directing them along the general course of the ridges. A moment later he saw the tented arch pattern begin to develop, and a moment after that, he smiled.

The print was only a partial, but unless he missed his guess, there would be enough to use.

He moved back to the larger brush, using it again

to "search" for latent prints. When he came across what appeared to be a whorl pattern, he returned again to the smaller tool.

Lyons glanced up when Blancanales said, "He's lifting them right now" into the phone, and knew Pol had to have Kurtzman on the other end by now. Schwarz moved over to the bed, set the fax machine on the bedspread and knelt to plug it into the wall socket.

The Able Team leader went back to his dusting, covering the rest of the glass with a light residue of fingerprint powder. Several smudges appeared, but none worth lifting, so he shook the brushes again, then returned them to the kit.

Pulling two clean white fingerprint cards and a roll of what looked like extrathick transparent tape from the box, Lyons set the cards on the table. He carefully placed the tape over the prints on the glass, and even more carefully patted it with a piece of soft cloth to remove the air bubbles. Slowly pulling the tape off each print, he placed the whorl on one card and the tented arch on the other.

Lyons heard the buzz as the fax machine warmed up. "Aaron ready, Pol?" he asked.

Blancanales extended the receiver. "He wants to talk to you."

Lyons stood, walking the print cards to Schwarz, then taking the phone. "Yeah, Bear?" he said.

Kurtzman cleared his throat. "I'll run these things

through AFIS just as soon as you get them to me," he said. "But you know its limitations."

Lyons nodded. The Automated Fingerprint Identification System was one of the true law-enforcement computer breakthroughs of recent times. It could search all files linked to it for prints similar to those under scrutiny, then select the top ten possibilities for fingerprint technicians to examine. In essence, it did in minutes what would take a team of skilled technicians their entire careers to accomplish by hand.

"You have any other leads as to who the guy might be?" Kurtzman asked.

"I heard him speaking Japanese, Bear," Lyons said. "Of course, that doesn't necessarily mean he *is* Japanese. But along with the samurai topknot, that would be my first guess."

The Able Team leader knew why Kurtzman wanted more info if he had it. The downside of AFIS lay in the fact that it was too new. So far, no national system had been initiated, and most states operated on their own system. That meant that if matching prints didn't show up in the files checked, they had to be "hand carried" to all other AFIS programs.

"I'll check the U.S. systems first," Kurtzman said. "If nothing pans out—"

"I've got a feeling it won't," Lyons cut in. "Mr. Topknot has 'foreign' written all over him. I'd be real surprised if his prints are on file in the U.S."

"Then I'll try Japan next. Everybody is on file there."

Lyons heard a click, then Barbara Price said, "Ironman, I've got Hal on the other line. I'll connect you."

The Able Team leader waited for a quick series of clicks, then heard Hal Brognola's voice from the man's office at the U.S. Department of Justice. "Ironman, we've gotten a body count from Oklahoma City," Brognola said.

Lyons held his breath. He and the other members of Able Team had done their best to keep the demonstration from turning into a riot, but they had been too late. Part of him didn't want to know how many innocent civilians had died.

The other part knew he had to know.

"Seventeen men down for the count," Brognola said. "Five Caucasians who appear to be your Aryan Brotherhood yo-yos and an even dozen Orientals of unknown origin. Four more men wounded. No women."

Lyons let his breath out slow. "Got IDs on any of them?" he asked.

"Nothing positive yet, but no one's claiming any of the bodies. Which leads me to believe they were all Topknot's men. One of the men wounded was an undercover OCPD detective. He took a round through the upper arm, but it's not much more than a burn." Brognola paused. "Good job, Ironman," he finally said. "It could have turned out a lot worse."

The Able Team leader glanced to the fax machine Schwarz had set on the bed. Gadgets nodded.

"I'm hanging up now, Hal," Lyons said into the phone. "Gadgets has the fax ready."

"Affirmative, Ironman. As soon as you send it, head out for Wiley Post Airport. Know where it is?"

"Not far from the main Will Rogers airport. We were there with Striker a few months ago." He paused to breath. "Grimaldi on his way?"

"He is," Brognola said. "Should be there in another thirty minutes or so. We'll contact you en route if Kurtzman comes up with an ID on Topknot."

"En route to where?" Lyons asked.

"Did I forget to tell you? You're on your way to Austin. Kurtzman's probability program has been working overtime. The Texas governor came up as the number-one choice for a retaliation hit by the Chinese."

AARON KURTZMAN RAN both hands through his hair as he listened to the hum of the fax machine. The light finally came on, indicating that the transmission was on its way. Feet padded up the wheelchair ramp behind him, but the computer ace didn't bother to turn. He knew who the light footsteps belonged to— had heard them hundreds—no, thousands—of times in the past.

A moment later Kurtzman saw Barbara Price's reflection in the blank monitor screen in front of him.

Stony Man's mission controller reached a lithe arm around his chair, set a cup of steaming coffee on the console to one side of the screen and straightened.

"Thanks, Barb," Kurtzman said.

Price chuckled. "Just don't ask me to do windows," she said, then her tone turned serious. "How long will it take? Once you get the prints, I mean."

Kurtzman shrugged, still looking at the woman's reflection in the screen. "Just depends, Barb. AFIS itself is like greased lightning. Almost boggles the mind if you understand what a tedious procedure searching for print matchups by hand used to be. But the problem is that we don't even have a central data base for the entire U.S., let alone the world." He picked up the coffee cup, took a tiny sip that burned his lips and set it back down as the fax machine began coughing out a hard copy of the fingerprints.

Kurtzman lifted the white paper. What he saw made him smile. Two prints—and both impressions had come out clean. The ridges were clear, and you could even vaguely make out the light gray lines that indicated the boundaries of the print cards Lyons had used. Kurtzman stared at the fingerprint on top: a tented arch. The one below was a loop...no, the ridges circled back on themselves. A whorl.

Tapping the keys, Kurtzman accessed the hard drive and activated another of the many programs he'd developed himself. This one, which he called Flash Class, provided near-instant classification of fingerprints. Instead of poring over the impressions with a magnifying glass, he could enter the same fax Schwarz had forwarded and have a complete extended Henry System classification in seconds.

Kurtzman opened the lid to the scanner, inserted the page and closed the lid again. His fingers danced across the keyboard, and a moment later the prints appeared on the monitor screen. Typing briefly, the computer ace then sat back and lifted his coffee cup to wait. Still the coffee was too hot to drink.

Setting the cup back down, the computer man watched as the classification appeared on the screen. He typed again, then watched as the letters and numbers moved to a window in the upper right-hand corner. The image of the prints themselves disappeared, being stored in the memory of the machine.

"You going to try FBI's AFIS first?" Price asked.

"I guess. They're the biggest, so that's the most likely place to start."

"Then the different states?"

Kurtzman frowned. For a moment he sat motionless, thinking. Lyons didn't seem to think the Akira Tokaido look-alike who'd left the prints on the wineglass was "homegrown." If that was the case, Lyons was also likely to be right that Topknot's prints weren't on file with the FBI or anywhere else in the U.S.

"I was," Kurtzman said, "but I think I've changed my mind."

In the monitor's reflection, Kurtzman saw Price

frown. Waving his hand along the bank of computers and related instruments that ran from wall to wall in the Stony Man computer room, Kurtzman said, "You know, Barb, these things do stuff no human being— or any number of human beings—could do. But they can't operate on their own. They need humans to take care of them, to feed them, so to speak. It's a partnership of man and machine. But if I couldn't have both, I'd trade every one of these things for one seasoned screw-you-I-operate-on-hunches cop like our beloved Ironman." He paused. "And his latest hunch says that Topknot isn't on file in the U.S., and that he's Japanese."

"Don't trade the machines, Bear," she said. "You'd feel just like you'd gotten a divorce."

Kurtzman smiled. "I've never been married," he said, "but I suspect it would be worse."

"So you're going straight to Japan?"

He nodded. "Yeah. If we come up dry there, I'll come back to the U.S. or try the other Oriental nations." His fingers began to fly across the keyboard.

Five minutes later the Stony Man Farm computer genius had hacked his way through the access codes, traps and traces of the Japanese National Police's identification bureau. Two minutes after that, he gained access to their AFIS program.

Entering Topknot's fingerprint classification, Kurtzman sat back in his wheelchair and clasped his hands behind his head to wait. "We'll be lucky if the guy really is Japanese," he said. "Tokyo prints everybody. They operate on a guilty-until-proved-innocent basis."

"Think we should do that here?"

Kurtzman snorted. "Want to see the fastest armed rebellion in the history of the world?" he answered. "The Japanese police also have unlimited search-and-seizure laws. Not many Americans would stand for that sort of thing."

"You're talking to one of them," Price said.

Kurtzman had started to answer when the screen suddenly lit up. Ten names, in alphabetical order, appeared in amber against the black background. He tapped the keys again. Going down the list, he used his own system again to compare each of the ten candidates to Schwarz's fax, which was still in the scanner.

When he reached Tanaka, Ichiro, he got a match.

"Tanaka," Price said. "That name rings a bell somewhere. Electronics, right?"

Kurtzman nodded. "Computers and software. We've got some of their stuff right here." He cleared the screen, then reentered the Japanese police files. The photograph of a man in his late twenties, complete with samurai topknot, appeared. Again, even though Ichiro Tanaka had no criminal record, the Japanese government had a complete dossier on him. The file included not only facts but rumor and conjecture.

Kurtzman scanned the facts and figures. Then, re-membering what he'd just told Price about the com-puter "marriage" of man and machine, he swung his wheelchair to the side. "Akira," he called down the long bank of computers. When the young Japanese looked up, he swung his head toward the screen.

Tokaido's own topknot bobbed as he rose from his chair and hurried over.

"Besides the governor of Texas popping out first, how's the search for American likelies going?" Kurtz-man asked.

"Well, boss man," the young man said, "your probability program suggests that the Chinese won't choose senators or congressman as targets. They're the closest thing to a politburo that we have, and Bei-jing will expect them to be too well guarded."

"So who are they going after?"

Tokaido shrugged. "More governors, the program implies. Perhaps the mayors of large cities. We'll have it down to the shortlist within an hour." The young man turned his attention to the screen and squinted at Tanaka's picture.

"What do you think?" Kurtzman asked.

The topknotted cybernetics expert grinned. "Nice hair."

"That's great, but do you know him?" Kurtzman asked.

Tokaido squinted as he read the name below the picture. "Only by reputation," he said. "The Tanakas are an old family, dating all the way back to samurai times. The money is fairly new, though. Electronics—but you'd already know that. Ichiro is the youngest of three brothers. Yuji, the oldest, has run the family business since their father's death. Ichiro has a reputation as a playboy of sorts. Hotheaded. Before the family became wealthy—"

The phone in front of Kurtzman rang suddenly, cutting the young man off.

Price leaned around the wheelchair. "I switched my lines in here," she said. She picked up the receiver and said simply, "Price."

Kurtzman watched her as she listened to whoever it was on the other end, then she replied, "Affirmative, Striker...yes...yes...no. Grimaldi's tied up with Able Team at the moment, but I've had Charlie Mott standing by in Thailand in case you needed a lift. I'll activate him as soon as I hang up." She paused to listen again, then said, "Bear just came up with a name behind the riots here in the U.S. Considering what you just told me, I think it might interest you—Ichiro Tanaka." She paused again, then said, "Affirmative," and then hung up.

The Stony Man mission controller stepped out where she could face both Kurtzman and Tokaido. "Striker's hunch was right. The Golden Triangle warlords aren't financing the Confederation. Want to guess who is?"

"The Tanaka family," Kurtzman said. "Which is

why little Ichiro has been sent here to stir up protests against the U.S. taking action."

Price nodded. "That's right. We've been operating under the assumption that Striker and Able Team were involved in separate missions. But they're one and the same. Striker's heading for Tokyo as soon as Charlie Mott picks him up."

Kurtzman nodded. Turning back to Tokaido, he said, "You had started to tell us something else about the Tanakas when the phone rang."

Tokaido shrugged. "Just that before wealth brought respectability to the family, they had something of a dark past. They were a samurai family, remember, but not all samurai families are as principled as others."

"What do you mean?" Price asked.

"Well, rumor was that if you needed dirty work done, the Tanakas were who you went to. Not that they did it themselves. Samurai, as you know, operate under the code of Bushido. When they fight, it has to be out in the open."

Kurtzman felt himself growing uneasy as something in the back of his brain tried to move to the front. "Exactly what are you trying to say, Akira?" he asked.

Tokaido shrugged again. "The rumor was that they had close connections to several *ninja* clans."

Kurtzman's head jerked back to the screen. There, in the third paragraph beneath Ichiro Tanaka's picture, the same rumor was confirmed.

The Stony Man computer genius didn't speak as he whirled his chair around and rolled past Tokaido and Price. He didn't stop until he'd reached the computer where Tokaido had been running the probability program on who might actually be behind the assassination of the Chinese politburo members. Shoving the young Japanese man's chair to one side, he wheeled to a halt in front of the keyboard.

Price and Tokaido had followed him down the row. They stood silently as he entered the new Tanaka data into the program. As soon as the machine had digested the information, he cleared the screen and typed in "Most likely assassins of Chinese politburo members?" then hit Enter.

Starting on the left side of the screen, the letters appeared one at a time.

"NINJA."

Kurtzman twisted in his chair to face Price and Tokaido. "We thought we had three separate missions," he said. "Then we realized Striker's and Able Team's were connected, which made it two. But we've got only one mission going here, Barb. The Tanakas' *ninjas* are the ones killing the Chinese politburo members and blaming it on the CIA."

CHAPTER TEN

Austin, Texas

Oklahoma City to Austin, Texas, had been a short hop for Jack Grimaldi and Able Team. In the Learjet it took less than thirty minutes from takeoff to landing.

Lyons sat silently as Grimaldi dropped the plane through the air toward the isolated landing strip north of the city. One of Kurtzman's cybernetics team— Lyons didn't know who—had been running the Bear's probability programs and determined that Texas Governor Jack Rush was the most likely candidate for the Chinese assassins. A popular governor, Rush was known for two things: a quick, Will Rogers–style wit, and honesty.

That honesty included making no secret that a run for the presidency might lie somewhere down the line. And that run for the presidency made him a perfect candidate for assassination by the Chinese.

Lyons watched the runway as the plane touched down. At the end of the strip he could see two dark

Chevrolet sedans waiting on a stretch of gravel. Four men dressed in dark slacks, Western boots and hats, and sunglasses stood around the vehicles, their arms folded across their chests. Lyons could see gun belts on their hips, and small stars gleamed on their shirts.

"Stony Base to Able One," Price's voice said over the airwaves. "Come in, Able."

Lyons jerked the microphone from the mount in front of his seat and held it to his face. Pressing the red button on the side with his thumb, he said, "Able here."

"Affirmative, One," Price said. "Location?"

"Just touched down."

"You should find the Texas Rangers waiting for you," Price said. "They'll escort you to Governor Rush."

"Roger, Barb," Lyons said as Grimaldi slowed the jet to a crawl. Closer now, he could see that the men's gun belts held Sig-Sauer semiautomatic pistols. "I can see them. The Rangers in charge of Rush's security?"

"Negative," Price came back. "They've just been brought in to assist you, and for backup. The Department of Public Safety's executive-protection team handles the governor's bodyguard work."

Grimaldi brought the plane to a halt.

"We're home," Lyons said into the mike. "Able One out."

"Base clear."

Lyons opened the door and stepped down from the jet, feeling the heat radiate from the asphalt. He turned to see Schwarz and Blancanales descend to the tarmac.

All three of the Able Team commandos had executed a quick change of clothes on board the plane. Lyons now wore a conservative navy blue single-breasted suit. Schwarz and Blancanales wore similar suits but in gray.

All in all, the Able Team leader thought, inspecting the other two men before turning back toward the waiting Rangers, they looked more like U.S. Justice Department agents than most U.S. Justice Department agents did.

"Special Agent in Charge McKnight?" a slow Texas drawl called out behind Lyons. He turned to see a man in his early fifties, at least six and a half feet tall. The man ambled off the gravel and onto the asphalt. He was almost as broad as he was tall, and the short-sleeved white dress shirt beneath a colorful hand-painted tie threatened to pop around the chest and shoulders with each step. A small five-pointed star, fastened to the badge flap of a pen caddy in his shirt pocket, IDed him as a Texas Ranger. Dark brown Western-cut slacks fell over shining yellow full-quill ostrich boots, and the Ranger's Sig-Sauer .45 pistol hung from his hip in a *buscadero* rig.

"I'm McKnight," Lyons said, sticking out his hand. His other thumb hooked over his shoulder toward Schwarz and Blancanales. "Special agents Smith and Martinez."

The tall man grasped Lyons's hand in a firm grip. "Ranger Jim Campbell," he said. He hooked his own thumb now and said, "Garcia, Wesson and Jefferson."

Lyons glanced behind Campbell as he shook the man's hand, seeing a black man, a Latino and a Caucasian with short blond hair. All were dressed in Western gear similar to Campbell's.

The Able Team leader shook the man's big hand. Barely peeking around Campbell's side, and stuffed into his waistband at the rear of the brown slacks, were the grips of a Desert Eagle like the handcannon Mack Bolan carried.

Lyons had to hide a grin. A white Stetson on top of Campbell's head completed the look, making him the quintessential modern Texas Ranger. Campbell stuck to the proud Western tradition that had made the Rangers internationally known—but only so far that it didn't affect his work. His look might be that of a law-enforcement officer a century out of time, but the equipment that counted was on the cutting edge of technology.

"That's some serious firepower in the back," Lyons said, dropping the hand. "A .44 Magnum?"

Campbell chuckled. "You're in *Texas* now, boy," he said. "It's a .50 Action Express. Ever shot one?"

Lyons nodded. "I've got a friend who carries the

.44," he said. "Once in a while the .50." He glanced past Campbell to where the other Rangers were opening the doors of the sedans. "What do you say we get moving? You can fill us in on the way."

"You got it," Campbell said. He pivoted on a boot heel and led the way to the nearest car. "You Justice boys hop in with me," he said. "Garcia, ride back with Wesson and Jefferson."

Campbell adjusted the huge Desert Eagle in the back of his belt and slid behind the wheel. Lyons took the seat next to him as Schwarz and Blancanales slid into the back.

"I'm a little surprised they called us Rangers in on this deal," Campbell said as he threw the sedan into gear and tore away from the landing strip in a storm of gravel. The other sedan fell in behind them. "DPS handles the bodyguard chores for the governor, and they generally guard that duty like I'd guard a twenty-year-old girlfriend if I had one."

"This is a little different situation than usual," Blancanales said from the back seat. "Normally we wouldn't be needed, either."

Lyons watched for Campbell's reaction. The man's face betrayed nothing. Many law-enforcement agencies were as jealous of their jurisdictions as the Ranger had implied the Texas DPS was of its executive-protection role. But Campbell didn't seem to be bothered by the presence of Feds.

"Now, let me tell you," the man behind the wheel

said as they turned onto the highway leading into Austin, "most generally Governor Rush is one good ol' boy. Good-natured. Easygoin'. Hell, there ain't nobody likes a good joke any more than him, neither. But I understand ol' Jack's been actin' about half polécat on this one."

Campbell stomped a boot on the accelerator, and soon they were weaving in and out of traffic on the four-lane highway. "He's got a speech scheduled downtown on Sixth Street this afternoon. Y'all know that area?"

Schwarz leaned forward. "Near the university, if I remember right," he said. "Cafés, taverns, T-shirt shops and the like. Student atmosphere."

"That's a big 10-4 there, Smith," Campbell said. He leaned harder on the accelerator.

Lyons glanced over to the speedometer and saw the red needle floating near 110. He turned to look behind him and saw the other Rangers keeping pace less than ten yards from their back bumper.

"Sixth ain't a bad area really," the Ranger went on. "It's just one hell of a hard place to keep somebody safe. I understand Rush's team tried to talk him into calling the thing off. No go. Then one your boys called and suggested he cancel the speech. Brogzinski or something like that."

"Brognola," Blancanales said.

"Yeah, probably, I didn't talk to him. But there

ain't no way the governor's gonna back out. Got an election coming up too soon."

Campbell barely slowed as they reached the Austin city limits. A few minutes later they were burning rubber around the rear of the governor's mansion, then parking next to a steel door.

Jefferson, Wesson and Garcia pulled in next to them as Campbell and Able Team exited the sedan. The older Ranger rapped a fist on the steel door, and a moment later they were waved in by a man in a gray suit. Lyons, Schwarz and Blancanales followed Campbell down a short hallway to an elevator, rode it up and got off on the third floor.

Texas Governor Jack Rush's voice could be heard from down the hall as the doors closed behind them. "Dammit, Gordon, people are going to think I been eating Mama's mashed potatoes. I look like I gained twenty pounds in this thing."

Able Team followed the Rangers down the hall and through an open door to what looked like the governor's living room. Roughly twenty men—a mixture of gray suits and Western attire—stood around a man seated in a straight-backed wooden chair in the middle of the room. Rush had on the slacks to a navy blue pin-striped suit. An aide held his shirt, tie and jacket.

Rush slapped the Kevlar bulletproof vest he had put on over his white T-shirt. "Gordon, you know I don't like to make your job any harder than it already is," he said, "but isn't there any other way to do this thing? I've got an election coming up, and these are college voters. They're in the prime of their physical life. They aren't going to vote for Porky Pig."

"Jack," a bald man with a thick mustache said, "they aren't even going to notice the vest under your shirt and coat. We don't—"

"The thing's hot, too, Gordon," Rush said. "Even if I don't look like a pig, I'll be sweatin' like one." He seemed suddenly aware that the others had entered the room and turned toward where Lyons and Campbell stood. "Hey there, Jim," he said. "Good to see you boys. I always feel better with the cowboys around." He glanced quickly to the bald man he'd called Gordon. "Not that my team isn't top-notch."

"Governor, I'd like to introduce Special agents McKnight, Martinez and Smith," Campbell said. "You already know my boys, Garcia, Jefferson and Wesson."

The governor nodded and stood. He grinned, shook hands all around, then looked up at Lyons. "Special Agent McKnight," he said, "is it your expert opinion that I should wear this itching, scratching, heat-welt-instigating contraption?"

Lyons nodded. "You can't take too many precautions, Governor," he said.

He glanced around the room. "Gentlemen," he said, "I'm not at liberty to go into details. But I promise the threat is real. Don't any of you take it lightly."

"Jim, what do you think?" Rush asked the big Ranger.

Campbell cleared his throat. "Leave the vest on, Jack," he said. "And drop the steel insert into that pocket over your ticker."

Rush shrugged, reached out an arm and took the insert from Gordon. He fumbled trying to get it into the pocket, and Campbell stepped in and finished the job for him

"Thanks, Jim," Rush said. "I'll wear this hair shirt for you and Agent McKnight, here. But only because you boys have already shown such good sense and foresight."

"Governor," Campbell said, "we just got here. We haven't done anything yet."

Rush slipped into his shirt and began to knot his tie. "I beg to differ," he said. He tightened the knot and reached for his jacket. Walking between where Lyons and Campbell stood, he stopped in front of Gadgets Schwarz, who stood next to Ranger Wesson. "You brought this man with you, didn't you, Mc-Knight?" the governor said over his shoulder.

"Yes, sir," Lyons said. "Special Agent Smith."

Rush placed his other hand on the blond Ranger's shoulder. "And this young man's with you, isn't he, Jim?"

"You know he is, Jack."

The governor dropped his arms and turned back to Lyons and Campbell. "Well, hell, boys," he said.

"That's what I meant about good sense and fore-sight." His face broke into a wide grin. "How can anything bad happen to me when you bring along a Smith and Wesson?"

MCCARTER KNEW it would be only minutes before the Chinese cops woke up and called in what had happened. Hong, who they'd left conscious, might already have done so.

It didn't matter who made the call. The bottom line was that it wouldn't be long until every cop in the city was looking for the stolen police van.

The Briton turned the corner away from the hotel. Now out of sight of anyone who had witnessed Phoenix Force's escape, he dropped his speed to avoid drawing attention. "We've got to change vehicles," he said, thinking out loud more than informing the rest of the team. The Phoenix Force leader knew that his men would already be thinking the same thing. "As soon as we're out of this neighborhood, we'll boost another ride."

Glancing over his shoulder, he looked at Hawkins. "You know what to do, T.J. Get ready."

Hawkins nodded.

The Phoenix Force leader drove six more blocks, then spotted a red Toyota MR2 parked along the curb in front of a row of buildings. It would be a tight squeeze, getting all of the men inside, but McCarter

didn't intend to keep them there long. "There, T.J.,"
he said. "The red one." He pulled up next to the car.

Hawkins was out of the vehicle before it had rolled
to a stop.

McCarter continued down the block, then double-
parked the van in front of a drugstore. By the time
he and the rest of the men were out of the van, Hawkins had cracked the Toyota's steering column, started
the engine and pulled up alongside them.

With Hawkins behind the wheel, Phoenix Force
moved through the streets of Beijing. A mile later
Manning had his turn at hot-wiring when they traded
the Toyota for a Mitsubishi Montero. The small vehicle crowded them even more than the MR2, but two
miles later—and well away from the area where the
escape would have been witnessed—McCarter spotted a Toyota 4-Runner.

It wasn't ideal, but each man would at least have
a seat with a little room left over for equipment.

"As soon as I'm out, drive down to the alley and
turn in," McCarter said, indicating the passage between two buildings with a nod. "I'll meet you there.
We've switched enough times that our trail should be
dry by now. I don't want to blow it by someone seeing a bunch of round-eyes loading weapons."

A moment later the Briton had the Toyota up and
running and was pulling into the alley after the Mitsubishi. A moment after that, they were heading back
down the street with Encizo behind the wheel.

McCarter sat next to the Cuban with Manning, Hawkins and James in the back. The Phoenix Force leader reached over the seat. "Phone," he told Hawkins.

The younger man handed him the cellular, which he'd retrieved from the Chinese police.

The Briton tapped in the number for Stony Man Farm, making sure the scrambler and trace lights burned brightly on the instrument. As the line began to ring, he flipped the switch to speakerphone so the others could hear.

A moment later Price answered.

"Phoenix One, Barb," McCarter said. "We're blown and on the run."

There was a short pause, then Price said, "Location?"

"Downtown Beijing. We're okay for the time being, but we won't be going back to the hotel or showing our faces anywhere in the open. At least not until the heat dies down."

"Affirmative," Price said. "You need a place to hole up? I can get Aaron to check on safehouses the CIA or some other—"

They had holed up most of the time so far, and while it had been a necessary part of the mission, McCarter had had enough of it. "No, Barb. We can work out of the car. What we need is the name of another politburo member to go look after." It still came out more sarcastic than he'd intended.

But Price had known him too long to take it personally. "Hang on."

McCarter heard a click. The Stony Man Farm mission controller was off the line for maybe fifteen seconds, then returned. "Aaron's got that new name for you," she said. "Ku Mojo. He's the most probable next target."

"Do you have an address?" McCarter asked.

"Office only." Price read it to him. "He's more than likely at home by now, though we don't have that information." She filled the team in on the new Intel concerning the Tanakas in Japan and how they were tied in to both the riots in the U.S. and assassinations in China.

"There's one other thing you need to know," Price said. "Yuji Tanaka's men in Beijing are *ninja*."

"*Ninja,*" McCarter repeated. He knew that the famed Japanese assassins still existed, but like anyone with an IQ two points higher than that of a rock, he knew that they no longer pranced around in tabi boots or hooded black *gis*. The modern *ninja* actually practiced the art of *shinobi*—shadow warfare. "Any more Intel on the black-clad beauties than that?"

"Negative," Price said. "But Aaron's got Carmen checking Tanaka's payroll files for anything that doesn't look kosher. Something may turn up." There was a short pause, then Price said, "David?"

"Yes?"

"You're on the run from the police, you can't

change your looks and none of you even speak Chinese. How in the world do you plan to get anything accomplished?"

"I've got an idea," McCarter said. "If it doesn't pan out, I suppose I'll have to get by on my good looks." Without further explanation, he hung up.

McCarter could feel his adrenaline start to pump. It was time for battle, and it sounded as if Phoenix Force was about to take on some of the most well-trained, underhanded, ferocious and competent warriors the world had ever produced—the *ninja.*

Instead of fear, the Briton felt his heart suddenly leap with excitement. Well, he was up to it. He turned in his seat to the other members of the team. They'd heard everything Price had said.

And if their faces were any indication, they were up to it, too.

YUJI TANAKA LIFTED the knife from his desk, stood, and stretched his back. "Tell me as soon as the call comes through," he said into the speakerphone to Yoko, then tapped the phone's Off button and moved to the other side of the desk.

Tanaka rolled his head a full 360 degrees, loosening the tight muscles. The time when the Confederation of Southeast Asia would be one nation rather than just a pact between individual countries was nearing. Even now land forces were massing along the coast of the South China Sea, ready to be picked up by CSA ships.

Other ships—already filled with Confederation marines primed for a first strike that would take Manila, Olongapo, Cavite and Batangas—were edging closer to the Philippines in an ever-widening circle that appeared to be just a continuation of naval exercises.

Yuji twirled the knife deftly through his fingers and felt a warmth rush through his body as if he had just swallowed a double shot of sake. One nation. When that dream became reality, the CSA would emerge as the world's third greatest power, right behind the United States and China. When that happened, the world would be his playground. He would move into the Pacific and take the Philippines first, then push on all the way to Australia. Eventually the CSA would become the Republic of Tanaka and would stretch from Burma to Tasmania. And by then he should be ready to take on the U.S., China or any other country that stood in his way.

Gripping the knife firmly in his last three fingers, Tanaka let his thumb and index finger curl around the hilt without squeezing it. He had manipulated the blade through the twenty-six-step dexterity drill with both hands as a warm-up, and had moved into the *kioske,* or "attention" position to begin his *kata,* when the phone on his desk behind him buzzed.

He cursed under his breath. Nothing relaxed him like the performance of a good *kata,* either armed or unarmed. But business was business, and in the Tanaka family, business had always come first.

Twirling the Japanese blade as he walked, Tanaka moved back to his desk and tapped the speakerphone button again. "Yes, Yoko?"

"Ichiro is on the line."

The Japanese software magnate smiled. His hotheaded little playboy brother had done far better in America than Yuji would ever have guessed him capable of. The usual distaste he had when he dealt with Ichiro had gradually diminished. "Put him on."

A moment later the youngest of the Tanaka brothers said, "Good day, brother."

"How are you?" Yuji returned politely.

"I am fine," Ichiro replied.

"I have been following your progress with enthusiasm," Yuji said. "Ichiro, I am proud of your work." He paused. "I am proud of *you*."

Ichiro remained silent.

"Is anything wrong?" Yuji asked.

After a short hesitation, Ichiro said, "No, Yuji, I do not believe so."

Yuji frowned. A brief surge of anxiety shot through his chest, and he felt the muscles in his neck tighten again. His irritation toward his brother returned, and he rubbed his neck, but the muscles refused to relax.

He needed to move. Stepping out from the desk, Yuji returned to the attention position and said, "Your hesitation tells me you are not certain, Ichiro. Please explain." Bowing his head slightly, Yuji brought his hands up in front of him with the knife gripped in his right fist.

"I do not believe anything is wrong, but we encountered some unexpected resistance in Oklahoma City."

Yuji stabbed the knife straight forward at chest level and snapped his blocking arm back to his waist. "What kind of resistance?" he asked. "I have only had initial reports, but they have said that many people were injured."

"They were," Ichiro agreed. "But they were our people, Yuji, shot by men I believe to be American special police or agents of some type."

Yuji pivoted to face the other way and repeated the block and stab. "What makes you believe this?" he asked.

"One of them followed me from the march to where I met with the Aryan Brotherhood men to whom we contracted," Ichiro said. "I saw him later when the shooting began. He killed all five of the round-eyes before they could injure any of the demonstrators."

Yuji had started to twirl back toward the desk. Instead, he froze in sudden fury. "You stayed at the march when you knew the shooting would begin?" he asked angrily.

"I was a block away, Yuji," Ichiro stated calmly. "I was able to watch through binoculars from the top of a building."

Yuji's anger receded but by no means vanished. "Little brother," he said testily as he dropped into a low-horse stance and slashed at the hamstring of an imaginary opponent, "need I remind you that in addition to my concern for your personal safety, if you are killed, you will be identified?" Without waiting for an answer, he added, "And that if you are identified, our entire operation will be jeopardized?"

"I was far away," Ichiro repeated. "I was safe."

Yuji rose into a cat stance, leaped into the air and executed a front snap kick. Twirling the knife into an ice-pick grip, he came down with it sunk in the top of the some invisible enemy's skull. He paused. "If this man killed the round-eyes before they could shoot, who killed our men?"

"Others," Ichiro said. "I do not know how many. Perhaps a dozen would be my guess by the work they did."

Yuji executed a violent sequence of slashes, then went into a section of the *kata* that was performed in slow motion. His words slowed with his movement. "Do you perceive more resistance from these men?" he asked. "Did they have intelligence information before the march as to what you had planned?"

"It is impossible to know. But I do not think so. It is quite likely that they were simply lucky. I do not expect it to happen again."

Yuji finished the *kata* with a combination of cuts, stabs, kicks and elbow strikes. He bowed, then turned back to the desk. Leaning over the speakerphone, he said, "Is there anything else of which I should be aware?"

"No," Ichiro said. "What do you hear from Nori?"

Yuji felt the sweat start on his forehead and wiped it away with the back of his sleeve. "Vietnam has agreed to the unification," he said. "Nori's lobbying and, of course, a great deal of money placed in the correct hands, has succeeded."

"What of Laos and Cambodia?" Ichiro asked. "And Burma?"

"They will follow their big brother, Vietnam," Yuji said. "They would be afraid not to."

Ichiro chuckled softly at the mild ridicule of the weaker nations. "The newspapers here tell me that Kosuke is still having much success," he said.

Yuji thought of the *ninja*, and a bitter taste entered his mouth. "Yes. Ku Mojo is next. Have the Chinese retaliated with their own assassinations yet?"

"I do not believe so yet," Ichiro said. "Nothing has been in the papers."

"Then it has not yet happened." Yuji twirled the knife twice, watching the shiny steel blade flash by. "In America the newspapers are aware of events before the government. And they print anything that will sell papers." Turning away from the desk, he leaped slightly and took a seat on the edge next to the speakerphone. All of his life he had entertained mixed feelings about his little brother. He loved him as only the baby of the family could be loved. But Ichiro had been spoiled as those babies often were, and his temper and lust had often created problems for the family.

As if Ichiro could read his mind, he brought the subject back to the mysterious government agents. "Yuji," he said in a calm, confident voice, "do not worry about things here. I do not believe there will be more of the problems we encountered in Oklahoma City. And if there are, I will handle them."

Yuji wished he were as sure as he sounded when he said, "I am sure." He flipped the knife into the air, let it turn once and caught it by the handle again. "But be careful, little brother," he added. "Time is short. We are close to achieving our goal. In less than one week the Confederation of Southeast Asia will be one nation. Shortly after that, we will take over the Philippines and begin moving down the Indonesian archipelago."

"When will the name be changed?" Ichiro asked eagerly.

Yuji shook his head silently in disgust. Eventually, he had told his little brother several weeks ago, the Confederation of Southeast Asia would be changed to the Republic of Tanaka. Since then, it seemed that the name recognition had been more important to Ichiro than anything else. "Eventually," he said. "This kind of thing cannot be pushed, and is not that important." He let his voice grow stern, more big-brotherly. "Please do not ask me again."

Ichiro's voice held a tinge of embarrassment as he changed the subject. "I believe that the Americans are losing their stomach for intervention," he said. "But tell me one more time, older brother. You *are* certain that China will not intervene when the Confederation expands?"

"Nothing is ever certain," Yuji said. "But by then, China should have its attention diverted. They will be at war with the United States."

"Goodbye, my brother," Ichiro said. "I will contact you again soon."

"See that you do," Yuji replied, and hung up.

He stood from the desk and repeated the *kata* maneuver twice, his slashes and stabs more vicious each time. Nothing could be allowed to go wrong at this point. There could be no mistakes.

They were close. *So* close.

Walking back to the desk, Yuji breathed more easily. He had to stop worrying. Nori's diplomatic work in Vietnam had gone smoothly. He was good, and he rarely made mistakes.

Ichiro had done far better than was to be expected, and if the youngest Tanaka had made mistakes, they couldn't be serious.

And Kosuke Yamaguchi, for all his vileness and vulgarity, was as incapable of mistakes as Yuji Tanaka himself.

Relax, Yuji told himself, rubbing his neck. Soon the CSA would be a reality. The thought brought triumph to his soul, and he twirled the knife into an ice-pick grip and lifted it high over his head in victory. Driving it down with all his might into the desk, he felt the chisel point plunge into the wood with a solid thud.

Yuji knew what had happened immediately. He had forgotten to hold his thumb on the pommel at the end of the grip. Stepping away from the desk, he looked down at his little finger.

Blood dripped from the deep slice where his hand had slid down onto the razor-sharp edge.

Yuji examined the wound. He had been lucky. He could have easily lost the finger altogether, but as it was, a few stitches would repair the damage.

That wasn't what worried him.

What worried Yuji was that he had never made such a mistake before.

CHAPTER ELEVEN

Had it been a few hundred years earlier, and had the skyscrapers of Tokyo been shorter stone palaces, the black-clad man who darted from shadow to shadow, building to building and alley to alley might have been a *ninja*. He would then have worn the hooded black *gi* with a black mask hiding his face, and would have carried the straight-bladed *shinobigatana* short sword, or perhaps a long-range chain-and-cord weapon known as a *kusari dogu*. His pockets would have been filled with *shuriken* throwing stars, poison darts and other weapons of medieval Japan.

But the time was the latter part of the twentieth century, and the man wasn't even Japanese, let alone a *ninja*. He was, nevertheless, even more highly skilled in the killing arts than the invisible assassins had ever been.

Mack Bolan wasn't a *ninja*.

He was an executioner.

From the darkened doorway of an office building across the street from Tanaka Tower, Bolan stared up at the seventh floor of the twenty-story structure. Dressed in a black raincoat, black turtleneck shirt and matching slacks, he had found it easy to blend with the night as he made his way along the streets. Few people were still on the sidewalks in the city's commerce area. They were office workers who had been forced to stay late, or important businessmen who had stopped at one of the local bars or geisha houses on their way home from work. The secretaries and other assistants wanted only to get home to their families without further delay, and the movers and shakers of Tokyo appeared, almost to the man, to have indulged in a few too many glasses of sake. None of them had given Bolan a second glance.

Hanging from his left side on a shoulder strap, the big American carried a soft-sided black leather briefcase. Anyone who noticed it would assume it contained papers that related to whatever business the tall foreigner was conducting with his Japanese associates.

Which was exactly why he had chosen the briefcase and his clothes instead of wearing one of the combat blacksuits that would have in some ways been preferable for the mission he was about to undertake. During part of that mission, Bolan needed to be able to remain unseen in the shadows. During other parts, that would be impossible. And a man dressed in what was obviously a suit designed for battle and stealth would draw far too much attention on the streets of Tokyo, Japan.

Bolan glanced up and down the street, making sure there were no watchful eyes, then reached into the briefcase and pulled out a leather tube. Twisting the cap at one end, he produced an infrared telescope, removed the lens covers at both ends and dropped them along with the tube back into his bag. Aiming the scope at the fourth window from the corner on Tanaka Tower's seventh floor, he flipped the switch to activate the infrared feature.

Pressing the scope to one eye, he frowned. From the angle he was at, he could see only a small section of Yuji Tanaka's office. Occasionally an unidentifiable form moved quickly and gracefully through his field of vision, then vanished again. Which told him nothing about what he had come to find out.

Returning the scope to his briefcase, Bolan studied the entrance to the building across the street. Two uniformed security guards were visible through the glass doors and windows, and for a moment he considered trying to bluff his way through their sign-in sheet. He discarded the idea almost as quickly as it had formed. Even if he was successful, the clandestine entry stood a good chance of being discovered the next day. A man in Yuji Tanaka's position, with as much as he had to lose right now, was likely to check the records of evening visitors. Anyone he didn't know would generate suspicion.

And it was still too early for Bolan to play his hand and let the man who would be king know he was being watched.

Bolan turned, staring at the entrance to the building in whose doorway he stood. The lobby was dark, and the manager had seen no need to procure the services of a security company as Tanaka had done. Still, Bolan could see the faint telltale wires of an alarm system running through the glass. He could disarm the system, but first he would have to locate the main circuits, and that would take time.

Besides, thanks to John "Cowboy" Kissinger, Stony Man Farm's chief armorer, there was an easier way.

Reaching into his briefcase, Bolan pulled out another leather case. A moment later he had unzipped it and held in his hand an instrument that looked like a cross between an oversize flare gun and a deep-sea fishing reel. He took another quick glance up and down the street, then stepped out onto the sidewalk.

He turned to face the building across from Tanaka's office, then looked up, counting seven floors. He looked briefly at the strange instrument in his hand, smiling at the creativity that had gone into its design. Kissinger never rested in his quest to contrive new and better equipment for the Farm's operatives. This modern-day version of the ancient grappling hook, which Kissinger called the "climb-gun," was only one of his many recent creations.

Bolan raised the climb-gun over his head and pressed the button just to the side of the trigger guard with his index finger. A small red dot appeared on the window seven stories up as the laser sight activated. Inserting his finger into the guard, Bolan shifted the dot slightly, letting it fall on the wooden frame just above the glass. Gently he squeezed the trigger.

The climb-gun coughed not unlike a sound-suppressed pistol as the folded grappling hook shot up, the steel cable attached to it spooling out behind it. Bolan heard a quiet thump as the dartlike missile shot through the wooden frame and into the office. He jerked quickly back on the cable like a fisherman sinking his hook into a fish.

The folding hook was designed to open up on impact. It did. Bolan felt the line tighten as it wedged back against the window frame.

He reeled the line in taut, then dropped the climb-gun, letting it dangle in the air at the end of the cable. He reached up with both hands, wrapping them around the steel cord and lifting himself up off the ground. He tugged hard, testing the line with both his weight and strength. It held, and he began the slow, laborious climb upward.

As soon as he reached the seventh floor, Bolan squatted on the windowsill and turned to face the Tanaka building. Pressing a button at the end of the cable, he waited as the automatic rewind brought the climb-gun up from the ground. Another button in the grip of the instrument retracted the fins of the grappling hook.

The Executioner dropped to a sitting position on the windowsill directly across from Yuji Tanaka's office. He set the climb-gun next to him and pulled out the infrared night scope. Pressing it to his eye again, he stared across the street.

Tanaka stood in front of his desk, leaning back over it and speaking into what appeared to be a speakerphone. The Japanese businessman held a tanto fighting knife in his right hand. His expression was tight as he alternately spoke, then listened. Gradually Bolan watched his expression grow alarmed. A moment later Tanaka turned away from the desk and began the movements of a *kata* with the knife.

Bolan nodded. That explained the figure he had seen moving quickly in and out of his vision earlier. Tanaka had been practicing a tanto form.

The man continued to carry on a conversation with whoever was on the other end of the line as he slashed and thrust his way through the *kata*. Finally the conversation ended, and Bolan watched him tap the speakerphone off and return to his practice session. His movements speeded up now. He thrust furiously with the blade, adding kicks and punches with the opposite hand to his ritual.

Bolan watched him curiously through the scope.

The man was good with the knife. Obviously he had studied the art since childhood.

Tanaka concluded his practice session, and Bolan watched him bow and turn back to the desk. The Japanese smiled suddenly, then raised the knife high over his head, bringing it down furiously at the wooden desktop. Bolan watched the sturdy point wedge itself into the wood, then saw blood suddenly spurt from under Tanaka's grip.

Leaving the blade in the top of the desk, Tanaka jerked back to an upright position. His left hand grasped his right, cutting off the flow of blood. As Bolan watched, he disappeared through a door at the side of the room.

Tanaka returned a moment later with his hand bandaged. He tapped the speakerphone again, spoke briefly into it, then turned off the lights in his office and exited through another door.

Two minutes later a limousine appeared outside the lobby of the office tower. Tanaka, now wearing a beige trench coat, walked out and let the chauffeur open the door for him.

As soon as the limo had driven away, Bolan rose to a squat on the windowsill. Through the scope, he studied the frame around the windows leading into the businessman's office. Steel. Kissinger had warned him against trying to use the climb gun's folding grappling hook on anything harder than soft wood.

The spring system was of a design that might cause it to jam on impact rather than open.

Bolan lifted the climb-gun from his side and unscrewed the folding grappling hook from the end of the cable. Digging into his briefcase again, he removed what looked like a tiny mason's drill on the end of a threaded bolt. Screwing the end of the bolt onto the climb-gun's cable, he aimed the red laser dot across the street at the concrete just above Tanaka's window.

Reaching out with his left hand, he threw a tiny toggle switch in the bolt behind the drill. A soft whir sounded as the drill began to rotate. A moment later it was flying across the street seven stories in the air, tugging the bolt and cable behind it.

Bolan heard the thud as the drill struck the concrete with just enough force to penetrate and stick. The whirring continued for several seconds as the drill bored its way into the face of the building, pulling the threaded bolt in after it. As soon as the head of the bolt came flush with the concrete, the whirring sound stopped.

The soldier attached the folding grappling hook to the other end of the line, then shoved the compressed hook back through the hole in the window frame behind him and flared the fins outward once more to secure the hook.

Bolan's eyes followed the angle of the cable now stretched across the street. It angled downward slightly, just enough to let gravity pull him across the street.

Turning to face the office tower, Bolan rose to full height. With the barrel of the climb-gun in his right hand and the grip in the other, he thrust away from the window and went sailing out into the air.

The cable made a soft whooshing sound as the Executioner slid across the street. The wind was heavy this high up in the air, and it swayed him to the right as he slid. His feet hit the face of the tower to the right of the sill, and he had to walk them across the concrete to find purchase.

But a moment later he was reeling in the line again, recharging the climb-gun and replacing it in his briefcase.

Bolan studied the window to Tanaka's office, which consisted of nine panes. The small rectangles were positioned in rows of three and divided by metal slats. As he'd suspected, little caution had been taken as to security this high up. His eyes spotted motion detectors but no sound or breakage devices.

Which would make his job easy. As long as the frame wasn't moved, the window could be disassembled.

Bolan pulled a small aerosol bottle from his briefcase and angled the sprayer up to the glass. Spraying the dissolving solution into the caulking around the top row of glass panes, he watched the material disintegrate. The panes loosened, and he worked them carefully out from the frame and set them on the sill next to his feet. From there it was a simple matter of removing the remaining slats and glass.

When the opening was complete, Bolan lowered himself into the office. Carefully he pulled the slats and glass panes in from the sill and stacked them on the floor. Unless he wanted Tanaka to know that his office had been invaded, he would have to replace them when he left.

Drawing the shades to help camouflage the hole, Bolan pulled a miniflashlight from his briefcase and twisted it on. He scoured the dark office until the light fell on what he was looking for—the computer. Making his way across the room to the wooden hutch, he switched on the machine and let it warm up.

When the computer buzzed ready, he took a seat in front of the monitor. The specifics of the model took him a few seconds to figure out, but within a minute he had routed a simple message to Stony Man Farm.

"Hello, Mr. Kurtzman," he typed into the machine.

Bolan sat back and waited. Kurtzman didn't know where he was or what he was doing. An unexpected message making its way through all the security checks and traps the computer genius employed would surprise the man. At least for a second or two.

It turned out to be three seconds. Bolan had barely quit typing when the return message appeared on the screen in front of him.

"How's it hangin', Striker?"

Bolan smiled. Kurtzman had already traced the Executioner's communiqué back to Tokyo, knew exactly where he was and what he was doing. The burly expert was the consummate computer man, and you didn't beat a man at his own game.

"Had to hang to get here. You know where that is—tell me what to do," Bolan typed.

As he waited for the return message, he glanced across the room to the door. Next to it, against the wall, he saw a hard-shell attaché case. The case had been positioned as if someone had wanted to make sure he didn't forget to take it when he left the office.

Bolan frowned. That someone had to have been Yuji Tanaka, and he had forgotten the attaché case anyway—probably due to being distracted when he cut his hand. Would he be back for it this night? There was no way to know. But it was too late to do anything now but proceed with the transfer—and hope that the Tanaka files would be on their way to Stony Man Farm before Yuji's return.

A few seconds later a list of computer entries appeared on the monitor. Bolan followed them chronologically. Working as quickly as possible, he linked the files to those at the Farm. Five minutes later he hit the Enter button, and every bit of data stored on Tanaka's hard drive began making its way across the Pacific to the Farm.

Bolan waited until Kurtzman had typed "Transfer

complete'' on the screen, then exited the files and flipped off the computer. He glanced once more to the attaché case against the wall, then slung his own briefcase over his shoulder, moved to the window and collected the panes of glass and metal dividers.

The Executioner studied the gaping hole for a moment. He would have to recaulk the individual panes from outside—tricky, but it could be done. Hauling himself up onto the ledge, he stepped back out onto the windowsill.

Which was where he was when the door to Yuji Tanaka's office opened behind him.

LIKE ALL MAJOR American universities and most smaller colleges, the University of Texas at Austin had a large number of Orientals on its rolls. Most were Americans, and many—like those of Chinese and Japanese descent—had family histories in the U.S. that dated back several generations.

Others, most commonly those of Vietnamese, Laotian and Cambodian extraction, were first- or second-generation citizens whose relocation to the U.S. was either a direct or indirect result of the war that had rocked the cultures of both America and Southeast Asia during the late 1960s and early 1970s.

Still other Orientals were exchange students who came to take advantage of the education offered by American universities. They were there to learn and obtain degrees in their chosen fields. With that accomplished, they would face a difficult decision: would they return to their homelands or make new lives for themselves in the United States?

Regardless of how long they had been in the U.S., Oriental students had at least one thing in common: they were, with few exceptions, always near the top of their classes. They were good students who added hard work to the intelligence God had given them and stood out as fine examples to be emulated by other scholars.

Carl Lyons knew all this and wasn't surprised that a large number of the faces gathering in front of the platform, which had been set up on Austin's Sixth Street, bore Oriental features. That didn't worry the Able Team leader in the least.

What worried him was that each young man or woman just might be a well-trained Chinese assassin instead of a sophomore philosophy major.

In the impromptu orchestra pit just beyond the front edge of the stage, members of the Texas University band broke into a brassy rendition of "The Yellow Rose of Texas" as Lyons and Jim Campbell escorted Jack Rush up the steps. The crowd, still gathering along the street and on the sidewalks in front of the stores, let out a roar of approval, which mildly surprised the Able Team leader.

Rush was a hard-as-nails conservative, and college students weren't historically known to readily embrace conservative thought. The words of Winston

Churchill concerning the fact that any man who wasn't a liberal at the age of twenty, and a conservative by the time he was forty, had something wrong with him at both ages, crossed Lyons's mind. But the students of the University of Texas had seen too much violence result from indulging criminals, and they were tired of the fear they felt when they walked through the parking lots at night after class. The frequency of assaults, rapes and even murders had caused most of them to grow up fast.

But that was only part of the reason behind Rush's popularity. In Jack Rush, people sensed an honesty for which they had all but given up hope in politicians. Rush had done the unheard-of during his first term as governor—he had kept the promises he had made during the campaign.

Lyons, Rush and Campbell reached the top of the steps, and the governor paused long enough to hold up both arms and face the crowd. Rolling his fingers into fists, he extended the thumbs and little fingers on both hands in the famous Texas University "Hook 'em Horns" gesture. Now the crowd went wild.

The big ex-cop led the governor across the stage toward a row of chairs at the rear. On a personal level the Able Team leader had learned to like the governor during the few minutes they had spent together at the mansion. The man's basic sincerity came through on a gigantic wave of charisma. Rush was a likable, down-to-earth, intelligent good-ol'-boy politician that

Lyons himself would vote for were the Able Team leader a resident of the state.

But Jack Rush was first and foremost a politician, and Lyons had grown irritated with him only a few minutes before when the man had allowed his quest for votes to override common sense.

Lyons reached the row of chairs where several of Rush's executive-protection team already stood. He started toward the end, his eyes sweeping left to right, right to left and in and out. As he let his subconscious mind search for potential threats to the governor, his conscious returned to the unoccupied storefront across the street from the speech site.

The vacant structure had been rented by Rush's staff to serve as a central command post and final dressing room during the speech. Rush had worn the ballistic nylon vest during the limo ride from the governor's mansion to the store, then taken a final look at himself in the full-length mirror after the makeup artist had done her work.

"Jim," Rush had said, shaking his head at his reflection, "I just can't do it. Image is everything in this business, especially to a bunch of college students. I'm already fighting thirty years of wrinkles and a bad hair transplant the way it is, and this thing has to go."

Without further comment, Rush had removed the vest.

Lyons stopped at the end of the chairs, his eyes

continuing to scan the cheering crowd of college students. Now it seemed that *every* face he saw was of Oriental descent, and he had to remind himself that the assassins sent by the Chinese to kill Governor Rush might be of any race.

The Able Team leader waited for Rush to wave to the crowd again, then sit down before taking a seat next to him. He watched Ranger Jim Campbell take the seat on the other side of the governor, then turned his eyes toward the crowd, scrutinizing the assembly as his brain looked for anything that might even remotely be considered suspicious activity.

The assassins would probably be Chinese, but the operative word was *probably*. The fall of the Soviet Union had sent many former KGB specialists looking for a new place to sell their talents, and more than a few had found a home in Red China. And contract assignments had been part of the espionage game since time immemorial—Beijing could have hired anyone from Iranian terrorists to local Texas outlaws.

"The Yellow Rose of Texas" concluded, and the band went into a soft instrumental version of Marty Robbins's famous song "El Paso"—the governor's hometown. Rush's aide, Gordon, rose from his chair on the other side of Jim Campbell and walked to the podium. "Ladies and gentlemen," he began.

Lyons only half listened to Gordon's introductory speech as he continued to inspect the students who had come to hear their governor. A half block from

the stage, making his way through the throng in front
of a clothing store, was Rosario Blancanales. Pol,
along with the other Rangers Campbell had brought,
had been assigned roving patrol duty within the
crowd. Schwarz, and a combination of Rangers and
executive-protection team members, were working
the perimeter.

Along with the Austin PD and Travis County Sher-
iff's Department deputies assigned to the speech,
there were close to two hundred uniformed and plain-
clothesmen working the function.

"...and now, that very same little boy who grew
up in that two-room shack fifty yards from the Mex-
ican border," Gordon said into the microphone, "a
man who pulled hard on his own worn-out bootstraps
to work his way through this same institute of higher
learning that you people now attend, a man whose
life has had ups and downs, but who never allowed
himself to be kept down...ladies and gentlemen...Governor Jack Rush!"

Rush rose with both hands in the "Hook 'em
Horns" sign again, smiling broadly as he walked to
the podium. The governor began his speech with his
trademark opening. "Where's the biggest, best, finest
place to live in all the universe?" he shouted into the
microphone.

"Texas!" three thousand voices screamed.

Rush let the roar die down, then shook his head.

"Don't know what I'm going to do some day if everybody decides to yell 'Missouri,'" he said.

The kids loved him as Rush went on, telling a few opening jokes that were carefully tailored to offend no one, then launching into an impassioned oration on the sad state of the criminal-justice system, not only in Texas but in every state across the country. He promised not to rest until the entire Texas penal system had undergone a complete overhaul, and implied that someday, given the chance, he'd do the same for the rest of the United States.

Again Lyons listened to the speech with one ear and added the other to his search for potential threats. He heard only a few boos and catcalls, and those were quickly quashed by students who agreed with the governor's hard line.

Halfway through the speech, the Able Team leader saw Schwarz a block away at the edge of the crowd. The electronics ace entered what appeared to be a sandwich shop. A rail ran around the walkway on the floor above the shop, and several outdoor grills could be seen through the iron. Apartments, no doubt.

Rush's speech was winding down when Lyons saw Blancanales again. Less than a hundred feet from the front of the stage, Pol suddenly tackled a young Oriental man wearing a red bandanna as a sweatband. Using his cane in a come-along hold, he gained control of the other man, and Lyons saw a revolver fall to the ground. Then, suddenly, several other students jumped in to help their friend. The crowd turned its attention from the governor and onto the fight.

Lyons's antennae shot up with lightning speed. He wasn't worried about Pol—the Able Team commando could take care of himself. What worried him was that the word *diversion* had suddenly shot into his brain like giant letters on a movie screen. A split second later the unmistakable sound of a rifle shot rang out.

The big ex-cop saw the wood at the top of the rostrum in front of Rush splinter as he leaped to his feet. The governor froze, his fingers clamping on the edges of the podium. The Able Team leader took two steps and dived into the air. It was impossible to pinpoint the sniper's location from the lone shot, but the big ex-cop had recognized not only the caliber of the weapon, but the make. The distinctive sound had come from an M-16 capable of full- or semiauto fire. The sniper had missed, and another round would be on its way.

The Able Team commando heard the second explosion and could tell now that the round came from down the block, from the same direction where he'd seen Schwarz enter the sandwich shop.

The big ex-cop twisted in the air, turning to face the source of the attack as he fell over the podium between Rush and the sniper. As his side hit the top of the wooden rostrum, he felt the round strike him full in the chest.

McCARTER HAD TO ADMIT that Phoenix Force was in a predicament.

As Price had so aptly summarized, they were on the run from the Chinese police, their Caucasian features stood out and none of them spoke the language.

So they needed someone who did, someone they could trust.

And the Phoenix Force leader knew only one man who might fit that bill.

Encizo pulled the vehicle to the curb a half block from the men's dormitory at the People's Security Institute. With his darker skin, blue baseball cap and sunglasses, he came the closest to passing for an Oriental of any of the Phoenix Force commandos.

But McCarter had to admit that wasn't very close. They'd be lucky to pull off what he had in mind, even if Encizo kept his distance from suspicious eyes.

After his conversation with Barbara Price and the new Intel that had come from Stony Man, McCarter had known beyond a shadow of a doubt that if they were to locate Ku Mojo and keep him alive, Phoenix Force would need help. That knowledge had prompted a bold decision.

McCarter, Manning, Encizo, James and Hawkins would have to engage the services of a Chinese-speaking ally. Preferably one who also understood the intricate workings of the Chinese National Police, which meant Hong Chei.

With all but Encizo hugging the 4-Runner's floorboards, Phoenix Force had returned to the Beijing Plaza in time to see the same officers they'd escaped from throw Hong into a car and whisk him away. At first they had feared the young man was suspected of being part of the plot to kill the politburo members and would be placed under arrest, but as they followed the vehicle through the streets, it had become obvious that the men in the dark green uniforms were taking him back to the People's Security Institute.

Hong wasn't being arrested, just kicked out of the cadet program for showing poor judgment in the way he had handled his American charges.

"Here he comes," Encizo said. "Side door."

McCarter shifted his gaze and saw Hong come down the steps outside the dorm. Gone was the light green cadet uniform; the young man now wore jeans, a white T-shirt and a light nylon windbreaker. He carried a suitcase in each hand, and the weight slowed his steps. But the bags weren't the only burden the young man carried. Hong trudged along the sidewalk toward the street, his head hanging forward against his chest with the heavy heart of remorse.

"You know it's a damn shame," James said. "The kid got caught up in the middle of all this, and there goes his career."

"Maybe, maybe not," McCarter stated. "If we pull this off, there may be a way to get him back in everyone's good graces."

"And if we don't pull it off?" James asked.

"Then Hong Chei's police career will be the least of anyone's worries, including his." The Briton turned to Encizo as Hong started down the street away from the campus. "Looks like he's heading for the train station. Let him get a couple of blocks before you take off."

Encizo nodded.

Phoenix Force watched the young man walk away. They were surprised when he stopped next to a panel truck parked on the street, set his bags next to the driver's door and stuck a hand in his pocket.

"That's *his* vehicle?" Hawkins asked out loud.

"Looks like it to me," Manning agreed.

"David, are you thinking what I'm thinking?" James asked.

McCarter nodded. "More room and no windows. Let's go, Rafe. Time it so we get there just as he gets behind the wheel."

Encizo nodded and started the engine. He waited until Hong had found his key ring and unlocked the door before throwing the 4-Runner in gear and starting down the street.

Hong glanced up at the approaching vehicle, but the young man's mind was too preoccupied to pay it much attention. He stepped up into the cab just as Encizo hit the brakes, pulling across the street to block the truck's forward movement.

McCarter, James, Manning and Hawkins leaped

from their vehicle as the Cuban threw it in Park. McCarter jerked open the door next to Hong as Manning slid the side door back and the others dived inside. Then the big Canadian jumped in himself and slid the door shut.

Hong turned to face McCarter, his face a total blank.

The Briton couldn't stop the sardonic smile that came over his face. The kid had seen it all in the past few days during his stint as Phoenix Force's escort. Nothing surprised him anymore.

"Better put it in reverse and back out, Hong," McCarter said. "The 4-Runner's blocking your path."

CHAPTER TWELVE

Kenji Takaka disliked holding hands with the woman as he walked along the sidewalk at the edge of the park. Her hands were rough and callused, and the knuckles were permanently swollen from punching bags filled with rice and *makiwara* boards to toughen them.

But what he disliked about holding hands the most was the fact that the woman wasn't a woman.

Kosuke Yamaguchi, dressed this evening in a lavender skirt and coordinated orchid-print blouse, leaned closer to Takaka, resting his head on the other man's shoulder. To anyone watching, they appeared to be nothing more than one of the many young couples in love who had chosen to take an early-evening stroll through the park. Even though he knew it was only for show, the intimacy made Takaka uncomfortable.

A bench appeared just off the sidewalk ahead, and Yamaguchi tugged the undercover Japanese Defense Force agent toward it. They took seats next to each other, and Yamaguchi pulled Takaka's arm around his shoulders and snuggled in close. The two men looked across the street at Ku Mojo's mansion.

Yamaguchi leaned up to whisper in his companion's ear. "Do you see any security alarms?" he asked, his voice soft and feminine.

Takaka shook his head. "No, it would be unusual if there were."

"Yes," Yamaguchi agreed. "In a country that executes criminals for serious crimes and gives serious prison terms for lesser offenses, such things are not necessary. Entry will be easy. Almost an insult to our skills."

Takaka nodded again. "How will we enter?"

Yamaguchi leaned back slightly and slapped playfully at his face the way a woman might do to a lover who was teasing her. "We will go through the door, silly," he purred. "I do not want you trying to look up my skirt while I climb through a window."

Takaka turned his face away and didn't answer.

"Did you know Ku Mojo has four children?" Yamaguchi asked, breaking the silence.

Takaka nodded. "Yes. The two eldest are boys. Fourth and fifth grade. The girl is three years younger, and they were surprised only last summer with an unexpected baby."

"Naughty, naughty Ku Mojo," Yamaguchi whispered.

Takaka tried to laugh but couldn't force himself to

do so. "How will we do it?" he asked. "We will have to enter the house without waking Ku Mojo's wife or children. If he sleeps with his wife, that will be difficult."

Yamaguchi reached up to fondle a button on Takaka's shirt, making the undercover man uneasy. "Why worry about waking them?" he asked.

"Because if they see us, Kosuke, they could identify us later," Takaka said impatiently.

"Dead people cannot identify others, Kenji."

Takaka froze, horrified at the suggestion. "They are children," he said. "The youngest is less than a year old. We cannot kill them, Kosuke!"

"Keep your voice down," Yamaguchi threatened in the tone of a man. "We can and will kill them," he said. "If we do not, they might not only identify us—they could grow up to hunt us down and kill us."

Silence descended again, and Takaka sat paralyzed. His orders were to collect intelligence only, and not interfere with the plans of the *ninja*. But orders be damned. Being part of the assassinations of the politburo members had been bad enough. He wouldn't be party to the slaying of an innocent woman and her children. He would make contact with his superiors in Japan when Yamaguchi went to sleep tonight and make certain that Ku Mojo and his family left the country under guard.

Finally Yamaguchi leaned away from him and stood. When he spoke, his voice was that of a woman in love. "It is time to go," he said, reaching out for Takaka's hand. "I have seen what I needed to see."

Takaka stood and took Yamaguchi's hand. "Then we will go tomorrow?" he asked.

"Tomorrow?" Yamaguchi asked. "What is wrong with later tonight?"

The secret agent felt the chill of ice in his veins. If Yamaguchi insisted on carrying out the mission this night, Takaka would have no opportunity to contact his superiors. Ku Mojo, his wife and children would be murdered.

Takaka's throat felt dry as he nodded and started down the sidewalk with Yamaguchi's arm looped through his.

The sidewalk circled the park and led them back into a commercial district. Yamaguchi dropped Takaka's hand as they crossed the street in front of the stores but kept with his feminine walk and speech. "Dressing as a woman has aroused me," he said suddenly, and stopped.

Takaka stopped with him, glancing past the *ninja* to see that they were in front of a pharmacy. A small telephone booth stood just outside the entrance against the glass window.

"I am going to visit a brothel," Yamaguchi said. "Would you care to come, Kenji? It will be my treat." The words sounded strange in the feminine voice and coming from what appeared to be a woman in an orchid-print blouse.

Takaka wasn't fooled. He knew the offer was a further test to see if he was gay. But what was the best response to ensure that Yamaguchi continued to believe the diversionary illusion? Should he go along, then fail to perform? That plan might blow up in his face. He wasn't certain he could fail to achieve an erection with an attractive prostitute.

But there was an even more important reason he couldn't go with Yamaguchi to the brothel. It might be the only chance he would have to contact his Japanese Defense Force superiors and get word of the assassination to Ku Mojo.

"Well?" Yamaguchi asked, smiling slyly. "Would you like to come?"

Takaka shook his head. "I am not in the mood."

"It will not take long to *get* in the mood," he said. "That is, if you are capable of such a mood."

"I am capable," Takaka said, faking irritation as he knew a man subtly accused, as he had just been, would. "But I am not like you, Kosuke. I cannot make love one moment and kill children the next. I must deliberate on what we are about to do."

"You are not certain?" Yamaguchi asked, his voice threatening again.

"I am certain I can and will assist you as always," Takaka said. "I am certain I will perform my duty. I am not certain exactly how I will get into the right frame of mind to murder babies, however." He paused for effect, then added, "But I will."

Yamaguchi reached up and patted him lightly on the cheek. "You still have much to learn as a *ninja*," he whispered. "But I will help you." He nodded toward the pharmacy. "We will need adhesive tape to bind their wrists and ankles and to fashion gags," he said. "I think we should have a little fun with Ku Mojo's family before they are killed. Finding their bodies mutilated will instill even more anger at the CIA. Please purchase the tape while I am gone." He glanced at the thin gold watch on his wrist. "I will meet you back here in front of the pharmacy in two hours," he said. "Do not be late." Without another word, the *ninja* turned and started down the sidewalk on his high heels.

Takaka watched him disappear around the next corner, then looked at the telephone booth against the pharmacy's front window. He glanced back down the street to where Yamaguchi had disappeared.

No, not yet, he told himself. The *ninja* might return with some item of forgotten business. Takaka would buy the tape first, giving him plenty of time to get out of the area. Then he would use the phone to call Japan.

Takaka entered the pharmacy to find it deserted except for the elderly proprietor. The man stood behind a counter wearing a soiled blue lab coat buttoned to the throat. The garment almost matched his gray-blue hair and beard. So bent was his spine that his chin hunched forward almost to the counter as he handed

Takaka a roll of adhesive tape, opened the cash register and made change.

Takaka dropped the tape in his pocket, shuddering as he tried to imagine what "fun" Yamaguchi might have in mind for Ku Mojo's wife and children. He stepped back out on the street and looked carefully up and down the sidewalk. He saw no sign of Yamaguchi.

The Japanese Defense Force undercover man's heart beat madly against his chest as he ducked into the phone booth. His fingers trembled as he tapped the numbers into the phone. He would be criticized, perhaps disciplined, for taking such a chance and breaking cover. But he had no choice. He couldn't allow children to be murdered.

The phone was answered on the second ring, and Takaka identified himself through a series of codes, then related what Yamaguchi had planned for the Ku Mojo family. His contact wasn't as angry as Takaka had expected, and assured the undercover man that the Chinese authorities would be alerted within the next few minutes.

Takaka breathed a sigh of relief as he set the receiver back in the cradle. He had kept both eyes scanning the street and sidewalk during the conversation, fearful that the master *ninja* would somehow appear by magic to find him in the booth. Now he chuckled softly, realizing that he had fallen prey to one of the very tactics he had learned to use in his own *ninja* training: to create magic, one had only to convince others that he was capable of doing so.

The undercover man had started to push the phone-booth door open when he heard tapping on the glass behind him. He turned to the pharmacy window to see the disfigured pharmacist smiling into the booth. But now the man stood straight and erect. He still wore the light blue lab coat, though it had been un-buttoned. In the gap Takaka could see orchids. Away from the counter now, the undercover man could also see the old man's legs.

They were encased in beige silk stockings beneath a lavender skirt.

As reality struck Takaka like a baseball bat be-tween the eyes, the old man straightened and lifted an automatic pistol that had been threaded with a sound suppressor. Takaka's last thoughts were that Yamaguchi hadn't suggested the brothel to test his sexuality but rather to see if he would attempt to alert Ku Mojo, and that maybe *ninja*s really were magic.

At least some of them.

TWO OF THE UNIFORMED MEN who entered Yuji Ta-naka's office gripped Shin Chuo Kogyo Model 60 New Nambu revolvers. The other two wore the same company's 9 mm parabellum submachine guns slung over their shoulders in assault mode.

Standing on the window ledge, Bolan turned to face them as one of the men screamed an order in

Japanese. He watched them fan out across the room to cover the window from different angles, and as they spread, he saw the tall, slender man in the dark blue suit standing in the doorway.

Yuji Tanaka. His right hand was bandaged.

"What is your name?" Tanaka barked.

Bolan stared hard at Tanaka, who stared back.

Tanaka repeated his question.

"It's not important," Bolan said. He threw a quick glance over his shoulder to the building across the street. There was no way he'd be able to draw the climb-gun from his briefcase, shoot the bolt and slide across without taking a few rounds in the back.

At least not without a diversion.

Tanaka drew the knife from a sheath on his hip and took a step forward. "We will speak English," he said. "Who are you and why are you here?" He twirled the blade in his fingers and started forward again.

Bolan reached into the briefcase, and the security men raised their weapons higher. The Executioner shook his head. "I wouldn't if I were you," he said. "This thing is set to go off on the slightest impact."

"What thing?" Tanaka demanded.

"Oh, a pretty simple thing really," Bolan answered. "Almost primitive by today's standards. C-4, a blasting cap and a remote-controlled electronic detonator."

For a moment Tanaka and the four guards froze. Then the businessman snarled, "You are lying."

"Maybe. Want to find out?"

Tanaka's face revealed his answer.

"Okay, guys," Bolan said, "here's the plan. I'm going to set this thing down and leave the way I came in. I suggest you go out the other door as fast as you can when I do because just as soon as I'm far enough away that the blast won't get me, your office goes up."

Tanaka took another step forward, but this time it was hesitant.

Bolan pulled the briefcase strap over his shoulder and set the soft-sided bag on the ledge. His hand went to his wristwatch. "One more step, Tanaka," he said, his index finger pressing lightly against the watch, "and we all go up together."

The Japanese's snarl returned. "You are lying, American dog."

"You said that before. And like I said, we can find out."

"No!" one of the guards with the subguns shouted.

Tanaka turned toward him and raised the tanto over his head. He brought down the butt end of the grip on top of the man's head. The guard slumped to the floor. The businessman cut the sling from the unconscious man and lifted the subgun. "I will shoot you myself," he snapped as he turned to Bolan.

For a brief moment their eyes met again, and the soldier saw that Tanaka was serious.

Bolan had tried his bluff, and it had been called.

Tanaka raised the weapon to eye level, aimed at Bolan's chest and pulled the trigger. Nothing happened, and the Japanese cursed, looking down at the unfamiliar weapon for the safety.

Bolan grabbed the briefcase, turned away from the office and opened the latches as he dived from the ledge. He drew the climb-gun from the case, aimed across the street at the corner of the building he'd climbed earlier and squeezed the trigger.

The drill-and-bolt combo shot across the street, boring into the building as Bolan continued to fall. He released his grip on the briefcase and reached up, grasping the barrel of the climb-gun with the other hand.

As he did, he heard the distinctive sound of the Japanese submachine gun from the window above. The rounds blew past, one close enough to rip through his jacket, before the rest ricocheted off the building across the street in tiny clouds of concrete dust.

Bolan was still two stories off the ground when the slack in the line tightened. The force of the fall and his own weight threatened to rip both shoulders from the sockets, but he held on. He swung down, and as he neared the ground, he saw that his feet would still hit the pavement roughly ten feet in front of the building's corner.

The line had taken much of the force from his fall, but he was still traveling fast enough to break an ankle or leg. The automatic fire was continuing above and behind him, and the only thing that had saved him from being shot so far had been the erratic movements of being jerked by the line.

If he came to a sudden stop on the pavement, particularly with an injury, he'd be a stationary target, which meant he'd be dead.

A split second before his feet hit the ground, Bolan pulled up with all the strength left in his arms. His chin rose over the climb-gun like a man doing pull-ups. At the same time he curled his legs back behind him, the heels of his boots brushing his buttocks.

His knees touched the sidewalk as he swung past, then started back upward into the air. As he reached the corner of the building, his legs unfolded and his feet shot out to break the impact.

Bolan's boots struck the concrete, his bent knees acting as a shock absorber. He pushed back and to the side as the enemy gunfire continued behind him, shoved away from the building, then swung around the corner.

The big American released his grip on the climb-gun and dropped the short distance to the ground. He moved to the edge of the building and peered around the corner.

Seven stories up he could see Yuji Tanaka still

holding the smoking subgun. His voice was faint in the distance, but Bolan could make out his words.

"We will meet again!" the outraged Japanese shouted.

"Count on it," the Executioner said before slipping away into the night.

FOR A MOMENT Carl Lyons thought it was Mack Bolan standing above him, blasting away at some unseen target with the Desert Eagle. Then, as his vision began to clear, the cowboy hat and small star on Ranger Campbell's chest came into focus.

The Able Team leader lay flat on his back, the roar of dozens of pistols filling his ears. He tried to move, but his arms and legs refused to obey his brain, and he realized he had been knocked unconscious for a few seconds by the force of the 5.56 mm round that had struck the steel-plate insert in his ballistic nylon vest.

Lyons concentrated hard as feeling began to return to his limbs, forcing himself to roll onto his stomach, then rise to his knees. Silently he congratulated himself for slipping into the vest Rush had refused to wear. It had been little more than an afterthought on his part, but it had saved his life.

And the life of the governor of Texas.

Drawing the Colt Python with a hand that still felt numb, Lyons looked out at the crowd. What he saw was pandemonium, pure and simple. The college students had begun racing for cover and were now running into one another. Terrified cries and screams pierced the air above the explosions of the gunfire, and several students lay on the ground either shot or knocked unconscious by the stampede.

Thirty feet in front of the rostrum, Lyons saw Blancanales and the men who had caused the diversion for the sniper. He realized suddenly that they had been sent to do more than simply create a distraction. They were a backup plan, as well, there to step in and shoot the governor if the hidden sniper failed, which he had.

The dozen assassins around Blancanales had turned their attention toward the stage and were battling it out with Campbell and the other defenders. As the Rangers and executive-protection team stood firing down, the assassins fired up.

Three of the assassins still kept Blancanales busy. The Able Team warrior was still fighting with his fists, feet and cane, obviously not having had time to draw his Beretta since the skirmish began.

As he tried to will the unfeeling hand that held up the Python, Lyons saw a short, muscular black assassin pull a Browning Hi-Power pistol from his blue jeans and shove the barrel into Pol's back.

The sight sent new life into Lyons's arm, and the Colt rose of its own accord. Still on his knees, the Able Team leader double-actioned a 125-grain semijacketed hollowpoint from the gun that drilled into one of the would-be killer's temples and out the other.

Lyons rose to unsteady feet, his eyes scanning the stage for the governor. He finally spotted the man's legs beneath a pile of executive-protection men near the rear of the platform. There had been no time to whisk Rush away, and the brave bodyguards were living up to their name, protecting the governor with their own bodies.

As Lyons continued to try to coax sensation back into his arms, he saw a round strike the back of the man at the top of the pile. A singing sound reverberated across the stage as the round bounced off another steel vest insert.

The big ex-cop turned in the direction from which the round had come and saw an Oriental in a black leather jacket and jeans. That man, too, held a Browning Hi-Power and was preparing to fire at the pile of humans again.

Lyons dropped the red insert of the Python's front sight on the man's chest and squeezed. The trigger traveled backward, first cocking the hammer, then releasing it, and the Colt jumped in his hand.

Another of the fierce hollowpoints streaked from the four-inch barrel and cut its way through leather, then flesh. The assassin's eyes rolled back in his head as he fell to his back.

Feeling had all but returned to the Able Team leader's arms now, and his movements picked up speed. Swinging the Python to the side, he double-actioned another round into the face of a hardman who had produced a sawed-off shotgun. The killer crumpled to the ground.

Next to him Campbell ran his Desert Eagle dry, slammed it back in his belt and drew his SIG-Sauer pistol. As Lyons fired a double-tap of .357 Magnum rounds into the chest and throat of another assassin, the Texas Ranger pelted the killers with .45s.

By now Blancanales had had time to draw his Beretta and the Able Team warrior stood his ground in the middle of the killers, tapping 9 mm parabellum bullets into their bodies from the very eye of the hurricane.

Lyons used his last revolver round on another Oriental, then switched to his .45. The Gold Cup leaped into his hand as the Python returned to leather, and he thumbed the safety down as his fingers curled around the beavertail.

The weapon bucked twice in his hand as he squeezed the trigger. The first of his rounds took the chin off another of the Oriental assassins. The second caught the same man behind the ear as he spun with the force of the first.

Below the stage, two of the killers tried to run. A .45 from Lyons's Gold Cup chewed flesh between one of the men's shoulder blades. The same-caliber slug from a different weapon worked likewise on the other gunner when Campbell pulled the trigger.

Suddenly silence fell over Sixth Street, and all that

remained was the hum in Lyons's ears and the smell of cordite in his nostrils.

The Able Team leader looked down to see that eleven men lay dead in front of the stage. Five were Oriental, undoubtedly Chinese Intelligence agents sent from Beijing. The others looked like local talent recruited there in Austin.

Campbell confirmed Lyons's suspicion by clicking his high-heeled boots down the steps, slipping the toe of one under a body lying facedown and flipping it over. "Well, well, well," the big Ranger said. "Charlie Pratt. Looks like I won't have to arrest you anymore."

Behind him Lyons heard movement and swung the .45 that way. He lowered it again when he saw the men who had formed the human wall of protection over Rush getting to their feet and brushing off the governor. Several of the team had bullet holes in their clothing where rounds had penetrated only to be stopped by their vests. One of the guards had taken a flesh wound through the upper arm, but looked little worse for the wear.

The governor's limousine screeched from its parking spot, knocking the wooden sawhorses lined up as barriers into the air. For a moment it looked as if the driver would take the front bumper right through the stage, but at the last instant he skidded to a halt.

Out of the corner of his eye, Lyons saw a man

running down the street toward the platform. He turned to see that it was Schwarz.

"You missed all the fun, Gadgets," Lyons said as the governor's guards began herding him toward the waiting car.

"I wouldn't say that," Schwarz replied. "I got the sniper."

"Tell me about it on the way in," Lyons said. "Pol, come on." Pushing into the center of the protection team, Lyons piled into the middle seat of the limo with the governor and Ranger Campbell. Schwarz and Blancanales took the back.

Campbell turned to face Schwarz. "How'd you know where the sniper was, son?" he asked.

"Luck," Schwarz said honestly. "Plus the oldest dumb move in the world on his part. I caught a glint of sunlight off steel and looked up. There he was." Gadgets paused for a moment, took a breath, then said, "I got upstairs to the apartment and kicked the door. He must have heard it, and the sound threw his first shot off. But he was a pro. He ignored me running to him and fired again. Accurately this time, it looks like."

Lyons saw that Schwarz was looking at him and glanced down to see the huge tear in his shirt where the round had struck.

"Where's the shooter now?" Campbell asked.

"Still in the apartment."

"Do I need to send some boys over for him? You cuff him to something?"

"No," Schwarz said, "I didn't cuff him. But he's not going anywhere."

Campbell's face lit up with understanding. "Good job, son."

The driver tore away from Sixth Street. They took several turns down side streets as a precautionary measure, then shot up the ramp to the freeway. Suddenly the red light on the radio mounted under the dash flashed on.

"Department of Public Safety Base to EPS. Come in, EPS," a female voice said over the airwaves.

The officer riding in the shotgun seat jerked the microphone from the dash and held it to his lips. "EP 447 here," he said. "Go ahead."

"Are the Justice Department agents with you?"

"That's affirmative, Base."

"Advise them to public service their offices immediately. Repeat, tell them to call their offices. Stat."

AARON KURTZMAN WHEELED away from the keyboard and took a deep breath. Leaning forward, he lifted the telephone receiver and pressed it to his ear with one hand while his other tapped in Barbara Price's extension number. As soon as the mission controller lifted the phone, he turned to the glass wall that divided the computer and communication rooms and looked at her. "Is Hal on location?" he asked.

Price nodded. "Affirmative. He's out in the armory with Kissinger right now. You need him?"

"Yeah. Have him meet me downstairs." The computer wizard paused, then added, "You'd better come, too, Barb."

The woman could read the seriousness of his tone. "What's up, Aaron?" she asked.

Kurtzman glanced back at the screen. "We've scanned the Tanaka files, and things are even hotter than we thought. There are some other new developments, too."

"They must be serious."

"In short, and at the risk of sounding crude," Kurtzman said, "it's nut-cuttin' time."

"I'll buzz Hal," Price said, and hung up.

Kurtzman turned away from the bank of computers and started down the ramp, his callused hands riding the tops of the wheels at his side to slow his roll.

Price was waiting for him by the time he reached the bottom. "Hal's on his way in."

Together they made their way to the elevator in the corner of the computer room.

The doors stood open on the ground floor of the main house. Kurtzman wheeled inside, turned and reached up to the row of buttons just inside the door. The car started down. The doors opened again in the basement, in a large room known as the War Room.

Kurtzman rolled off the elevator and stared at the wall as he moved on to take a place at the large conference table. How many times had he been in this room during his years at Stony Man Farm? He couldn't remember, but knew only that each time he rolled into the room, he felt the adrenaline pump through his veins so hard he could almost feel it in his lifeless legs.

Kurtzman wheeled into the table, leaned forward and folded his hands on the top. Along with the adrenaline, he always got a mildly queasy feeling in his stomach. That, he knew, was normal.

A meeting was never held in the War Room when the fate of the world didn't seem to be in the hands of the personnel of Stony Man Farm.

Price took a seat next to him and sat quietly waiting. A moment later they heard a buzz, and Hal Brognola came in through the coded access door across from the elevator. He dispensed with all formality. "Okay, Bear," he said. "What have you got?"

"Four items of business," Kurtzman replied, meeting Brognola's gaze. "Item one, we've intercepted an unprotected phone call from Beijing to Tokyo, from a Japanese Defense Force operative named Kenji Takaka. He's identified the head *ninja* in Tanaka's employ as one Kosuke Yamaguchi." He paused, waiting to see if the name rang a bell with either of his colleagues. When he drew blank expressions from both, he went on, "I've run him through our files and those of every other government agency I had time to tap into. There's nothing on him, Hal. Not here, not Japan, not anywhere. Not just no file, there's not even a reference to the man.'' He paused, then added, ''But the Tanaka files show him on the payroll. Listed as a salesman, and he makes some mean commissions.''

''Then it's either a mistake on this Takaka's part, or Yamaguchi is very good,'' Brognola said. He pulled a half-chewed cigar from the breast pocket of his sport coat and jammed it into his teeth.

''My guess is he's good, Hal,'' Kurtzman said. ''I found plenty on Kenji Takaka. He is a good agent, *ninja* trained himself.''

''Is the Japanese Defense Force in contact with Takaka?'' Brognola asked.

Kurtzman shook his head. ''No. Evidently it was a breach of policy for him to even make contact yet. Let me go on, and you'll see why he did.''

Brognola nodded.

''We were right on the Ku Mojo hit,'' Kurtzman said. ''Yamaguchi plans to do it later tonight.'' He glanced at his watch. ''And it is later tonight over there. But get this—Yamaguchi wants to take out Ku Mojo's entire family while they're inside.'' He paused to let it sink in. ''According to Takaka, Yamaguchi is one emotionless son of a bitch except when it comes to some pretty oddball sexual perversions. That's what Takaka thinks he has planned for Mama and the kids. Besides, if you think China is mad at the U.S. now..." He let his voice trail off.

Next to him Kurtzman felt Price stiffen with anger. In Brognola's eyes he saw a fiery flash of controlled rage. Both the director and mission controller were hardened warriors, but nobody, no matter how hard, could stomach the idea of hurting children.

"What else?" Brognola asked around the cigar.

"Item two, I've had Carmen monitoring everything coming into the CIA," Kurtzman stated. "I guess the ChiComs are pretty mad that Lyons and company ruined their party in Austin."

"Let them be," Brognola said. "Go on."

"Beijing sent the spooks a subtle threat that mentioned nukes."

"They always do that," Brognola said. "It's the bluff of the twentieth century."

"I hope so, but if it is, they're bluffing in a big way."

Brognola chomped down on his cigar. "How's that?"

"Item three is the fact that the Navy has picked up three Chinese nuclear subs less than a hundred miles from Honolulu," Kurtzman said.

The big Fed's cigar almost separated in the middle. "Where there's three fish," he said, "there can be a whole school."

"If Yamaguchi gets Ku Mojo and his family..." Price said. There was no need to finish the sentence.

She reached for the phone on the table. "I'll try to get Phoenix Force."

She had reached for the phone when it rang. Holding it to her ear, she said, "Yes?" then handed it to Kurtzman.

Kurtzman heard Huntington Wethers on the other end. "Aaron, Beijing police found a Japanese man shot in a phone booth. It just came in. Want to guess who it is?"

"Takaka."

"Bingo."

Kurtzman hung up and relayed the Intel to Price and Brognola.

The big Fed nodded. "Make sure McCarter knows that," he said, turning to Price, "then call Lyons. I want Able Team in the air and headed toward Hawaii with Grimaldi pronto."

He turned and started for the door, then whirled back. "You said four items, Aaron?" he said.

Kurtzman shrugged. "Number four is kind of an anticlimax after all that."

"I could use an anticlimax after all that," Brognola said.

"Just that the Confederation has expanded its naval exercises and is moving closer to the Philippines. According to Tanaka's files, that's where they plan to start. They've worked out a timetable to take everything up to and including Australia, and there are inferences that they'll move on from there."

Brognola nodded. "And if they can keep the U.S and China busy blowing each other up, they might just pull it off." He walked to the trash can in the corner, let the stub of tobacco fall from his lips and pulled a fresh cigar from his coat pocket.

"Get Striker in Tokyo, Barb. An army is no better than its general, and Yuji Tanaka is the money behind the Confederation. That puts the stars on his shoulders."

Price stopped tapping numbers into the phone and held the receiver away from her ear. "What do you want him to do?" she asked.

"What he does best," Brognola said as he punched the exit code into the War Room door.

Another sentence that didn't need finishing, Kurtzman thought as he wheeled himself back toward the elevator. He, and everyone who knew Mack Bolan, knew without being told what an executioner did best.

CHAPTER THIRTEEN

"Let's go, Hong," McCarter said as he slid into the passenger seat of the panel truck.

The young police cadet didn't speak. He just stared.

"Hong, come on," Manning said from the rear of the truck.

"No."

McCarter glanced out through the windshield. It didn't appear that anyone had noticed them jump from the 4-Runner into Hong's truck, but he couldn't be sure. But there were cadets walking the grounds, and now and then a real cop in the darker green National Police uniform appeared. It was only a matter of time before they were discovered if they didn't move.

"One more time," McCarter said. "Drive."

Hong shook his head.

The Phoenix Force leader drew the Chinese 7.62 mm pistol he had jammed in the waistband of his jeans. "Drive!" he ordered.

Hong stared at him for another second. His face showed little fear and no anger at all. Just sadness.

The young cadet threw the truck in reverse, backed away from the 4-Runner and pulled around it.

McCarter stuck the pistol back in his belt. "Hong," he said, "I'm sorry I had to do that."

"You are not sorry," Hong replied, staring straight ahead and refusing to look at the Phoenix Force leader as he drove down the street. "You deceived me from the very beginning. You *are* CIA. And I suppose now you will kill me like you have been killing the politburo members."

The Briton blew air through his clenched lips. "Hong, for the last time, we haven't been killing your people, we aren't CIA operatives and we aren't going to kill you."

"You just drew a gun on me," Hong countered.

"I had to get you moving."

"And if I had still refused to drive?" Hong asked. "Will you tell me now you would not have shot me?"

McCarter didn't answer.

James leaned between the seats from the back. "Hong, listen to me," he said. "We didn't want anything bad to happen to you, and we're all sorry you've been kicked out of the institute. If there's any way to get you back in after all this is over, we will."

Hong laughed sarcastically. "When this is over? When *what* is over?"

McCarter took over again. "We've come to protect your people, Hong, not to kill them."

The truck came to a traffic light, and Hong stopped. He finally turned to look at McCarter, but the look was suspicious. "Your voice sounds British now," he said. "Before, you sounded like that American colonel in the white suit." He frowned. "The one who sells the chickens."

James smiled. "Colonel Sanders."

"Yes, Colonel Sanders," Hong said. The light changed, and he drove through the intersection. "So what am I to believe?"

"The British part," McCarter said. "I'm English."

"Then you are with the MI-6?" Hong asked. He shook his head. "The others seem very American to me."

"I'm British, Manning is Canadian, Encizo is Cuban and Hawkins and James are as Yank as hot dogs and baseball."

"But how is it then that—?"

"Let me finish what I was about to say," McCarter said. "I'm going to explain what I can, and what I can't, you're going to have to trust me on." He waited while Hong turned to avoid a one-way street and then went on. "We represent an institution that is based in America, but we'll fight for freedom and just causes anywhere, for anyone. That's all I can say about that. Right now we're trying to locate a man named Ku

Mojo. He's the next politburo member who is about to be assassinated. And we need your help."

Hong's hands tightened on the steering wheel. "How do I know you do not want my help so you can kill Ku Mojo?" he asked.

"Look at me, Hong," McCarter said.

The young man turned to face him.

"You have my word."

Hong turned his gaze back to the road.

The men in the truck sat in silence for a few seconds. McCarter could appreciate the kid's situation. He didn't know what to believe, and a wrong decision could cost Ku Mojo, and perhaps other politburo members, their lives.

Finally Hong turned back to him. "Suppose, for the sake of argument," he said, "I believed you. What would you want of me?"

"To help us locate the man," McCarter said. He glanced at his watch. "Take us to his house. Run interference for us. Do the things that five round-eyes who don't know Mandarin from Manchurian can't do."

Hong had started to speak when Hawkins interrupted from the back. "Call coming in."

McCarter turned to the rear of the truck, an idea striking him. "Switch it to speakerphone, Hawk," he said.

Hawkins's eyebrows lowered slightly.

Stony Man Farm was the best-kept secret in the

world of clandestine operations, and allowing Hong to listen in on a call to the Farm itself was a breach of security. There was always the chance the young man might pick up some piece of information that could be costly at a later date.

And, after all, McCarter had to remind himself, Hong Chei represented China—Communist China.

On the other hand, the Phoenix Force leader knew, the call might be the only way to convince the young police cadet that the intentions of the commandos were honorable.

McCarter sat silently for a moment. Should he risk it? He could always advise Price that they had company listening, but that in itself might lead Hong to believe that the call had been prearranged for his benefit. If the young man was to be convinced, he would have to be allowed to listen without restriction.

"Do it, T.J."

Hawkins shrugged. Pulling the cellular phone from under his shirt, he switched it on. "Hello."

A short pause on the other end indicated that Price had picked up on the fact that Hawkins hadn't answered with the customary "Phoenix Force." Stony Man's mission controller might not put two and two together and infer that someone outside of the team was listening, but she would realize something was unusual and double her guard against giving away anything about the Farm.

"T.J.?" Price finally said.

"That's me."

"Are the others where they can hear?" she asked.

McCarter knew there was more in the question than what met the ear. Price was no dummy, and she was trying to ascertain exactly what the peculiarity was to the situation.

"Speaker's on, Barb," Hawk said, "so speak away."

"We've got new Intel that just came in," Price said. Her voice sounded as if she were still "fishing."

"Go ahead," McCarter said from the front seat.

There was another short pause during which the Phoenix Force leader knew Price was trying to decide exactly what she should say. That was the way it was with so much of the world of clandestine ops, McCarter knew. So many things came in shades of gray rather than black and white. So many decisions had to be made on instinct rather than policy because they didn't fit into existing policy.

"Okay," Price said finally, making up her mind to go ahead. "The *ninja* behind the assassinations is one Kosuke Yamaguchi. He's been working with a Japanese Defense Force undercover man named Kenji Takaka. Who, I might add, he discovered was one of the 'good guys' and killed." She stopped talking for a moment, then went on. "Now I'm going to skip to the chase. Yamaguchi plans to kill Ku Mojo tonight, *and* his wife and four children. Of course, he'll make it look like a CIA hit again, too."

McCarter had kept one eye on Hong as Price spoke. He couldn't tell if the young man believed what he'd heard, but Hong's interest had definitely been aroused. Anyone would get upset when children were in danger, but Hong looked almost as if it were his own family that was in danger from the *ninja* assassin.

"There's more," Price added. "Your Stateside counterparts stopped an assassination attempt on the Texas governor a few hours ago, and the Chinese authorities not only aren't happy, they're embarrassed. They've got nuclear subs circling Hawaii and they've hinted that one more politburo kill means mushroom clouds over Honolulu."

"Got it, Barb," McCarter said. "Anything else?"

"Negative, David," Price said. "Have you gotten Ku Mojo's home address yet?"

"No. You have it?"

"Negative."

"Then we'd better get rolling, and fast," McCarter said. "We'll get back to you as soon as something breaks." He nodded at Hawkins, and the other man killed the phone.

McCarter turned to Hong. Until now the young man had been driving idly through the streets of Beijing but the Phoenix Force leader now noticed he had sped up. "We need to stop somewhere," McCarter said. "I doubt Ku Mojo will be listed in the phone book. Is there anyone you could call to find out where he lives?''

Hong turned a corner, then looked at McCarter. "Before I answer," he said, "I must tell you something."

McCarter waited.

"I believe you and have decided to help you by leading you to Ku Mojo. But if I am wrong, and it turns out that you have deceived me again, I advise you to kill me." The young man's face tightened, making him suddenly look years older and far more worldly than he had only moments before. "Because if you do not, I will do my very best to kill you."

"Fair enough," McCarter said. "Now, is there someone you could call and get Ku Mojo's address?"

Hong turned back to the street and made another turn. "There are many people I could call," he replied, "but the call would be wasteful." When he turned to face McCarter this time, the hardness had disappeared from his features. "I know where Ku Mojo lives. I have been to his home many times. Comrade Ku Mojo is my uncle."

THE TWO-STORY HOUSE looked like many others up and down the darkened street in the fashionable residential area of Tokyo, a mixture of both Eastern and Western architecture.

Bolan moved quickly through the bushes just outside the iron perimeter fence. The front gate was locked, the guardhouse deserted in the early morning hours. Scaling the fence and dropping down behind the hedge on the other side was no problem.

Keeping low to the ground, the Executioner crabwalked toward the house twenty yards away. His eyes scanned the ground for trip wires or other alarm devices, but he saw nothing of that nature. He reminded himself he was in Japan, not America. The Japanese needed no expensive and complex security systems. They had long relied on repressive laws that took away the individual rights of citizens to control crime, and that thought brought the words of Benjamin Franklin to Bolan's brain: "They that can give up essential liberty to obtain a little temporary safety deserve neither liberty nor safety."

The soldier rounded a swimming pool at the rear of the house and moved quickly to a glass door. Through it, he could see a kitchen inside. He inspected the door frame for any signs of an alarm and, seeing none, reached into his pocket to produce a small leather kit not unlike a manicure set. But beyond the zipper lay a set of locksmith picks.

The picks had the door open in less than ten seconds.

Closing the door behind him, Bolan moved quickly through the kitchen to a hallway. The interior of the house was decorated in traditional Japanese style with thin *shoji* screens serving as walls. Following his instincts, he turned right and soon found himself in the living room. Moonlight drifted through the windows at the front of the room, leading him to a staircase.

He moved swiftly and silently up the steps, pausing when he reached the top. Again he found a hall leading both ways. Soft snoring came from both directions, and he walked silently across the thick carpet to a break in the screens on his right.

Inside the open door he saw the lace curtains of a canopy bed. Snuggled under the covers was a girl of perhaps ten years, hugging a stuffed panda bear.

Bolan moved back down the hall, passing two more bedrooms that were empty. When he came to the end of the hall, he stopped, peering slowly around the screens into the room.

Two people were asleep on the mat on the floor. One was female, dressed in a short baby blue nightgown, and the other was Yuji Tanaka. Flat on his back, the Japanese business magnate wore a lightweight white karate *gi* as pajamas.

Bolan drew the Desert Eagle and moved swiftly into the room. He dropped to one knee next to Tanaka, clasped his left hand over the man's mouth and shoved the barrel of the big .44 pistol under his chin.

Tanaka opened his eyes.

The Executioner waited until the eyes focused and Tanaka had time to grasp the situation. "Keep quiet," he whispered. "I'd hate to upset your wife by drenching her with your blood." Slowly he removed his hand and stood, keeping the Desert Eagle aimed at the man's head.

"Come on," Bolan whispered.

Tanaka stood.

The big American pushed him out of the room into the hall. "You've got an office in the house somewhere," he said. "Take me to it."

Without a word Tanaka led Bolan down the same staircase he had come up, then back through the living room to another short hallway. Sliding a screen out of the way, he reached in and flipped on the light switch.

Bolan followed him inside to the elaborately decorated office. "Take a seat in your chair," he ordered, then followed him to the side of the desk.

"May I speak now?" Tanaka asked.

"When spoken to," Bolan growled. "Now listen carefully. You're going to lift the phone and call whoever it is you need to call to put a halt to the Philippine invasion. Tell them to pull their ships back all the way across the South China Sea and into Vietnamese waters." Bolan paused to give him time to comprehend, then went on, "Your first thought, Yuji, is going to be that you could call anyone—even the time-and-temperature number—and mouth those orders and I'd never know the difference. Don't kid yourself. As soon as you hang up, there's a number I can call to see if the withdrawal has started."

"I am sure there is," Tanaka said. "But what if I refuse?"

"Then you, my friend, will start dying the slowest and most painful death anyone has experienced in this part of the world since the Mongols were run out."

Tanaka had appeared emotionless so far, but now his face lit up with glee. "As you wish," he said. He lifted the telephone receiver with his bandaged hand, pressed it to his ear, then tapped in a number. "It will take a few minutes. The connection will have to be routed on board ship."

"You don't seem all that upset about it," Bolan said. He could see by the smile that the man had something up his sleeve.

"I am not." Tanaka shrugged. "I can always call back and reverse the orders as soon as I kill you." His voice took on a mocking tone now. "By the way, the Cambodian admiral in charge of the Confederation fleet speaks fluent English. Would you like me to speak in that barbaric language for your benefit?"

"That would be accommodating," Bolan replied. He kept his gaze focused on the man's every movement, regardless of how small. Something was coming. He just didn't know what yet.

The line evidently connected because Tanaka turned his attention back to the phone. "Yes, Admiral Wat," he said pleasantly. "Yes, this is Tanaka. Please recall all of your forces and return them to Vietnamese water immediately." He listened for a moment, then said, "No. There has been a slight change of plans. Keep your ships in harbor until you hear from me again. Do nothing until then. That is my order." He hung up and smiled at Bolan.

"And now," Tanaka said, reaching behind his back with his bandaged hand, "it is time that I killed you so I can reverse the order." The back of his *gi* rose slightly, and when his hand returned, he held the tanto Bolan had watched him practice with earlier that evening.

It was Bolan's turn to smile. A good fifteen feet away, he shook the Desert Eagle in the air. "If I'm not mistaken, there's an old joke about the guy who brings a knife to a gunfight."

Tanaka stood but made no effort to move forward. He held the knife at his side as he said, "I know the joke, but it does not take into account extenuating circumstances. And in this case, I have an advantage of which you are not yet aware."

Bolan kept the Eagle's front sight centered on the man's chest. "Care to share it with me?" he asked.

"Yes. You saw my wife earlier. Are you aware of my daughter in the other bedroom?"

The soldier nodded. "Sleeping peacefully with her panda," Bolan said. "I saw no reason to disturb her. It's hardly her fault she was fathered by you."

"Precisely! And although you do not know my wife, rest assured that Keiko is equally innocent. She knows nothing about what my brothers and I have planned." He paused. "But she is the wife of a samurai and comes from a samurai family herself. She is well trained in the martial arts, and as soon as she hears your gunshot she will come running with her short sword." Now Tanaka chuckled. "You will be forced to kill her, as well as me."

The man had a point. His wife would mistake Bolan for a burglar, and if she was the fighter Tanaka said she was, would come at him with her *wakizashi* slashing. He'd have no choice but to kill the innocent woman.

"And you are not the kind of man who would do such a thing," Tanaka said. "As I, a samurai and follower of the code of Bushido, would not be." He began to step slowly forward.

Bolan stepped back away from the desk. His left hand moved toward the Beretta under his arm, then stopped. The 9 mm pistol was equipped with a sound suppressor, sometimes erroneously called a silencer. It didn't make the weapon silent by any means, and while it did lower the roar enough that the walls of a normal house would stop the sound before it reached Tanaka's bedroom upstairs, he doubted that the thin screens would do so.

With one smooth movement Bolan holstered the Desert Eagle and unclipped the Benchmade knife from his pocket.

"Ah," Tanaka said. "It will be as it should be, as it was in the days of the samurai. Two men facing each other with steel, man to man." He moved from behind the desk and began to circle to his right. "I hope you are good. As a samurai I have studied the blade since childhood."

Bolan began to move with him, careful to keep his knife hand out of reach. The other arm he held in front of him to block the tanto. He would sacrifice a slash on his blocking arm to protect his weapon if it became necessary.

Tanaka feinted with the knife and drew it back. "We are alike, you and I," he said as he continued to circle, "men of honor. That is why you would not risk the life of my wife."

"I believe in honor," Bolan replied, "but I'm nothing like you."

The Japanese feinted again, then shook his head. "No, we are the same," he said. "I am a samurai, and I follow the code of Bushido. Perhaps your code is not as well defined, but it is much the same. You are a warrior."

Bolan feinted now, moving the knife in a half-speed slash in order to watch Tanaka's reaction. The man slashed out with his tanto, trying to cut the knife out of his adversary's hand.

Bolan got his arm and weapon back out of range a split second before the tanto would have made contact with his wrist. "There's a big difference in our codes," he said as he continued to circle. "Mine doesn't allow underhanded techniques like killing innocents."

"Nor does mine," Tanaka replied, feinting again.

"No, but you hire *ninja* to do it for you. You'll forgive me if I don't see the difference."

Tanaka's expression changed slightly, and Bolan knew the discrepancy in the samurai's code had hit home. It was the diversion he needed—the *suki,* or momentary lapse in concentration—that might bring Tanaka's guard down long enough for him to strike.

The Executioner slashed out again, letting his arm hang for a split second like a worm wiggling on a fishhook.

Tanaka took the bait.

With a loud *kiai,* the Japanese brought the tanto around in a horizontal cut toward Bolan's wrist and the knife.

Bolan dropped his hand slightly and held the blade straight up, the edge facing Tanaka's oncoming attack. The Japanese saw the countermove too late to stop. His arm passed across the razor edge of the knife at the wrist.

Blood spurted from the severed arteries and veins as the soldier stepped in and sent a short left jab into the man's temple. Tanaka's head rocked back behind Bolan's fist. Following through Bolan raised his knife high above his head, then plunged it into the Japanese's chest.

Tanaka fell to the floor, his chest heaving up and

down as he gasped for air. He tried to speak, but blood poured forth instead of words. A moment later he was dead.

Bolan leaned over, grabbed the man's arm and hoisted him over his shoulder in a fireman's carry. Turning, he walked quietly out of the room, back through the kitchen and out the door through which he'd entered the house.

Tanaka had been right about at least one thing. The Executioner lived by a code. It was a code of right and wrong that not only covered combat, but the rest of life, as well. This night wasn't the first time that code had caused him to risk his own life to avoid hurting innocents.

But his code went even deeper than that, Bolan realized as he jogged back across the lawn with Yuji Tanaka on his back. The man had been responsible for the deaths of dozens, if not hundreds, of innocent people. Had his invasion of the Philippines, and other imperialistic plans, been carried out, the body count would have risen beyond reckoning.

But regardless of how ruthless, underhanded and despicable Tanaka had been, his wife and daughter weren't. And Bolan had no intention of letting them see their husband and father dead on the floor in the home they had shared as a family.

FROM THE THICK STAND of trees in the park across the street, McCarter could see no lights in Ku Mojo's house. He held the cellular phone to his lips, whispering into it. "We're on-site, Barb," he told the Stony Man mission controller. "Can't tell if Yamaguchi is here yet. We'll be going in as soon as I hang up."

"Affirmative, Phoenix One," Price replied. "Be advised that approximately one half hour ago, Yuji Tanaka was eliminated. Before that happened, Striker forced him to call back the invasion."

"That's one pain in the arse out of the way," McCarter said.

"Roger that, David," Price agreed. "But the U.S. Navy has now picked up six fully equipped Chinese nuclear subs circling Hawaii within firing range. Able Team is en route on the USS *Georgia*."

McCarter recognized the name of the American submarine. An Ohio-class sub with twenty-four Trident 1 SLBMs, it could provide an excellent second-strike attack. But a *second strike* would be of little value to the men, women and children of Hawaii if the Chinese subs sent their nukes over the islands first. "Let's hope we don't need them, Barb. It's pretty much go-for-broke time here. If we're able to save Ku Mojo, we'll get Yamaguchi, too, and with him and Tanaka both out of the way, it should be over. If we miss Yamaguchi, it will mean he takes out another politburo member and World War III starts in the Pacific."

"So don't miss him."

"Haven't the foggiest intention of doing so," the former SAS officer replied. "We'll get back to you."

McCarter turned to the four other Phoenix Force warriors and Hong. "Once we're inside," he whispered, "I want Manning and James to take the downstairs floor. Don't forget the garage area. T.J., you and Encizo head straight up the back stairs for the children's rooms. You remember where Hong said they were?"

Hawkins nodded.

"I'll go directly to Ku Mojo's bedroom and check on him and his wife. If all is well, we'll set up inside the house and wait. If Yamaguchi is already there..." He paused, then said, "You know what to do. And don't hesitate. The man's a well-trained killer. Let's go."

McCarter had turned to start across the street when he felt the hand grab his arm.

"You did not give me my assignment," Hong said.

"Stay here."

"No. You will need my help getting in. I know where Ku Mojo hides a key to the back door."

"Just tell us where it is," McCarter said.

"No, I must go with you. I must redeem myself in my own eyes for being asked to leave the institute. I will not tell you where the key is unless you agree to take me with you."

McCarter shrugged. "Then we'll get in through other means."

For the first time since Phoenix Force had met their amiable young cadet guide, they saw another side of him. Hong's face suddenly became a mask of rage. "I stood by you when the police regulars wanted to throw you in jail!" he whisper-shouted. "I was kicked out of the academy for it, and even then I brought you here when there was no solid proof that you were not the enemy!" His voice grew even more angry as he continued. "Ku Mojo is my uncle! His wife is my aunt, and his children are like my own! Now, I am going with you, I want a gun and I want it now!"

McCarter grinned at the young man. "When you put it that way, I'd have to say you've earned it," he said as he drew the pistol from his waistband and handed it to the young man. "Lead the way to the key, Hong. Then stick with me."

Phoenix Force and their young Chinese recruit hurried across the street. Hong took the lead as instructed, hurrying around the front of the house to the rear and stopping at a row of large stones that divided the yard from a flower bed. McCarter watched him start at the end, then count to nine before rolling the stone out of the way and bending to retrieve the key.

He held the key in his left hand, the Chinese pistol in his right as he moved to a door off the patio. Phoenix Force crowded in behind him, and a moment later the door swung open.

McCarter knew the *ninja* was already in the house the moment he stepped through the doorway. An almost tangible evil seemed to hang in the air, as if Satan himself had taken up residence. The Briton turned to the others. "He's here," he whispered.

Manning, Hawkins, James and Encizo nodded. They could sense the presence, too.

James and Manning split to begin their search of the downstairs floor as Hawkins and Encizo started up the rear stairs. Hong led McCarter across a dark den area to the staircase next to the front door. The Phoenix Force leader now took the lead, starting quietly up the steps, the Type 85 submachine gun held at the ready. The belief that Yamaguchi was in the house grew even stronger as he reached the top.

A soft light drifted in through a large glass window at the front of the house, and more came down through the skylight. The effect distorted what could be seen in the hallway.

What *could* he see? the Briton asked himself. What exactly was he looking for? A *ninja*, he answered, a descendant of the ancient Japanese assassins who were such masters of disguise that they were rumored to have the power of invisibility. Trained in the arts of death since childhood, they were reputed to develop their senses to levels beyond belief. If one believed the legends, the *ninja* could hear the ocean waves from ten miles inland and see at night like a cat.

The Phoenix Force leader stared through the distorted light down the hallway. Only one door appeared at the end of the short passage. It had to be Ku Mojo's bedroom—right where Hong had said it would be. It was the only room in this wing of the house.

With Hong following behind him, McCarter started toward the door. He flipped the safety off the subgun and slipped his finger inside the trigger guard. The sinister sensation continued to grow as he neared the closed door, and the Briton knew that it would be him and Hong who confronted the *ninja* rather than the other Phoenix Force commandos.

McCarter was ten feet from the closed door when it opened. He brought the subgun to his shoulder, and his finger started back in the trigger. It stopped halfway through the stroke when he saw a woman in a long robe running down the hall, frantically whispering in Mandarin to McCarter.

"She says he is in there," Hong translated, "about to kill her husband!"

McCarter pushed past her, the Chinese subgun leading the way. Behind him, he heard the woman repeating her words to Hong.

The Briton skidded to a halt and swung back around, his finger pulling back on the trigger as he did.

A stream of fire shot from the Type 85, hitting the woman in the chest. She jerked and spasmed, her hand clawing inside the robe as if searching for a hidden weapon. McCarter let up on the trigger, raised the sights and fired again.

The new rounds took the woman in the face.

Hong stood holding his pistol at his side, his mouth agape. "You killed her!" he accused. "You killed my aunt!"

McCarter walked back and stooped over the body. Most of the woman's face was gone. What little wasn't, was too hard to see in the strange light.

Hong lifted his pistol and jammed it into the Phoenix Force leader's side. "You *are* CIA!" he shouted.

The Briton reached out and snatched the weapon from the inexperienced young man. "Hong," he said, "cut the CIA crap once and for all. This wasn't your aunt, it was Kosuke Yamaguchi."

"No! That is my aunt's robe!"

McCarter loosened the belt of the robe and reached in to grab the corpse's hand. He pried a Type 51 Chinese pistol from the dead fingers and said, "The gun hers, too?"

"It could be!" Hong said, tears running down his cheeks. "My uncle kept a gun for protection."

McCarter had run out of patience. Grabbing the hem of the robe, he flipped it up over the corpse's groin. "Okay, Hong," the Phoenix Force leader said, "does *that* belong to your aunt, too?"

Without another word McCarter turned and entered the bedroom. A man and a woman lay tied to the bed, their arms and legs secured with thick adhesive tape.

The woman was roughly the same size as Kosuke Yamaguchi's body in the hall, and the Briton had no trouble seeing how the well-trained *ninja* had been able to fool Hong.

"Uncle Mojo!" Hong cried. "Aunt Kimi!" He raced to the bed and pulled the tape from their mouths. Turning to McCarter, he said, "But how did you know?"

"The woman in the hall didn't recognize you," McCarter said. "Even in the dim light, she should have known her own nephew."

Hong frowned. "But I should have known my own aunt, as well. She did not get close enough for me to see. How then could you be sure she had seen *me?*"

The Phoenix Force leader shrugged. "She—or he, I suppose we should say—kept to the shadows so I couldn't get a good look at him, either. He did it very low-key, very well. That's because he was a *ninja*, Hong. Kosuke was a *shinobi*—a shadow warrior."

The lights in the room suddenly came on, and Manning, James, Encizo and Hawkins raced in with their weapons ready. Seeing things under control, they lowered the Chinese submachine guns.

McCarter took a deep breath. Only one thing still worried him. "The kids?" he asked.

James grinned. "Asleep and fine. We tried not wake the baby."

As if to prove him wrong, the sound of a crying infant suddenly came from the other end of the house.

Ku Mojo's wife burst into tears of relief.

While McCarter and James had been talking, Hong had cut the tape that bound his uncle and aunt. Now Ku Mojo rubbed his wrists as he looked from his nephew to McCarter, to the other Phoenix Force warriors and back to Hong. "Hong Chei," he said, confused, "what has happened? Who are these men? Are they with the American CIA?"

The Chinese police cadet laughed. "No, Uncle," he said, "they are not CIA. I do not know who they are." He turned to David McCarter and smiled. "Only that they are our friends."

EPILOGUE

Nori Tanaka took a seat under the umbrella nearest the water and looked out over the waves toward the island of Little Cayman, seven miles in the distance. He had arrived in the Caymans less than an hour earlier, coming in on a flight routed from Vietnam to Brazil, with several other stops and plane changes before he finally arrived on Grand Cayman. From there it had been a short flight to Cayman Brac. The flights had been long and boring. He was exhausted, but it had been worth it.

The middle Tanaka brother was taking no chances of being followed. He hoped Ichiro was being as careful.

A tall, dark-haired waiter came over to where Nori sat and stopped at the edge of the table. "May I bring you a drink, sir?" he asked in the Caribbean accent peculiar to the Caymans.

"Do you have any sake?"

"Of course, sir," the waiter said. "Cold or hot?"

"Hot, of course."

The waiter left, disappearing into the rough stone building that served the outdoor restaurant and bar. Nori shifted slightly, let the sun beat down on his face for a moment, then leaned back under the protection of the umbrella. A moment later the waiter returned with his drink and set it down on the table.

Nori stared at the waves as they beat against the iron shore in front of him. He would miss Yuji. The eldest brother had been the leader of the family ever since their father's death, and Nori had gladly followed him. Hardly a leader himself, the younger man had recognized that fact early on and developed political and bureaucratic skills instead. No one was better at what he did, he knew. He was the best second-in-command imaginable, but he would never steer the ship.

He took a sip of the hot rice wine and set it on the table. He wasn't ambitious like Yuji had been, and would be content with the money he and Ichiro had been able to smuggle out of Japan before the government took over the family business. There were millions of dollars at his disposal, and that was enough for him.

For Ichiro, Nori wasn't so sure. The youngest Tanaka brother was much like Yuji, although more prone to impulse. Ichiro might well try to regroup someday and carry on where Yuji had failed. And who knew? By then he might have matured enough to be successful. If so, Nori might even come out of retirement and follow a new leader, helping the Republic of Tanaka become a reality.

Nori heard a car pull up and stop behind him. He turned to see a taxi driver jump from behind the wheel, hurry around the hood of the vehicle and open the passenger door.

As if he had been summoned by Nori's thoughts, Ichiro Tanaka stepped out of the vehicle. He paid the driver and turned toward the umbrellas, spotting his brother immediately. The topknot bounced and jiggled as he made his way to the table and took a seat.

The waiter appeared almost immediately.

"Beer," Ichiro said. "Red Stripe, and be fast about it."

"Certainly, sir," the waiter replied, and hurried off.

"It is good to see you, little brother," Nori said. "For a while I did not know if I ever would again."

Ichiro turned and spit on the ground. "We must carry on," he said. "We will avenge Yuji by making his dream come true."

Nori shrugged. "Perhaps someday. But now is not the time. We must allow things to cool down."

The waiter brought the Red Stripe beer and set it in front of Ichiro. "Will there be anything else?" he asked.

Ichiro took a sip and spit it on the ground. "It is warm!" he shouted. "Bring me a cold beer!" Looking up at the tall waiter, he jerked the bottle and splashed beer in the man's face.

The waiter pulled a bar towel from his belt, wiped his face and said, "I'm sorry, sir." He took the bottle and hurried away.

Nori glanced around to see that the other men and women sitting under the umbrellas had taken note of the incident but were now returning to their conversations or drinks. "Little brother," he said, "this is no good. You must not draw attention to us while the world is still talking about what happened."

"I am sorry," Ichiro said, looking down at his hands. "But our brother is dead, and we do not even know who is responsible."

"And we will never know."

"*I* will know," the man with the topknot snarled. "I must know. The men who foiled our plans in Oklahoma City," he said, "and the big, dark-haired American Yuji found in his office. These men are behind our brother's death. And as soon as I learn what agency they work for, I will hunt them down and kill them like dogs."

The waiter returned carrying another bottle of Red Stripe beer on a silver tray. He set it on the table and took a half step back. "Please try it, sir," he said. "Make sure it is all right."

Ichiro waved him away with a hand. "Go," he said. "My brother and I have business to discuss."

The waiter didn't move.

"Go!" Ichiro shouted, suddenly enraged. "I told

you we had business to discuss that does not involve you!"

"But it does involve me," the waiter said.

"You imbecile. Do you not know who you are dealing with?" As Ichiro uttered the words, he reached under his jacket to the small of his back and unleathered a pistol that had been holstered there.

The "waiter" flung away the tray to reveal a .44 Magnum Desert Eagle.

Nori watched helplessly as the big waiter fired a shot that struck his brother between the eyes. Ichiro's trigger finger spasmed before death claimed him, the one round from his automatic drilling into Nori's chest. He collapsed, dead before he hit the ground.

The Tanaka family's dream of its own empire lay dead in the dust. Mack Bolan turned and sauntered away, putting the death zone behind him before the frightened tourists recovered enough to make an ID.

This battle was over, but the war was far from won.

When all is lost, there is always the future

JAMES AXLER

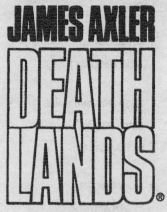

Skydark

It's now generations after the firestorm that nearly consumed the earth, and fear spreads like wildfire when an army of mutants goes on the rampage. Ryan Cawdor must unite the baronies to defeat a charismatic and powerful mutant lord, or all will perish.

In the Deathlands, the future is just beginning.

Don't miss out on the action in these titles featuring
THE EXECUTIONER®, STONY MAN™ and SUPERBOLAN®!

The Red Dragon Trilogy

#64210	FIRE LASH	$3.75 U.S.	☐
		$4.25 CAN.	☐
#64211	STEEL CLAWS	$3.75 U.S.	☐
		$4.25 CAN.	☐
#64212	RIDE THE BEAST	$3.75 U.S.	☐
		$4.25 CAN.	☐

Stony Man™

#61907	THE PERISHING GAME	$5.50 U.S.	☐
		$6.50 CAN.	☐
#61908	BIRD OF PREY	$5.50 U.S.	☐
		$6.50 CAN.	☐
#61909	SKYLANCE	$5.50 U.S.	☐
		$6.50 CAN.	☐

SuperBolan®

#61448	DEAD CENTER	$5.50 U.S.	☐
		$6.50 CAN.	☐
#61449	TOOTH AND CLAW	$5.50 U.S.	☐
		$6.50 CAN.	☐
#61450	RED HEAT	$5.50 U.S.	☐
		$6.50 CAN.	☐

(limited quantities available on certain titles)

TOTAL AMOUNT	$
POSTAGE & HANDLING	$
($1.00 for one book, 50¢ for each additional)	
APPLICABLE TAXES*	$ _____
TOTAL PAYABLE	$ _____
(check or money order—please do not send cash)	

To order, complete this form and send it, along with a check or money order for the total above, payable to Gold Eagle Books, to: **In the U.S.:** 3010 Walden Avenue, P.O. Box 9077, Buffalo, NY 14269-9077; **In Canada:** P.O. Box 636, Fort Erie, Ontario, L2A 5X3.

Name:_____

Address:_____ City:_____

State/Prov.:_____ Zip/Postal Code: _____

*New York residents remit applicable sales taxes.
 Canadian residents remit applicable GST and provincial taxes.

GEBACK17

The Destroyer takes on a plague of
invisible insects—as the exterminator

THE Destroyer

#107 Feast or Famine

Created by
WARREN MURPHY
and RICHARD SAPIR

Is the insect kingdom mobilizing to reclaim the planet…or
is something entirely different behind it all? Unless the
Destroyer can combat this disaster, a whole nation may
start dropping like flies.

Look for it in April wherever Gold Eagle books are sold.

Don't miss out on the action in these titles!

Deathlands

#62530	CROSSWAYS	$4.99 U.S.	☐
		$5.50 CAN.	☐
#62532	CIRCLE THRICE	$5.50 U.S.	☐
		$6.50 CAN.	☐
#62533	ECLIPSE AT NOON	$5.50 U.S.	☐
		$6.50 CAN.	☐
#62534	STONEFACE	$5.50 U.S.	☐
		$6.50 CAN.	☐

The Destroyer

#63210	HIGH PRIESTESS	$4.99	☐
#63218	ENGINES OF DESTRUCTION	$5.50 U.S.	☐
		$6.50 CAN.	☐
#63219	ANGRY WHITE MAILMEN	$5.50 U.S.	☐
		$6.50 CAN.	☐
#63220	SCORCHED EARTH	$5.50 U.S.	☐
		$6.50 CAN.	☐

(limited quantities available on certain titles)

TOTAL AMOUNT	$
POSTAGE & HANDLING	$
($1.00 for one book, 50¢ for each additional)	
APPLICABLE TAXES*	$_____
TOTAL PAYABLE	$_____
(check or money order—please do not send cash)	

To order, complete this form and send it, along with a check or money order for the total above, payable to Gold Eagle Books, to: **In the U.S.:** 3010 Walden Avenue, P.O. Box 9077, Buffalo, NY 14269-9077; **In Canada:** P.O. Box 636, Fort Erie, Ontario, L2A 5X3.

Name:_____

Address:_____ City:_____

State/Prov.:_____ Zip/Postal Code: _____

*New York residents remit applicable sales taxes.
 Canadian residents remit applicable GST and provincial taxes.

GEBACK17A